THE SILVER PROMISE

by

WILLIAM C. WALKER

This book is a work of fiction. Aside from actual city names in North Dakota, names, characters, places and incidents either are products of the author's imagination, or are used fictitiously. Any resemblance to actual events, locales or persons is entirely coincidental.

Cover by the Scarlett Rugers Design Agency
www.scarlettrugers.com

ACKNOWLEDGEMENTS

Thanks to the helpful personnel in the office of Clerk of The Circuit Court, Indian River County, Florida.

Also thanks to the officers of the Indian River Shores Public Safety Department, Vero Beach, Florida, and the Indian River Sheriff's Department.

For Maureen

THE SILVER PROMISE

1

Doris Blackwell rubbed a nicotine-stained index finger over the corners of two facedown cards flattened against the green felt baize of a blackjack table. She eyed the dealer, a sloe-eyed Korean or Chinese girl—hell, they were all the same—who probably came over smuggled inside a trailer on a container ship. The young woman gave Doris a hard stare while waiting for a sign.

Doris focused on the dealer's dilated pupils, wells of shiny blackness absorbing all light and giving nothing in return. Lustrous ebony hair was pulled tightly behind the girl's head, and a black-vested whatever worn over a white ruffled blouse made her look like someone lording way above her station in life.

An icy tumbler of Chivas appeared at Doris' shoulder, this offering from a buxom young girl stuffed into a ridiculous white T-shirt imprinted with lines of a tuxedo. She ignored the server and thumbed up the corners of her cards. The queen of clubs lay atop the king of hearts, a royal coupling that gave her a twenty. Doris palmed a veined and liver-mottled hand over her cards, shook her head to emphasize no further hits, and helped herself to a very generous swallow of twelve-year-old Chivas, courtesy of the house. Let the slant-eyed breed beat this one.

The dealer moved to successive players on Doris's left, dealing cards to some, pulling discards from others. She returned to Doris, exhaled a labored breath, and tapped her fingers lightly on the deck in her hands, there again with that patronizing demeanor, as if this squalid Indian casino in North Dakota was some high-end establishment in Monte Carlo.

"Your cards, ma'am," the dealer said with an uptick of her head. "I have to see them." Her words had the ring of an order, not a request.

Doris touched her tongue to the corner of her lips and allowed a smile to form into a smirk. She'd been doubling the ante for the past few minutes, grinding her way through another losing streak dished out by this immigrant from hell. This corner location in the casino was one of her favorites. Otherwise, she would have switched tables when the new dealer appeared. She'd actually come away with money in her pocket a time or two.

She flicked the cards face up. The odds were high that the dealer would bust going after her, and Doris celebrated this certain outcome with another long pull on her scotch. Her hand shook, but only because one-hundred dollar chips were stacked in front of her like cordwood at the back door of a north wood's cabin.

The dealer raised one eyebrow and turned her down card face up to reveal the five of diamonds alongside the ace of clubs. That gave her sixteen and a long way to go. The pit boss strolled over and cast a casual glimpse at the table. He gave Doris a smile. She damn well deserved one, as many times as she'd been here.

The man made a quiet remark to the dealer that Doris didn't catch. There was too much noise in the background. Ranch hands and oilfield rowdies were hooting and yelling alongside truckers and drifters. The computer generated ding-dongs of a hundred slot machines rode over the splattering racket of coins spilling into metal troughs. She could go deaf in a place like this.

The Asian woman flipped a card from the deck, her hands a blur of motion faster than a thought. The five of hearts appeared lying atop the ace and the five of diamonds as if it had been there forever. A flicker of the impossible gripped Doris. A twenty-one? No way!

She did the simple math again, counted the five flame-red blooms stamped on the glossy surface of the card. Her mouth fell open in disbelief as she caught the curl of the dealer's smile, one that barely cracked her lip gloss. The bitch was laughing. A white-hot pulse of anger flared in her temples. The house was cheating. Had to be!

The pit boss leaned over with a plastic smile, as if he could read her thoughts. "The tables are just off for you today, Mrs. Blackwell. You're welcome to stay over. Same deal as always, everything on the house. Your luck will turn. You know that. Give it twenty-four hours."

Doris pushed back from the table as her chips were raked away. A cotton-wool numbness came over her. This was by far the largest pot she had lost. The money was actually Cliffy's, so there was more where that came from. But still...what the hell? She drained her Chivas, swapped her empty glass with an icy replacement that quickly appeared, and slowly shook off the loss. Maybe no real damage, and in twenty-four hours she might feel better. She looked across the room. Drifters were pawing bargirls at the roulette wheels. The blond in the black leotard and heavy pancake makeup looked vaguely familiar. She realized that she had seen the woman up close, closer than most. Cosmetics were pasted over her rough complexion as thickly as mayonnaise on a sandwich. Yep, that was the one. After a moment, Doris nodded to herself and walked toward what could be a definite possibility.

2

The difficulty lay in the slope of the yard as it fell way from the house, although yard was a misnomer since the plot of land was five miles from the nearest neighbor. The barren ground was fixed with a hard pan of ice that reflected gray from the leaden overhang of clouds. Juliet Driscoll stepped carefully. The slightest misstep could break a kneecap or twist an ankle, and the bone-chilling wind didn't help. She glanced back at the house. One of the cellar doors was sprung, and gusts were pulling against the loose boards and rusty hinges rattling things, a warning again to watch her movements on the steep incline.

Juliet caught a wave, a fluttering hand from her brother. He was tending the remnants of a brush fire in the lower clearing, alternately disappearing and reappearing behind a dense boil of sooty, black smoke, which the wind dispersed as the column rose out of the depression. Juliet pinched her features and felt her eyes water as she faced the blast of air scouring the frozen land. She knotted her green quilted hood tighter and extended her arms for balance.

The house was tucked into an isolated corner on the northern border of North Dakota. The climate was hot and windy for three months of the year, freezing and windy for the other nine. The handful of survivors—for that was how she thought of herself and others—staked out a miserable existence in this barren moonscape. A few bars, several small grocery stores, and a handful of hardscrabble businesses sprouted from the crossroads like stubborn weeds in a parched land. It was not enough and never had been enough. Winnipeg was closer than any decent-sized U.S. city. She'd been there for a time, other places too.

She yelled as she made her way closer. "What are you doing here, Lenny? I thought you were working at the R & J?" She dodged the smoke and watched her brother work the base of the burn pile with a heavy garden rake. He shrugged, though the gesture seemed more associated with his raking than in response to her question.

"They said they didn't need me anymore."

She stepped toward him. " 'Cause you were late every day? Think that mighta had something to do with it?" She touched her swollen jaw. It would really be sore tomorrow.

Her brother shrugged again.

"Where'd Aunt Doris run off to? She's not in town and her car is gone. Lu flagged me down coming up the road with the mail. Wondered if she was sick or something."

"Haven't seen her," he said.

"Since when?"

"Since I saw you last, I guess. Five, six days? I'm not responsible for her whereabouts. Maybe she went into Bismarck to see her brother." He glanced over. "One of those truckers git you again? I wondered where you were." He punched at a charred branch buried at the bottom of the pile. Sparks flew. "Sis, I told you to stay away from those truckers. They're a mean bunch."

"They come into the saloon. I have to wait on them. That's my job. And Lenny, I can't be coming around here all the time anymore. You gotta understand that."

"Yeah, well..."

"Anyway, Doris couldn't care less about her brother. Just waiting for him to die in that nursing home."

"So maybe she's up at the casinos in Belcourt." He worked the rake handle again. "You know what she's like."

Juliet nodded toward the brush fire. "So how come you're out here burning this time of year?" She hoped the answer was something simple, like he had nothing else to do, which was probably the truth since he was just fired from a decent job.

"Gotta keep the place up. Doris said." He had that look, the one that had come into his face at an early age, a childlike naiveté that went with his normal, underachieving self. They had never been alike inside, even though they were twins. Outwardly, aside from obvious gender differences, they did bear a faint fraternal resemblance with their thin, reedy frames. A premature birth—or so they'd been told—almost thirty years before had created big problems for her brother. Juliet counted herself lucky in that regard. She had inherited a quick wit and the shell of a pretty face, but unfortunately her cheeks and lips had never quite filled out to compensate for her deep-set eyes. She could still become quite attractive by taking better care of herself, maybe by putting on a few easy, extra pounds, but lines of worry and disappointment continually worked their way into her complexion. In marked contrast to her brother's slack-jawed listlessness, she had pushed at life, always in conflict for the sake of conflict, and usually unhappy with herself at the outcome. Juliet still didn't know who she was. She only realized that if she could not solve the equation very soon, she would end up with the worn-out look of an old country music singer, a Tammy Wynette, in her final years.

She puffed out a swirl of condensation. "She give you extra again?"

"What? Whataya mean?"

"Extra, Lenny. You think I don't know? Like that two thousand you squandered last month across the state line. It's not safe for you to be carrying all that cash in your pockets, and I worry about you, especially when you go to establishments like that."

He glanced down and swiveled the bill of his dirty ball cap toward her. A logo of a chain saw company sat on top of a poor haircut and a week's worth of stubble. "Come on, Sis. Whataya going on about that for? It's personal, and I get lonely out here." He waved his arms to indicate the wide, gray-white expanse of frozen lakes bordering the rear of the property.

She followed his eyes and took in the land that no one wanted, at least until the oil companies came, and that was only recently. During the years following World War II, the Great Northern Railroad promised growth and development at the railroad junction six miles to the west. The company had big plans: a downsized Chicago full of commerce and industry. The growth never came. Rail and truck shipping bypassed them to the south, and the Great Northern merged into Burlington Northern. Their small town of Sherwood was left with a spur line that had been covered with rust for decades.

"She does that to keep you here, Lenny, under her thumb. You realize that? So you won't go out and get a steady job. She knows about that, how to manage us. Always has."

His head was down low on the rake. He straightened and looked at her. "You got away."

"It wasn't easy."

"She's got you too, Juliet. Remember that car last year she paid for? You let your boyfriend tear up the transmission."

"I didn't let him. Didn't know he was going to wreck it. And he wasn't a boyfriend."

"Then you had to go back and ask her for a loan, like you were begging for the money."

"It's not even her money. It's Cliffy's. We both know that." Juliet stared into a middle distance and shivered at the bitter syllables of the name. Uncle Clifford (he made her call him 'Cliffy') was no more a relation to them than Doris herself. A door opened somewhere in her mind, just a crack, but behind it existed sharp, ugly images just waiting to come out. She caught herself, folded her arms over her chest, and tried to ignore the twist of bile in her stomach.

"Well, I won't miss her if she never comes back," her brother said. "And you know that's the truth."

"Maybe she passed out drunk in a ditch somewhere."

He grinned. "And froze to death?"

"Yeah, maybe." She caught his expression and smiled. They'd talked about things before, more him than her. The conversations never seemed real, but the fantasies had been a background to their lives for as long as she could remember.

"Wouldn't that be nice?" he finished.

She peered into the blaze. The heat registered on one side of her face. "So what happens to her house if she doesn't come back, let's say?"

He shrugged. "Well, I guess I'll just keep living here, like always."

Juliet turned her attention toward the small clapboard dwelling in the final stages of its useful life. The east corner of the porch had fallen in and most of the siding needed paint. The barn was in about the same shape. An old-fashioned well in the back yard arose from the hardened topsoil. They'd actually drawn clear, fresh water for a few years after the pump was put in. Now the small structure looked as worn down as the house. For the last five years or so Doris hadn't put a penny into keeping the place up. Lenny had worked around the property, and she had helped in years past, but neither of them had a handyman's ability at fixing things, and money was always an issue according to Doris. "If she never comes back I wouldn't want you out here alone," she said. "You need someone, Lenny. I'd have to think about moving back." She reached out to ruffle his cap and thought better of it.

"I'm grown up now, Sis. I can handle things."

Really? Juliet stuffed her hands into the insulated belly pouch of her parka. Everything about the place was a mess. She focused on Lenny's pickup truck sagging on worn tires a short distance away. The tailgate hung down and gusts of wind swirled into the bed lifting bits of paper and garbage. The vehicle was a rusted-out piece of junk. Her brother, now moving around to the other side of the fire, was equally unkempt with his bad teeth and scruffy, dark stubble. She thought about herself, her failed attempts with men, her failed life. God, if they weren't a pair. "Anyway, that old woman is too tough to freeze in a ditch," she said. "I'm betting she'll be back in a day or two."

His cap dipped up and down with the movements of the rake. His short attention span had been exceeded and he turned his concentration to the fire.

"I'll be up at the house," she said in a louder voice.

Aunt Doris' house was always cold in the winter. Lenny had turned up the heat, but it didn't seem to make any difference.

Juliet watched her brother going through drawers in Aunt Doris' bedroom. A fragrance of bath powder filled the air along with the musty scent of old clothes.

"She's not dead yet, Lenny," she said. "We shouldn't be going through her things like this."

"She might be. She's never been gone this long."

There was a mood to her brother, a sleepy contentment that was not normally present. He smelled like wood smoke, not that Doris would ever pick up on any lingering odor in the room. Nothing could cut through the reek of stale cigarette smoke imbedded in the coverlets and drapes.

Lenny held up something white and elastic with half a dozen straps attached to the fabric. He poked his tongue out of the corner of his mouth, furrowed his brow, and tossed it to the other side of the bed.

She avoided her brother's look and focused on the bleached, white landscape of Dakota through the large corner window. They knew each other too well, and his easy temperament would be crushed as soon as Doris made an appearance. She pulled two government checks from her pocket. "These were in the mailbox," she said. "If you're searching for them you can give it up."

Lenny looked up sharply. "The Social Security checks!" He stepped over and snatched them away. "Maybe I'd better hang on to these."

She straight-armed a hand in front of him. "Give 'em back, Lenny."

"You're always gone anymore. What do you care? And what if she really did freeze to death out there somewhere?"

"You're still not going to sign 'em. You want to go back to James River? This time it'd be for more than a month, I guarantee you."

He scratched his head through the top of the ball cap. "Sis, couldn't we use some of this money? The last coupla days I was thinking about the checks, thinking maybe we needed the money more than Aunt Doris. She was always spending it on all that mail order stuff. Wasting it."

"Lenny?"

The knock on the front door froze both of them. Juliet was the first to move. She quietly pushed a drawer closed, yanked the checks from her brother, and went to the bedroom window. The sheriff's cruiser was outside. An individual was standing on the porch steps.

"Nick Olsen's at the door," she said to Lenny. She looked down on a wide slab of a man's shoulders covering a large, trim torso. He was hatless, and his hair was a blond shock of Norwegian DNA that most people took for the white of early aging. She knew better; he'd had it all his life.

Lenny's eyes widened. He took a step forward, then back. "What's he here for?"

Juliet turned from the window. "Relax. He's not going to bother you unless you've done something stupid again. There was a fight at the Roads last night." She touched her jaw and considered the possibility. "Could be about that."

Lenny trailed behind her as she moved toward the stairs. She had a thought. It could be that Doris actually *was* lying in a ditch somewhere. Juliet made it into a prayer and refused to feel badly about it.

Nick Olsen was a big cop with a fair complexion. She had always found his face pleasantly shaped with angles that were vaguely complimentary. They reminded her of geometry classes long ago: a rectangle of a forehead, a triangle of planes leading to a square jaw, and cheekbones that appeared chiseled from a Norwegian glacier. His mouth hardly ever curled upward anymore, at least it seemed that way when she spied him around town. She had heard him laugh, but that was more than a few years in the past when his countenance seemed softer.

He stood before her in a sleeveless, quilted-green hunting vest that covered his uniform top. The rest of his outfit consisted of his wide, black leather gun belt and his starched khaki pants.

"Afternoon, Juliet," he said as she opened the door a crack. She watched his eyes track her brother in the background. He pressed his lips into a line and nodded around her. "Lenny."

Juliet stepped out onto the porch and braced the cold air. She was wearing a thin cotton blouse over a pink scooped-neck T-shirt. Her pants were a pair of gray exercise sweats looped at the waist with a drawstring. "This about the fight at the Crossroads?"

"Yeah." He looked at her, leaned over and regarded the side of her face. "That fellow got you, didn't he?" He lightly touched her bruise.

"Yeah he got me." She twisted away and crossed her arms over her chest.

Olsen took a stance and stuck his thumbs into his belt. "I've got him locked up if you want to press charges, Juliet. You weren't the only one he hit."

She shook her head after a moment. "I guess not."

He studied her face. "I'll just have to release him then. That's not fair to you."

"So? I've learned how to take life now. I don't want any more to do with the jerk."

"I can't talk you in to coming down? Wouldn't take long."

"I don't think so, Nick. You didn't have to come all the way out here. You coulda just called."

"I didn't mind the ride. Haven't seen you in a while anyway." He turned to go and scanned the house and yard with a lingering cop's look. "Everything okay here? How's Doris?"

"Don't know. She's away somewhere."

"Bismarck? Her brother's not going to last much longer, what I hear."

She shook her head. "My guess is the casinos in Belcourt."

He backed down the porch steps and gave the loose boards a little up and down shift of his weight. "Yeah, well..." His gaze steadied on her for a long moment. "Juliet, we've known each other a good many years, since grammar school."

"I'm not sure you ever really knew me, Nick."

"We went out a few times..."

"You were older. A senior. I was only in the ninth grade."

He narrowed his eyes. "I understood that. I was polite, if you recall. Didn't try anything. And anyway, you were distant, hard to warm up to."

He did try something, as she remembered. They had driven over to Devil's Lake for the evening to watch the Trojans play the Muskies for the regional finals. Doris had permitted her to go only because the entire school and community seemed to be in on the excitement.

The nighttime ride home stuck in her memory, mostly because the couple in the back seat seemed to be having such a good time with each other. She allowed Nick to pull her close on the bench seat of the old Ford, circle her shoulders with his free arm. His legs were open and bent at the knees in a relaxed kind of way, one foot on the accelerator, one hand on the wheel as he hummed to the music on the radio.

He seemed content to ride that way. She was not, and her body stiffened with apprehension, especially after they dropped off his friends and completed the remainder of the ride together.

She kept her mouth closed when his kiss came, her lips sealed in a line. He tried a second time, a gentle nuzzle on her cheek, a slide of warm breath against the corner of her mouth. She went rigid, a bar of cold steel countering the warmth of his embrace, and he backed away, as if he knew or sensed something off-center.

Juliet hugged herself against the cold and turned partially away from Nick on the porch. The man in front of her would never suspect the truth: that she had never been able to open her mouth to a man's kiss, to tolerate the slightest intimate contact between her lips. That she opened herself up in other ways on rare occasions was her own problem, a puzzle she could never figure out.

Nick heeled his boot into a loose board again, stamped it several times. "You were the pretty girl who decided long ago to let life run her over. And you were smart, Juliet, really smart. I've never figured it."

"So? I still am smart, Nick. That doesn't go away."

He nodded. "I guess that's right."

"But I didn't make A's like you did: the valedictorian an' all."

"You could have."

Her facial muscles slackened with a sense of loss. A disconnect existed somewhere in her past, separating what she was from what she could have been, and she had no idea how to repair everything. She wasn't even sure what she was supposed to reconnect, and the lack of that knowledge left her in a depressed silence.

Nick appeared to consider his words. "Maybe it wasn't that easy for you and Lenny, orphans and all. Lord knows…"

"No one promised us anything, if that's what you mean. You know the old saying about a rose garden."

Nick stepped off the bottom tread onto the hard ground. "It's not too late, you know, to get going, turn your life around." In a firmer tone, "You need to stay out of those motels and take better care of yourself. I want the best for you, Juliet. Always have."

The life force within her seemed to come and go as it pleased, a wave action that washed in and out. It receded at this moment. She was left expressionless, her face as barren as the empty landscape. "Yeah. See ya, Nick." She stepped back into the house.

After dinner it began to snow. Flakes swirled in from the night and gathered into small drifts on the porch and on the windowsills around the house.

Lenny reached forward and put a thumb on her bruise. "You don't look too good with that swollen face, Sis. That hurt yet?"

"Ouch! Of course it hurts." She pulled away, reached for a dish, and swished it in the sink a couple of times. The plate was cracked and badly chipped around the edges, hardly useable anymore. Like her.

She placed the worn piece of crockery in the rack and slowly picked up a wet, yellow sponge. She squeezed it several times with dull awareness. The action created thousands of tiny, iridescent blue and purple soap bubbles that slid through her fingers. She leaned forward against the counter and let the sponge fall into the water. Tears came to her eyes. The kitchen window in front of her was black and opaque with the night outside, and she stared into the void. Nothing in her life made a difference anymore. She was used up. If it wasn't a trucker beating on her, it was somebody else.

Juliet let out a long breath and held herself completely still. Sometimes she could find peace this way, a type of quiet inside, but tonight she couldn't seem to unlock whatever it was, to find the right way in. The pulse of her heartbeat was visible on the inside of her left wrist just below the two white scars, and she let her eyes rest on the vein for a moment. The fact that her heart kept beating at all was slightly ridiculous. She shook her head, took a deep breath, and looked back at her brother. "What happened to us?

Lenny leaned back against the counter, eyed her sideways, and worked a fingernail against a bit of a pork chop lodged between his back molars. Juliet had explained flossing, all the things that he should be doing every night, but most nights he forgot. If the tooth ever became loose he could use the doorknob again, but only if it really had to go. He'd tie one end of a string to the knob, and the other end he'd fix around the base of his tooth. This time he'd slam the door himself, and the tooth would fly away. Aunt Doris had plucked four or five teeth out of his head that way and he had hated her for it. He'd stand there and wait while she tied a string around his tooth. Then she would laugh and make jokes and pretend to slam the door while he waited for the sharp instant of pain, and he'd cry and dance around with nervous pee in his seven-year-old body. It was the *anticipation* of the thing that set his nerves a jangling. He realized that now. Back then he was convinced he was just a disappointment to Aunt Doris, and he wanted so much to be good. He'd put a gun to his head before he went through those days again. He took in his sister standing at the sink and frowned. "I don't know. I don't know what happened to us, Sis."

3

Nick Olsen leaned back in his chair, swung his feet up on his desk, and chewed on a yellow, number two pencil. He crushed through the enamel with his incisors, breaking the surface into rows of tiny pits. After each series of punctures he'd inspect the pencil, rotate it a quarter turn, then start the process again. It was an old habit he'd picked up in college. He was a smart man, but he often found that his mental processes were a thing apart; they could somehow work on their own as long as he relaxed, let them go. Right now he was letting them go, and nothing helped the process so much as chewing on a number two lead pencil.

"Nick, we can't hold him," George Murphy said from his desk. His deputy was parked by the corridor leading to the cells. There were only two lockups down the hallway and Butch Kellam was in one of them. "If that girl is not going to press charges, well then, we gotta let him go."

"Her name is Juliet," Olsen said. "And you know that." He tossed the pencil on the desk and looked over at Murphy. The deputy was reading a textbook on contracts, readying for another law school exam at the university extension. The guy was a holdover from the previous sheriff's administration and Olsen had more or less put up with him. Murphy was maybe into law enforcement on a good day. Otherwise, the deputy counted the semesters until his bar exam, while at the same time bragging about his upcoming career as a hot shot lawyer to anyone who would listen.

Olsen knew a thing or two about careers, and there was something decent about working the job at hand.

He stepped to the window. His office was in the back of the county courthouse, and when the sun was bright in the Dakota sky he looked out on a vista of prairie scrub. One thousand acres of that scrub belonged to him, courtesy of his late mother, but his property was a thirty-minute drive from the sheriff's office in Sherwood.

His morning visit to the Blackwell place troubled him. Something nagged at the gut level about the brother and sister at that run-down house. "Murph, what's your take on Doris Blackwell?" He was talking to the window. Snow was beginning to drift down in the night sky, phosphorescing around the hooded pole lamps arcing high overhead. The flakes were small and dry-looking, signifying a clearing weather system coming down from Canada. It would be a cold night, but since he lived alone he was in no hurry to leave. His house was well maintained and snug, and it would be there when he returned.

"Old Lady Blackwell?"

"Yeah, you've known her almost as long as I have." He turned and watched as his deputy closed the outsized legal volume and put some thought into the comment.

"I don't know. An alcoholic, I guess, like a lot of people out here. Don't think we've ever picked her up on a DUI though, so how bad could it be?"

Nick moved back to his desk, leaned against the edge, and picked up the pencil. He twirled it baton-like for a moment in his fingers. "Maybe not so bad, if that's all there is."

"You've got to keep in mind what she's done. She didn't have to take in those good-for-nothing kids years back. She gets credit for that in my book, especially since there was no family around."

"Don't forget her brother in Bismarck. He helped out."

"Lotta good it did," Murphy replied. "You think they would have been raised properly. Looking at those two, I'll tell you, there's something to be said for the 'bad seed' theory."

Nick examined the pencil. There was no smooth place left to bite. "Ever think we might've had it backwards all this time?"

"What do you mean?"

"That Doris is the bad seed, and I mean the really bad seed."

The deputy shook his head slowly. "I don't figure it. Marge got to know her a little during one of Doris' needlepoint workshops a few years back. Said she was always polite to everyone, courteous. Had a hurt and kinda distracted look that would come over her when any reference to the kids came up. You could tell she was torn up by the way they behaved, according to Marge's take on things anyway. Nick, you were away in the army, then your college and med school when all this crap came down the pike. Lenny got thrown in jail for kiting checks, and the girl was a runaway. Had to be hauled back from Canada once, maybe twice."

"I heard it all."

"I know you have. I'm just saying I'd put Doris in the category of a fairly solid citizen."

Nick stared back out the window.

"So what are we going to do about Kellam?" Murphy asked.

"Who?" Nick lost the connection for an instant.

His deputy nodded toward the cellblock and the one prisoner it contained. "Butch Kellam."

"Right. Well, let him go. He can beat up someone in another town, someone else's town." Nick threw down the pencil and grabbed his down parka. He was through for the night.

Nick Olsen poured steaming coffee into a big mug and took it out to his enclosed porch. The area off the kitchen was originally screened, which opened it to the weather. He gave up on the cold breezes whistling through years ago. Now the porch was as warm as the rest of the house. He took a sip of coffee and looked out of the glassed enclosure. At six o'clock in the morning the light was steel gray from a sun not yet above the horizon. Snow was on the ground. He calculated three, four inches. Not enough yet to cause serious problems for the county, and he doubted they would get much more. The blanket effect of the white powder was soothing as long as one didn't own livestock.

He had thought about downsizing. The four bedrooms and roomy living areas were way too much for a single guy with no kids, and he doubted now that he'd ever have any. The legacy from his parents was large in terms of house and land, but when it arrived he had already left medical school and was in the middle of a divorce.

His father died first, a heart attack sitting in the air-conditioned cab of his John Deere 7600. With no income from the farm and his loans already maxed to the limit Nick had to cash out of med school in the middle of his final year, either that or lose the property. He came home to work the place for his mom, but within two years she was gone. She was not quite old, and in his opinion, still attractive for her age. She just didn't want to stay without her husband of thirty-five years. That was the best way he could think about it.

He blew a breath on the coffee and took another sip. Two deer were in a copse of trees a hundred yards from the house. They were camouflaged, but he could see the flick of their white tails as they pranced up and down with nervous energy. Early morning was the time of day for them. They'd be holed up and invisible in another hour.

He still carried a small amount of resentment at the way life had thrown a crowbar into the works. He tamped it down inside, tried not to let it grow into something larger. Med school was fascinating. He had been a determined and thoughtful student at the university, and he would have made a good doctor. He shook his head, exhaled with a small grunt, and let it ride again. Life was tricky enough without carting around a full load of bitterness on his shoulders.

And then there was Mary, a young woman with a sturdy, traditional name. However, his ill-chosen love was not sturdy or traditional or durable. This one was blond and willowy, and had a marvelous knack for covertly attaching herself to him in the most intimate manner, while in the most public places. Her behavior titillated and thrilled him. Why wouldn't it? He was only twenty-four, maybe twenty-five at the time.

He met her shortly after entering med school. She followed him on a bet and married him in his second year when the odds looked even better. Mary felt double-crossed, was how she put it, when he abruptly had to say goodbye to his future in medicine. He told her it was only temporary, that he'd finish out his remaining year when things were better at home. His new bride didn't believe him. Maybe she saw it coming, or maybe she was just playing the odds once again. At any rate, she hadn't planned on being a farmer's wife, and she never came out to the place. Not once.

So he reacted, kept his feelings inward and close, and maybe he was still in that zone somewhere. Fifty percent of marriages ended up just like his, or so he'd read, and that lessened the load slightly. In retrospect, he was more fascinated by the ability of a woman to divine what a man wanted and project those qualities that were necessary. He had been absolutely convinced of her love, a love that was never there. Looking back from his mid-thirties, he concluded that he'd been affected by her desertion more than he liked to admit. Nowadays, he was content to maintain a certain emotional distance from women. He had female friends in one or two of the larger cities in the state, women who at first welcomed the romantic connection, and only later grudgingly accepted his infrequent visits. The relationships never achieved any permanence.

Coffee was cooling in the cup, and he took a larger swallow. The medical books were still on the shelves: Guyton's *Textbook of Medical Physiology*, Moore's *Clinical Anatomy*, and others that were almost as heavy. He read through them from time to time, trying to keep the academics from slipping away. He kept telling himself he was going back to finish someday. Was he dreaming or lying to himself? They said it was never too late. Too late for what? And who were 'they'? Life was full of total bullshit sometimes. He finished his coffee. It was time to think about breakfast.

The sun hung just below the frigid Dakota horizon lightening the eastern sky with a milky-gray dawning. Juliet was wrapped in a thick wool blanket in the downstairs parlor. She had found a way into her quiet place, her best place. When she was younger she had tried to explain her special ability to leave. She could not find the right words, and even her best girlfriend never understood. It was a lot like sleeping, she said, only it wasn't. A small part of her was awake, but most of her was hidden inside a soft, cushiony place that no one could reach. She didn't tell her friend that she would go there when he came to visit.

When Clifford first stayed over she was young, not yet twelve years old, and she screamed and cried and begged, but he just stared with a feverish expression as he held her down. Then one day she just learned to leave. She went to a different place in her mind, somewhere away from what was happening to her, and that was how she found her place.

The room was bright with sunlight when she at last opened her eyes. The house had gone cold but she was warm inside the blanket. She pulled it tighter about her and absorbed the quiet tranquility of the room. She felt clean, refreshed, like what she imagined she would feel from a good night's sleep at a fancy resort with a nice big bed and lots of pillows. She touched her neck and flattened a palm in front of her throat, just as she remembered him doing. She could do that on a morning like this, when it was sunny and clear and the evil seemed to be gone from the old place. She pressed her thumb and fingers lightly in the soft hollows above her clavicle. This was the place where he would grab her and squeeze, and make her move up against him so he could press his sweaty hardness into her again and again. Once, Clifford almost choked her into unconsciousness. Doris was mad that time, and gave her some hot soup when she came around. She chased her brother out of the house.

Afterward though, Doris had hovered above her with a gray, pinched face and eyes as flat and soulless as a shark's. "Didn't mean for my brother to be so rough on ya, honey," she said with barely concealed irritation. "But, Juliet, you just gotta help out around here. That big boy…and that's all he really is, honey, just a boy. Nothin' to be scared of. He gives me a good bit of money to keep the place running, to put food on the table. And it's not too much if every once in a while I ask you to do something nice for him."

"He didn't have to hurt me so," she sobbed. She'd felt all bruised and dirty lower down. Tears ran down her face.

"Well now…" The woman placed a veined and liver-stained hand on top of hers, gave her a squeeze and a soft pat. "Maybe it's best when you finish that soup, if you go up and draw a hot bath. It'll make you feel better. You can stay in there 'til supper if you want."

Juliet rubbed a knuckle in her eyes. She had painted her fingernails light blue, a robin's egg color that she loved. She'd taken time to make small, squiggly lines over the polish. "What about Lenny? He didn't do anything. Uncle Cliffy was just mean to him." She could hear her brother crying upstairs.

Her aunt's face took on more severe lines. "That young boy's just gotta learn. He can't be making noise and trying to look in on you when uncle Cliffy wants his time and privacy with you. I've told him that before, and he just can't seem to get it straight."

God. Would those memories ever go away? Another ten, twenty years with those ugly episodes lingering like a black shadow? She remembered her uncle's last visit, when he tried to put his hands on her. She was bigger and stronger and she kicked out, caught Cliffy in the midsection, then in the face. He backed away, but afterward Doris made her pay. She was locked in her room. After a week she managed to escape through a dormer window. That was the first time she ran away. She discovered Canada wasn't that far from her lockup in North Dakota.

Juliet gathered the blanket around her and walked barefoot over the cold floor and up the stairs to her old room. Lenny's door was open and she looked in. He was asleep with his mouth open. Her brother couldn't breathe through his nose very well, hadn't been able to for a long time. He'd taken the worst of it as a boy. Even when he did everything Clifford wanted he still beat him, usually after he finished with her.

Her room was as cold as the rest of the house, but she still had warm winter clothes left over in the closet and plenty of hot water for a long bath. And that made a good start to the morning.

4

Doris Blackwell unglued her tongue from the roof of her mouth. After a carton of cigarettes and at least three complimentary bottles of Chivas over as many days, the action was akin to pulling apart a strip of Velcro. She attempted to breathe without moving. Her head was a block of pain. She cracked an eyelid and allowed her focus to wander around the beige prison-cell of a room that the casino had set aside for her. A pastel print of a sailboat—a crazed notion in this land-locked universe—was plastered inside a matted frame hanging from the opposite wall. The corners of the misplaced nautical scene moved clockwise in a dizzy shuttle until she opened her other eyelid and stabilized the motion.

She reached slowly and with excruciating discomfort toward the opposite side of the bed. Why the Tylenol had been placed on that side was a mystery until she took in the thick smudge of makeup on the adjacent pillow. Okay. The cocktail waitress. So what? She was over seventy years old, and by God she was going to take what she could get, especially since the casino assholes put her in this position in the first place.

She chewed through four tablets and washed the slurry down her throat with a glass of water. She was broke, truly broke. A day or two of rest was necessary. Hell, she could barely make her way to the john the shape she was in. In a few days she was going to lean on Cliffy, sit on his shoulders if she had to, remind him personally how much he owed her. He had lots of money and that was all that mattered.

Clifford Blackwell was waiting for cocktail hour. He was parked facing floor-to-ceiling casement windows in the corner library of a very exclusive nursing home. Ice pellets riding freezing downdrafts swirled toward the building and peppered the glass. Would sleet or more snow follow? He couldn't care less. The more pertinent question was why he had never purchased a condo in Miami, maybe something nice on the Bay of Biscayne. A little bare skin walking around wouldn't hurt either. At least it would give him something nice to look at.

He was accustomed to quite a bit more freedom than he was currently experiencing. The nose cannula was a pain in the ass, but worse was dragging the fucking oxygen canister behind his electric wheelchair, room to room, hallway to veranda, veranda to cafeteria, and so forth. Unfortunately, without the aggravating device close by he could barely breathe, and wouldn't for very much longer, according to the quacks in the nursing home. Didn't make much difference. If he could get his hands on a good Cubana cigar he'd smoke it and to hell with the consequences.

"Mr. Blackwell?" The voice behind him belonged to the irritating nurse who, on occasion, wiped his ass. She was none too gentle during the process.

"What?" His voice always came out pinched-sounding when the cannula was inserted.

"You have a visitor."

"Who?" He would be damned if he'd turn around and look at the witch.

"A Mr. Rhinehart. He said you were expecting him."

He toggled a switch on the chair and one wheel spun backward a full revolution. The contraption turned him around in a half circle and Ida Smith's unsightly countenance swam into view. She wore a stupid white cap that put him in mind of a busboy in an old-fashioned diner. The connection wasn't that farfetched, since she also doubled slinging hash in the cafeteria. Hopefully, it wasn't right after wiping his ass. He attempted to blank the thought. "I wasn't expecting him," he replied. "But I'll see him."

"He's in the Discovery Room. Would you like me to wheel you in?"

"I think I can manage to discover the Discovery Room all by myself," he said as he pressed the hand lever on the scooter. The voltage from the battery beneath his seat shot into the small engine and rotated the rear wheels at the maximum rate, which was not quite the speed of a normal walking pace. He roared from the library in a cloud of irritation, and certainly faster than the nursing staff permitted. Screw them. If only he could have spun a wheelie, laid a slick trail of rubber underneath Ida's horsey, black medical shoes, maybe she would have slipped and busted her pointy chin.

A whiff of lemon-scented disinfectant failed to cover the acrid spoor of urine that hit him as he cruised past a gated hallway to his right: The Memory Ward. This purgatory warehoused a group of lost souls who backed into the hereafter without knowing who they were, where they came from, or when their last carnal experience took place. He had seen the inside corridor when the double doors sometimes swung wide. The walls were covered with stark geometric figures. Circles and rectangles and triangles were painted in dazzling primary colors: reds and blues and yellows, all in obvious attempts to shock the fried neurons of the mindless inhabitants, to reboot the systems, so to speak. No thanks. He'd rather die of a heart attack, and he probably would since that event often accompanied death by emphysema.

The Discovery Room was richly appointed. Leather-clad sofas clung to the four walls. They were guarded by glass-top tables positioned like sand bunkers in front of manicured putting greens. Someone in charge of this ridiculous enterprise had to be a failed golfer.

His lawyer, wearing a typical black pinstriped suit, sat behind a ream of papers. Small rimless spectacles rested midway down the bridge of his sharp nose. He had the look of a ferret.

"Clifford! Glad to see you." The attorney came to his feet and held out his hand.

"Donald." Clifford extended an arm. He was actually pleased to see the man, an individual who in all probability remained as his sole friend on the planet. "You're early for drinks."

"I know. I called your room several times. The front desk told me you were usually in the library." He glanced about and made an apologetic sound. "I won't ask how you've been."

"I'll tell you anyway. Shitty."

Rhinehart grinned. "We've got to remember the good times, and there were plenty of those."

"Mostly courtesy of my trust money," Clifford stated.

The lawyer coughed lightly and returned to his position behind the table. He sank into the front edge of the sofa cushion and nodded at the documents. "Yes…well, remember, Cliff. The trust belongs to the Driscoll twins, not you. You're just the successor trustee. At any rate, that's why I came out today."

Clifford motored his chair forward and eyed the clutter arranged with colored paper clips. He shrugged. "What's to discuss?"

Rhinehart shuffled some pages and pointed to an underlined paragraph. "Do you recall that Juliet and Lenny will both be reaching thirty years of age on the fifteenth of May? That's a little over three months from now."

"Who gives a shit?"

"You should. Let me read this paragraph: 'After the children or the surviving child reaches the age of thirty, the Trustee shall distribute all or any remaining portion of the trust to the children or to the surviving child, and in such manner and proportions as the aforesaid may appoint from time to time by instructions signed by said children or surviving child.'"

Clifford ran a hand over his face. He was pleased that a white growth of stubble nearly covered the red spider webs of broken blood vessels that mapped his features. His normally fleshy cheeks had given way to a leaner vision of himself, thanks in part to the faux prime rib that Ida slopped on his plate. He had noticed during mealtimes that his fellow diners received much larger portions, ones that actually had the look of prime beef.

"You with me on this, Cliff?"

He threw a glance at the ceiling as a sign of annoyance. "Is this a problem? You've handled everything before."

Rhinehart seemed to choose his words. "What we've done before is use the latitude given to us legally by the original trustee, your brother Jonas, in accordance with the stipulations the Driscoll parents wrote into the document before they were killed in the plane crash." He cleared his throat. "When your brother nominated you as his *successor trustee* in the event he predeceased the Driscoll children, your rights under the trust agreement were the same as his. The fact that we interpreted those rights differently is not relevant."

"So can't we somehow get around this...difficulty? I'd hate to see all my trust money go to those kids."

Rhinehart injected a bit of the courtroom into his voice. "Once again, Cliff, it's not your money. It never was. Your ability to spend it was granted by one paragraph in the document, and I'll refresh your memory: 'The Trustee's discretion may be exercised for such purposes as the Trustee shall deem reasonable and appropriate for the welfare, enjoyment, and education of the beneficiaries'." He reclined against the back cushion. "We've interpreted that very liberally, as you know. Think of your huge house, for instance."

Clifford's voice rose with a sucking sound from the cannula. "The kids lived there for a while."

The lawyer smiled. "For two months, only for two months until you talked your sister into taking them. But that's okay. One could still argue that the money went for their benefit. You could easily testify that you had no way of knowing they would end up at Doris'."

"Who said anything about testifying?"

"I doubt it would ever come to that. For one thing, their counsel would have to prove that the funds you withdrew were not in any way tied to their welfare. Considering you never kept an account of anything that would be difficult in the extreme."

A smile squatted in Clifford's white stubble. "I remember a couple of cute, Spanish girls who gave us really good accounts of our activities that golf weekend in Columbia."

Rhinehart contrived a small grin. "As I said, we did have some good times."

For a long moment neither spoke. Then, "Am I right in assuming the Driscoll kids have no knowledge of this trust?" Rhinehart asked. "Would your sister have ever mentioned anything?

"Hah! Not on your life, Donald. This has been kept completely secret. Hell, I'm not even sure the kids know their real names."

"Their birth certificates and social security cards would have the name Driscoll. Doesn't the girl work somewhere?"

"Yeah. I dunno. They were the Blackwell twins in school. I know that much. If the Driscoll name registers...well, who in the hell knows what they think?"

"Well, from the legal end there is no way they would have any knowledge of this inheritance. Normally, they would have been required to sign off when you exercised your 'withdrawal rights', in other words, when you took money from the trust. However...let me find it here. It states: 'If the child is under legal disability, such withdrawal rights may be exercised on behalf of such child by a writing signed by the guardian of the estate.' You are the guardian of the estate, Cliff. And if you remember—"

"We made a big withdrawal when Lenny was in jail that time."

Rhinehart nodded. "As your attorney, I *suggested* you make the withdrawal. The boy was certainly under a legal disability."

"And when that little slut Juliet ran away..."

The lawyer tipped his head again. "Same thing, and if you recall, she ran away twice. That made a total of three big withdrawals that set you up rather nicely, I believe."

Clifford brightened for an instant before his features clouded. "But…so you're saying it all ends in a few months?"

"I think one could reasonably argue that I've provided as good a service as anyone could hope for in their wildest fantasies."

Clifford glanced at his watch. "Donald, let me buzz for a drink. They usually come right around, unless some of the bitches who don't like me are on duty."

Rhinehart stood and gathered his papers into a neat square. "Have to be some other time, Cliff. I've got another appointment. That's why I came early."

He was lying. Clifford knew it and he was aware that Rhinehart saw it in his eyes. He backed a quarter turn on the wheelchair. "Okay, then. Mind if I pose a hypothetical question?"

Rhinehart snapped the clutch on his briefcase and straightened. "Don't go there, Cliff. I know what you're thinking, and that's way outside the realm of my consideration. Period."

"I'm just asking." The cannula made his voice sound whiny again.

The lawyer ran a hand over his mostly bald scalp and looked down at the wheelchair. "Your brother Jonas—"

"He was a candy-ass lawyer."

"Doesn't matter. He was the Driscoll's closest friend and executor of their estate, and because of that relationship he was made the *contingent beneficiary*."

"Which means?"

"It means that had the Driscoll twins *both* experienced untimely deaths, and there was no *per stirpes* heir—"

"You mean no children."

"Correct. If the twins died leaving no children, then your brother would have inherited the mining company."

"But he's dead. The mining company was sold."

"Which is a long way around explaining that *you*, as the surviving trustee, will inherit the entire worth of the estate through your brother's relationship as the contingent beneficiary, *if* the twins predecease you before they turn thirty: if they die within the next three months. Is that what you're asking?"

Clifford bobbed his head and offered a look of thoughtful contemplation. "I was curious, is all."

"That's after all of the legal technicalities are resolved. Clear?"

"What about Doris?"

"She doesn't get anything, unless and until you die. Then she gets the trust if you own it."

"That's kind of what I thought."

"But hell, Cliff. Months, even years could elapse before anything like this would be settled out." He glanced away. "And you've got, well you know about how much time you've got left."

"Could be I'll last a lot longer than anyone thinks, you included, my friend."

5

Juliet wrapped an arm around a mini-bucket of beer—six bottles on ice dubbed the 'Crossroads Special'—and held the weight against her hip. She moved through a thin film of cigarette smoke. The haze wasn't as thick as in previous years, but the heavy atmosphere still left a stale, charcoal smell in her hair after a night's work.

Her jaw was not as sore as it had been, even though the bruises had turned yellow-brown. The coloration was hidden by a small amount of moisturizer and cream beige concealer, not that anyone could see much in the dim light. At eleven in the evening the Crossroads Saloon was a dark pit of spilled beer and peanut hulls.

She was bound for a table squared by four guys in jeans and parkas. They mainly wanted beer, but they'd cop a feel if they could get one. She had been pinched on the butt once during the evening, but she wore tight jeans and nothing much registered. In two hours her shift would be over. The night's work could actually be termed pleasant.

She deposited the bucket in front of the mullet head in the red parka. He'd paid for the last two, and he was obviously the leader of the pack. The man had a sullen expression as he hummed to a slow-moving dirge by Brooks and Dunn, something about whiskey and a lost love that was jacked up way loud on the overheads.

He looked up, seemed to take her in for a moment, and slid a hand around her waist. "Tell me you're free after the place closes," he said over the music.

She grabbed his arm and tried to swing away, but he held her.

"Not free and not interested," she said. "So you may as well let me go." She smiled and tried to be coy and pleasant. Guys typically just fooled around with her, strut their shit in front of their friends, did the macho thing.

The mullet head tightened his grip and pulled her in close. Her breast touched his shoulder. "I don't see no ring," he said with a grin. "You got a boyfriend? Bet I could whop his ass."

A round of laughter came from his tablemates. That was it. Mullet Head was damn near nuzzling her belly button the way she was cinched to his chest. She leaned into him, felt his arms relax—they always did that—and jerked away with a quick twist. She exhaled forcefully and managed a smile. "I'm sure that gets you laid all the time. You're so romantic and all. I'm just not your girl tonight."

The smile slid from his face. She watched his eyes flick to the others and return to hers. "You didn't answer, miss. You got a boyfriend?"

"None of your business, actually." Why did she always get these jerks in her face? "Now if you'll pay me for the bucket I'll be nice and bring you guys some more peanuts."

His arm flashed forward, a quick attempt to retake his prize. She parried with a faster half step to the side. Laughter came from the table again, but this time it was directed at Mullet Head.

He scraped his chair backward and came to his feet. "You're supposed to be nice to the customers." He was not smiling.

She gave him a stance, hands on her hips. "What? I'm supposed to go home with you because you're the answer to my dreams." She laughed. "That'll be the day."

He stepped toward her and she didn't back away. "What's your name, sweetie?"

"You're the last person who gets that."

He grabbed her arm. She yelped and tried to spin away. One of the guys at the table stood and slurred a laugh. "Hey, Tooley, let her go, for God's sake. There are plenty of other cunts around."

"Pete!" Juliet yelled in the direction of the bar.

A man with an average build emerged from behind a steaming row of dripping mugs. He dried his hands on a towel and tossed it behind his shoulders without taking his eyes from the group of men.

She tried to pull away again. Her captor tightened his grip until his fingers dug into her flesh. This time she screamed and the crowd in the saloon went quiet. Brooks and Dunn moaned through the hushed atmosphere in the room, still crying over their whiskey.

Pete approached with nothing in his hands. He didn't need anything. Juliet had seen him take down guys much larger and meaner than the individual planted in front of her. Her boss had once confessed to being in the military. He'd mentioned Iraq a time or two, but never said more. All she knew was that he was quick and knew where to hit a man.

The guy named Tooley shoved Juliet roughly to the side, and she turned to see him hold his palms upward in the picture of innocence.

Pete stepped up to the larger man and stuck a finger in his chest. "You boys are outta here, like, right now." His voice had a rough tenor, as if he had fine bits of gravel in his vocal cords.

The big man tried to slap his hand away and failed. "We got a bucket of beer to finish, so I reckon we'll just do that."

Pete smiled. "I reckon you won't."

Tooley appeared to assess the bar manager, as if he might consider a move. There was something. Juliet never quite got it, but guys seemed to know, man to man, who had the most steel inside. Pete had lots of it.

"Hey Tooley! No big deal man. Let's go." His buddies obviously sensed the uneven balance of power.

Tooley took a step backward and formed a smile that held no humor. "Next time then, I guess we'll see." He poked a finger toward Juliet. "You be careful, little girl. I'll see you again some time."

Juliet rubbed her upper arm and watched the humbled procession step toward the exit with an exaggerated swagger. The Tooley asshole turned and pointed toward her once more as he went through the door.

The crowd came back to life. A new song blasted from the speakers. Toby Keith was up and running now. Conversations returned to the subjects of truck tires and the oil boom that was just starting to rock and roll.

Pete remained close as a woman detached herself from the end of the bar and came up behind him. He nodded at her over his shoulder. "I think we're okay here, Darlene."

She stepped around him. "Juliet, can I help you, honey?"

"I'm all right. I'll probably have some bruises on my upper arm by tomorrow."

Pete looked closely at Juliet. "You want to finish out your shift? The crowd's starting to thin. You can call it a night if you want."

"Go on home, honey," Darlene said. "After that deadbeat hit you last week an' all. You've been through it lately, and that's a fact."

Juliet rubbed her arm and looked from one to the other. She shrugged.

"Tell you what," Pete said. "I'll take you home." When she started to object he cut her off. "Nope. Let's do it my way. If those guys happen to catch you out there by yourself…well, we don't want to take that chance. I'll even let Darlene time your card out when she leaves. That way you get the last couple of hours."

"I don't know."

He smiled. "That means you do know." And to Darlene, "Won't be long. I'll be back to close. Tell Hank to keep an eye out for those boys."

"I'll get my coat, I guess," Juliet said. "Thanks."

A few minutes later Juliet crunched over the frozen gravel in the parking lot. The cold air was sobering, even though she hadn't been drinking. How anyone maintained a buzz in these temperatures was a mystery. "What about my car?" she asked. Her ten-year-old Ford sat in the far corner of the lot.

"Give me your keys. I'll get Hank or Darlene to move it tomorrow. We'll figure something out."

She withdrew a jangle of keys from a small shoulder bag and detached one. "You're a good boss, Pete. I wanted to tell you that." She pulled her down parka tighter around her.

A moment later in the car, "And you're a good employee," he said to her, "And a friend. I want to tell you that." He switched on the headlights and put the vehicle in motion. Twin cones of white light stabbed through a black void and reflected off muddied snowdrifts on the shoulders of the pavement. The wheels crushed plate-sized fragments of frozen slush that would stay on the road until spring.

Her apartment sat on the northern outskirts of Minot, maybe forty-five minutes from the Crossroads Saloon. An industrial looking, two-story, brick rectangle was subdivided into twenty-four units. The structure originally housed transient crewmen from the big Air Force base nearby. Big jet bombers supposedly carrying nuclear weapons flew over once in a while, but the government for whatever reason was no longer in need of that particular housing unit. Her two-bedroom dwelling on the top level was not a perfect solution to her needs, but there were no perfect solutions, and the place kept her warm and reasonably comfortable. She turned in the seat and gave her boss directions.

He nodded. "I'll drop you off, wait till you're inside, then head on back."

There was no traffic. A silence came between them, a lapse of conversation that seemed to fit with the blank nothingness outside the white beam of the headlights.

After several miles of rough pavement Pete said, "You do draw a crowd, Juliet. I'll give you that. The good guys and the bad guys."

"Is it the way I'm dressed? I can wear baggier stuff."

He laughed lightly. "You look fine. If you don't mind my saying so, you've got a little bottom to die for. A great ass, as they say. That's not lost on anyone, Juliet, especially me. And you're nice to look at in other ways."

"Yeah. Thanks. Guess that's what gets me in trouble sometimes." She turned toward him and caught the dull blue reflection of the dashboard illumination on his features. "How come you've never made a pass at me, Pete?" She was not especially attracted to him, but the curiosity was there.

He shrugged. "Maybe it's best if we don't get into personals."

"Okay." Then after a moment, "I know you're not gay, not with you and Darlene living together."

The whirring drum of snow tires on rough pavement filled the empty space of another long silence. Juliet focused straight ahead and tried to peer over the bloom of the lights.

"I've heard things," he said finally.

Her stomach plunged. She tried to keep the thump of her pulse out of her voice. Was he referring to what happened a hundred years ago? He could not possibly know about that. No one could. "You could be more specific, Pete."

"Like you're a complicated person."

"That doesn't tell me much. Aren't most people complicated?"

He cleared his throat. "Maybe, but first things first. I'm not gay. I think Darlene would attest to it."

"Yeah. I was just… So, what have you heard?"

He went quiet for a while. She decided he wasn't going to answer the question.

"That you're—it's hard to explain," he finally said. "Maybe that you really don't want anything to do with men."

"I don't follow. I go with guys once in a while. You know…sex."

"Yeah, but I've heard it's like—remember playing with little magnets? Ever do that as a kid?"

She nodded in the dark. "I guess."

"When you touch the ends one way they really pull together. And then when you reverse the ends they push apart. Well, I'm told that's how you are with men. Once you're satisfied, well, it's like you swap ends of the magnet. I've heard you're out the door almost before the man finishes." He drummed his fingers lightly on the wheel. "Then you dodge your partner afterwards, never want to see him again."

She felt as if she was slipping inside. "Everyone has their own—"

"That's why I've never made a pass. I'd love to, Juliet—I mean, if I wasn't with Darlene. But you'd take off afterward for whatever reason and I'd lose you from the saloon. You'd never want to see me again, let alone work around the bar once we had sex."

"You've heard an awful lot, Pete."

"I run a bar."

She focused straight ahead. Thank God he couldn't read her face in the dark, or sense the shamble of her emotions as she strained to appear calm.

"And I want to keep my good employees," he said. "You bring in a good crowd. Besides, as far as sex goes, I'm not sure any interest on your part has ever really been there."

Wetness leaked from an eye. She turned her head to the side and touched her eyelash with a forefinger. Later, when she was alone, she could curl into a ball on her sofa and let everything bubble up again. Tears might run, although they didn't run for long anymore.

Ten minutes later they tracked through the rime-covered asphalt of her parking area. Curtained windows blocked patterns of diffused light in the units. People were indoors on a night like this.

Pete was as good as his word, a knight in shining armor. Maybe someday she could find one for herself. He watched until she turned the key in the door. She gave him a wave.

Later, she sat immobile in the dark. She stared through the partially curtained window and observed the yellow-orange streetlamps casting circles of light on the cold pavement of the parking lot.

Tears came, but not so many. Did that mean she was hardened now, or just exhausted trying to figure herself out? She assumed it was possible to love a man, truly love a man someday and have children, have the life that other woman had as part of a natural progression, something accepted as a given. Yet for her it did not seem to be a given, and she had no clear understanding why it was not. Counseling was off the planet, even if she had the money. Whatever person she would become was going to be up to her. Somewhere she would have to find the strength for that.

She showered off the smell of beer and cigarettes and felt better. A light scrub with a cellulose sponge cleansed the pores in her face. She applied a blow dryer to her hair and brushed through her shoulder-length auburn strands. Her cut was longish in the back, but long was better than too short. She could go for another two weeks.

Lenny's hair was a shade lighter than hers, and she had always wanted to trade. She wouldn't swap her eyes, though. Hers were light gray with flecks of green, always a pleasant reflection when she put on makeup. Lenny's eyes were dark brown and they made him look dull. She sighed. He didn't need that.

Thanks to the tussle at the bar she was home earlier than usual. Sleep would be a long time coming, but tomorrow was Sunday, a day of sloth. She slipped on a T-shirt and panties, threw on a robe, and padded toward the kitchenette. A glass of wine was definitely required on this evening, and she spied an unopened box of Pinot Grigio tucked inside the refrigerator door. Pete allowed employees to take wine or beer home from the saloon stocks occasionally. Juliet didn't abuse the system, and when she squirreled a bar freebie under her arm every so often he never said anything. This one had been in the fridge for two or three weeks, maybe longer, and the time had come to cut into the container. She snipped the top and leveled chilled wine one-third from the top of a fifteen-ounce tumbler.

Turner Classics featured the umpteenth rerun of *Casablanca*. After fifteen minutes Juliet realized she was bored. There was work to do, a problem to solve. She stepped into her bedroom. A straight-back, cushioned chair arranged in front of a small table and fast computer comprised her workstation. A nudge on the mouse brought the screen to life.

Years before, she had taken to working Sudoku puzzles, but she eventually found the exercises too easy, even ones in the hard categories. For a while she had been solving equations in physics. An unlikely online course provided by the state university gave her the escape she needed, an opportunity to grind against an obstacle that required no emotion and no feeling, just the application of an analytical process that sharpened her intellect. She was becoming better at toppling the intricate equations of fluid dynamics that the course syllabus required. The process created a pathway for a college degree, although to think of herself as an accomplished individual with a degree in engineering seemed a stretch. In any case, dealing with Torricelli's Theorem gave her the mental relief she needed.

The current problem involved something clean, something straightforward, and something that only had one solution. She had to determine the volume of oil, in cubic meters, discharged from an eight-centimeter outflow pipe exiting the bottom of a tank twenty-five meters high.

Math was a language of absolutes. Plug a square root function into one side of an *equals* symbol and one could rock and roll with the problem until the numbers popped like cherries in a slot machine. Only in this case there was no luck involved.

Thirty minutes later she emailed her solution and received an immediate green confirmation. Seldom anymore did the program throw back her equations with a burst of red corrections. Juliet gave herself high-five and exited the program. She'd forgotten all about the wine, and with three large swallows she put the contents of her glass and herself to bed.

6

Nick Olsen was south of the crossroads. He could've slept in and wanted to. However, someone had to come out on duty this morning. Two of his deputies were on vacation, the others had family responsibilities: church on Sunday morning, and probably bacon and pancakes stacked on a big platter with the dog licking the leftovers.

The accident, if one could call it that, was not something that either driver was too upset about. The pickup was just off the pavement with a damaged front bumper. The trailer rig was hulking motionless in the road, slightly ahead of the impact area. Its big diesel engine was ticking over in a lazy rhythm, punctuated by the hiss of the airbrake now and then. The scene was tranquil as traffic accidents go.

The EMT wagon was there with three medical techs he had known for years. Emma made rolling motions and pointed to his window as his cruiser crunched to a stop in the snow.

"Nick, sorry to even call you out on this one." She leaned on the Dodge Durango and puffed out a lungful of condensation. A handful of snowflakes swirled through the open window.

"That's what I'm paid for Emma," he said. He leaned forward to get a better view. "Where are the drivers? Anybody hurt?"

"Nah." She straightened and turned towards the trailer rig. Emma was a big woman. She'd come down the pipeline from heavy, Swedish stock. Her father had been a huge man, a pro football player back in the day. Standing the way she was, Emma completely blocked his view of the accident. "That's Wilber

Clarke's pickup," she said pointing. "He's sitting in the trailer cab with the trucker."

"I'd better have a look-see." Olsen ran the window back up, hauled himself out of the car, and closed the door. He checked the drivers alongside Emma, examined the plates, licenses, registration, and ran everything through the state database. He made a brief assessment of fault. That was not difficult. Wilber's pickup had run up the back of the trucker's rig, and he admitted as much.

Olsen tramped back toward the vehicles with Emma. The other techs were already in the wagon when he picked up the radio squelch on his portable. He thumbed the transmitter. "Sheriff Olsen here."

"Nick, Pete Haskett at the 'Roads Saloon got me at home. Someone slit the tires—all four of them—on a car in his lot. Gotta be vandals. I can take it if you want."

Nick recognized his deputy's voice. "Your kids up yet?"

"Nah, and Marge and I are gonna try and get 'em ready for services."

"You going to church?" He'd never pegged Murphy as a religious man.

"Nah. Marge is gonna take 'em."

"So go to church with them, George. Make the world a better place. I'll check out the Crossroads."

"Thanks, Nick. Later."

He turned to Emma. "Can you and Jimmy finish here? I've got to ride up to the Crossroads Saloon. Pete Haskett's got a problem."

She stopped and pulled back her parka hood halfway. Snowflakes melted on her plump cheeks. "Anything we can do?"

"Nope. Just try and enjoy your Sunday."

The parking lot of the Crossroads Saloon held two automobiles. One was a black, stiff-shouldered Ford pickup with oversized tires. The vehicle sat nosed to the front awning of the entrance, engine running. An individual opened the driver-side door and gave a backhanded wave as Nick pulled into the lot.

The cloud of white exhaust from the truck's tailpipe disappeared. A moment later Pete Haskett climbed down from his perch and walked to Nick's open side door.

"Didn't mean for you to have to come out, Nick." He extended his hand. "I called your deputy for this one."

Nick stretched, stamped in the snow. The emergency dispatchers were located in Bismarck and ran two counties. Local residents often cut through the bureaucracy and called public safety officers directly. He briefly gripped the other man's open hand. "I was already on the road. It didn't make sense to shake anyone else out of something warm and cozy."

"I know what you mean," Haskett said. He cocked his head. "Nice moves with that troublemaker last week. Don't think I've ever seen you take down a guy."

"I wasn't Special Forces but I picked up enough. And anyway, it's not that hard when they're beating up on women and swinging wild. Gets my blood going pretty fast."

Haskett nodded. "Think I'd agree with that. Where you been keeping yourself? I hadn't seen you much, until a couple nights ago, anyway. We did that turkey shoot last fall."

"I'm wearing a path from Sherwood to my place outside Park City. I can't seem to find time for much else." In Nick's opinion, Pete Haskett was one of the good guys. He ran a decent operation, made a little money doing so, and his employees liked him. Maybe that was the main thing. They'd swapped backgrounds years before, had a few beers together, and waited for a deeper friendship to develop that somehow never did. Their military backgrounds kept them close, easy with each other, while their separate vocational paths just fenced them off, was how Nick figured things.

"Doc, why don't you come by once in a while for a few drinks and a bag of peanuts. You won't drive off the customers."

Haskett was the only person in North Dakota that referred to him by his sidetracked ambition. Nick took it as a measure of respect, because he knew that's how it was offered. He grinned a little. "Maybe I'll sneak in around closing time. People will be leaving then."

"Hell, we'll keep the place open. Regulars would love that."

"I'd like to do it, Pete. And I will."

"Deal. And thanks again for your help the other night with that asshole. We get four or five of those a year and nothing's gonna change that."

Nick nodded at a weather-beaten Ford Taurus mashed into the pavement at the far corner of the lot. "You had another one last night, judging from the look of things."

They stepped toward the car. "That's Juliet Blackwell's. The poor gal just can't seem to dodge trouble. A guy tried to make a move on her again last night. She didn't like it. I had to shoo 'em out. They didn't like that either."

"The four tires are slashed. Guess they got their revenge." Nick moved closer. The damage was worse than that.

"Look at the hood. It's sprung," Haskett said. "That's trouble."

Nick nodded. "That means the boys tore up something inside." He grasped the cold steel latch and hoisted the dented sheet of metal covering the engine. A grating, metallic screech accompanied the movement." He peered at the remains of a once functional V-6 engine.

"They took a crowbar to everything, looks like," Haskett said.

Nick blew out a breath. "Car's definitely toasted. I'll call the tow truck, but Sammy won't come out till later. Sunday morning, and all." He let the hood drop with a clang. "Don't guess you saw anything? Video cameras?' He looked around.

"Afraid not. Been meaning to install them."

"Well then, there's not much we can prove, even if you suspect who did it."

"They must've come back after we closed. Juliet's was the only car on the lot. I was a little worried after I chased them out, so I gave her a ride to her place. They had to have been watching."

"I'll go by and talk to her, take a statement. At least I can fill out an offense report. It'll give her a case number for insurance," Nick said.

"You know where she lives?"

"The Blackwell place up north. I was there last week."

Haskett shook his head. "Then you must have caught her there by chance. She lives toward Minot now. Has an apartment near the military base."

He said, "Maybe I'd better call first. Has she got a cell?"

"Yeah, but I don't have the number. I can get it from a co-worker." Haskett glanced at his watch. "I'll have to wake up Darlene, but it'll give her a good excuse to get up on this beautiful Sunday morning."

"She'll hate you." Nick smiled.

Haskett caught his eyes with a glance. "Actually she loves me."

"Morning, Juliet," Nick said into the phone. He tried for a light touch as he gave his name. "Thought I'd call first this time," he said. "My visit up to your place seemed to upset you the other day."

"It's not my place anymore."

"Yeah, I know that now, but I'd like to come by and talk if I could. Your car was vandalized in the Crossroads parking lot last night."

"Shit. Ah, shit… How badly?"

"Pretty much totaled. Sorry, but insurance should cover everything. You've got to sign an offense report. I can bring one by. That's why I'm calling."

"God…" A long, drawn out breath ended in silence.

"Juliet?"

"Yeah. Whatever. You know where I live now?"

"Pete Haskett told me."

Juliet opened her apartment door wearing jeans, a heavy gray sweatshirt, and an expression that held no emotion whatsoever. Her eyes seemed to track him with curiosity, although it was possible he was reading too much; it could have been disinterest.

"Come on in, Nick. May as well not stand out in the cold," she said. She wore indoor cotton muffs on her feet.

He entered a small living area furnished with a pale green sofa upholstered in brushed cotton. Three cushions were set into a framework that had the look of wicker or woven sea grass, something that spoke of soft breezes and palm trees. A few side tables and lamps were dotted around, along with a single, cushioned chair opposite the sofa. The apartment had a simple, uncluttered, and intensely private feel to it.

"Here. Have a seat. May as well take off your coat." Her tone had the formality of a priest hovering over a communion table. She moved stiffly to the side.

"I don't mean to intrude, Juliet. Really, I don't. But you couldn't drive to the station, and I felt like this would be okay." He slipped out of his jacket and folded it under an arm. "The chair okay? All I really need is your signature. I can fill in the rest of the form if you've got the registration handy." He stepped onto a dark green area rug with thick pile insulation.

"The chair's fine." She took a position at one end of the opposing sofa and touched a small blue vase on a table close to her knees. She fiddled with a magazine, then sat back and stuffed her hands inside the pouch on her sweatshirt.

"Juliet—"

"I guess I should ask if you want something to drink. Do you?"

"A glass of water would be nice."

"Water?" She pronounced the word uncertainly, as if it might be an obscure foreign concoction. "I've got beer, or maybe some instant coffee."

"Just water." He made a motion with his shoulders. "If it wouldn't be any trouble. I'm still on duty until my deputy comes in."

"It's just from the tap."

"That's okay." A grin slipped onto his face, one that he instantly regretted. "Let me get it."

She rose. "Want ice?"

"I guess."

Nick allowed his jacket to drop to the floor and relaxed his hands on the armrests. The air in the dwelling had a lightly showered scent, a cosmetic fragrance that smelled as closely intimate as the tucks and creases on a woman's body. He had never felt so intrusive in his life.

A shatter of glass exploded with an almost musical boom. Her voice came from the kitchen. "Fuck!"

He jumped to his feet and crossed the short distance to the kitchen doorway. Shards of glass sprayed from the base of the refrigerator to a small counter opposite. Juliet stared at the broken slivers.

He said quickly, "Watch your feet! I can get this."

"Ah, Jesus."

He bent low. "You've got on cotton slippers. Don't step on anything. It'll cut right through." The kitchen floor was composed of tough, standard-issue terra cotta tile that could probably survive a nuclear strike. Most of the glass was atomized into tiny pieces, and he began collecting the larger shards.

A dustpan and a broom appeared at his shoulder. "These might help," she said.

He glanced upward. "I use mostly plastic glasses at my place," he lied, "because I'm so clumsy." He maneuvered the broom and plastic scoop, cornered the fragments into a pile, and swept the debris up and away. Microscopic particles still on the floor twinkled like stars in a void of space. "I can't get to all of it, so watch where you step."

A moment later he dumped the remains into a wastebasket and came to his feet. "Easy as pie," he said with a breath.

Juliet took the broom and the dustpan. A dishtowel nearby held a large, irregular red stain. Her hand was bleeding.

"Juliet? You've got a cut. Let me take a look."

She pressed the dishtowel into her palm and turned away. "For heaven's sake, I'm not going to die, Nick. The glass hit the counter first. I tried to grab it." Her voice wavered. "You wanted water, I believe. You'll have to get it yourself."

"*May I* examine your hand? That is, before I get my water?"

Her expression held the resistance of a patient consenting to open heart surgery.

"Let me look. *Please*." He reached for her hand. It was clear the wound was something more than a nick. She fixed her light gray eyes on his and released her palm to his touch.

"See? It's just a cut, Nick."

He pulled the dishtowel away and the blood flow resumed. The wound was in the palm of her hand, behind the thumb, and the cause was evident. A superficial branch of a blood vessel had been perforated, possibly an artery on the palmar side. He applied pressure again and steered her to the sink. "I'm going to rinse first, then I want you to hold pressure until I can grab my medical equipment in the truck. Okay?"

She nodded.

"This'll take a little bit more than a band aid to close." He turned the tap and held her hand underneath a stream of frigid water. Her fingers were slim, her nails unpainted. The stain of her blood ran into the edges of her nail beds. He pulled the wet cuff of her sweatshirt away from her wrist and blinked for a startled second at the two white lines of scar tissue running laterally over her wrist. She stiffened and tugged at her hand. He tightened his grip in response. "Juliet, I—"

"So now you're learning more about me. Like what you see?" Her voice held the tremulous effort required to hold back tears.

"I want to help you, if you'll let me. It's as simple as that. Now hold still."

"Bullshit, Nick." She turned to him with tears on her cheeks. "No one's ever wanted to help me, so don't tell me the world is going to change now over a little spilled blood."

He refused to release her hand, and her awkward, quarter turn drew her torso close to his. Her face was tucked a hand's width from his right shoulder. He had never studied her in such close proximity, at least not as an adult. Dark eyebrows were set over liquid eyes of translucent, pale gray. Motes of green reflected in her lenses, floating like chips of ice in a winter sea. She had a small, straight nose and expressive lips that were devoid of lipstick. Her features were fine-boned and even. Her parents, whoever they might have been, passed patrician lines to a child raised in a culture that camouflaged those genes. He imagined they would be heartbroken, looking down from wherever they were, to know the anguished state of their daughter. "I'm going to get my med kit," he said. "Promise you won't lock me out." He tried for humor. "Remember, I'm a doctor."

She squeezed the wetness from her eyes with the palm of her free hand. The corners of her lips moved slightly upwards. "Yeah, and I'm a nuclear physicist."

He smiled in return. "Just hold the pressure. I'll be back in a sec."

The shard of glass had missed the superficial volar arch— a flashback to his textbook on anatomy—but the wound was still deep. The flesh was sliced in a one-quarter inch line. A scalpel couldn't have done a cleaner job.

They sat across from each other at her three-foot-square kitchen table. Her back was to the small window. His back was to the wall. He faced the refrigerator diagonally to her side and noted the neat line of magnets on the door. "Well, you missed the palmar arch," he said. "That's a good thing. Otherwise you'd have been in deeper trouble."

She aimed a level stare. "Maybe I'd better go back and try it again."

He met her eyes but they revealed nothing, and he held back a response. The woman was tough inside with a dry sense of humor that went deep. That was a positive. "First I'm going to irrigate with hydrogen peroxide, then apply a bit of ointment, maybe a bandage or two," he said, "and we'll have this wound fixed in no time." He glanced at her face at intervals as he inspected her hand. More than a bandage was required, and that meant primitive and rudimentary sutures inserted and tied by a one-time newbie intern. He explained as much.

"You going to charge me, doctor?"

That deadpan humor again. He concentrated on the project. "This'll sting a bit, even with the Lidocaine."

"So?"

"So you can cry if you want. I'm going to put in two sutures—two stitches—and there'll be just a little more blood."

She took a breath. "Should I ask how many times you've done this?"

He changed the subject. "So what's with your refrigerator magnets? There's one I don't understand."

"Let me guess, the one with the North Dakota state flag." She gave him that steely look once more.

"Very funny. I'm talking about the one with the chicken head and the Greek symbol for *pi*—the little figure that looks like a two-legged stool."

"I'll let you think about it for a while," she said. "But you've got to look at it more closely."

A few minutes later Nick elevated her newly repaired wound. "*Voila*," he announced, and then, "You *are* the prettiest patient I've ever operated on."

"So how many times have you done this? You didn't answer."

"A half a dozen times."

She examined the completed project. "So I'm patient number seven?"

"Yeah," he said, and smiled with a different thought.

"What's so funny?"

"I've got to ask," he said. "It's the most important question of the day"

She cleared her throat and said nothing, but he could sense the rise in tension.

"Want to know what the question is?"

She relaxed a bit. "I have a feeling you're going to tell me, whether I want to hear it or not."

He nodded. "The question is: Are you right-handed or left-handed?"

A corner of her lips came up. Flecks of green lightened her eyes again. She nodded at her packed and bandaged appendage. "What do you think?"

"Since you've temporarily lost the use of your left hand, you must be left-handed. Welcome to that most refined level of society."

She released a small laugh, a tinkling wind chime of a sound that hit him with pleasure. Had he ever heard her laugh before?

He went serious. "Juliet, you can't do anything that'll pull your thumb from your fingers, or put stress on the inside of your palm, like gripping something. Your injury is not critical, but the cut is bad. It'll heal on its own, but the piece of glass went through blood vessels that will separate again very easily, and if that happens they tend to retract. It's a natural phenomenon, but it makes re-connecting everything that much more difficult."

She nodded and examined the dressing once again. "How come you didn't finish medical school? I never heard."

He sat back. "My dad died. Mom couldn't afford the bills without income from the place. The GI Bill didn't pay for everything. I already had loans to pay off from college…"

"You got married."

"Yeah. And divorced." He added, "The woman wanted to marry a doctor. Not specifically me, just a doctor. So I discovered a tad late in the arrangement."

She seemed to allow the information to settle. "You said I have to sign something?"

"It's the offense report. I can fill in the other blanks, but if you want to file a declaration for insurance you have to have a claim number."

She glanced at her bandaged hand. "I can't hold a pen, can I?"

"Actually, I guess you shouldn't."

"So?"

"Can you sign with your right?"

"No. I think it's harder for left-handed people to use their other hand."

"Grip the pen in your right and I'll move your hand for the signature. It'll be easy."

"But then, it'll really be your signature. Is that legal?"

"I haven't a clue."

She laughed again. This time her own sound of amusement seemed to take her by surprise. "I don't remember you being funny like this, when we were younger and all."

He released a completely relaxed sigh. "Maybe I don't either."

Sitting beside Juliet didn't work. In that position Nick found that moving her right hand with his left was an easy concept to consider, yet difficult to actually accomplish. She doubled her fingers tightly into her right palm with the pen in the middle. He changed his procedure and leaned over her left shoulder from behind, extended his left arm in front of her face, then placed his hand over her closed fist and allowed the pen to pass between his thumb and forefinger. He tried to keep his chest from pressing against her thin shoulder blades, but essentially he was drawing her into an embrace from behind.

"Are you okay with this?"

"Let's just do it, Nick."

"How about once for practice. The 'B' will be hard to make."

"I don't have a 'B' in my name."

"Blackwell?"

"My last name is Driscoll."

"It's...I thought it was Blackwell. Come on, Juliet, you're joking. I've known you since high school." He released her hand and straightened.

She eased back in the chair. "It's complicated, Nick. I always thought my name was Blackwell until I took Driver's Ed at school. The day we applied for our licenses Aunt Doris showed me my birth certificate, and we went down to the DMV office together. She never did actually let me keep the photocopy, but I saw that my last name was Driscoll."

"Your parents' first names would have been on the certificate, and your place of birth."

"Yeah, I was pretty nervous and excited that day, my license and all. I couldn't tell you where I was born, just didn't notice. I do remember seeing my mom's name, Lyra."

"Well, that's… and all this time… Ever try and find them, your real parents?"

"They were killed in a car crash when Lenny and I were toddlers, or so I was told."

"And your birth certificate? Whatever…"

"Jesus Christ, Nick! Is this an inquisition? Legally I'm a Driscoll. Okay? That's all I know. I kept Blackwell just because everyone knew me as Juliet Blackwell. You know, just like the celebrities in Hollywood sometimes have different names."

He firmed his voice. "All I'm saying is that, if you get the chance, you need to try and find your birth certificate. Something doesn't seem right about that. I assume your brother doesn't have his either?"

"You assume correctly." She stopped speaking and seemed to fall into herself.

He gave her a moment. "Okay, then. Want to try your signature one more time?"

She nodded and he encapsulated her loosely in his arms, as a teacher might lean over a student with a homework problem. Together, working into a lengthening interval of silence, a readable signature was transcribed onto the paper.

"There," he said.

She spoke in a quiet voice, "You're learning quite a lot about me today."

"It's about time," he said.

Nick halted at the door after a few minutes of formalities. Their conversation was not as stilted as before, but he didn't consider it easy going. Words were minefields with this woman. "We didn't get to everything, Juliet. You don't have a car, for one thing."

"I can borrow my brother's pickup. He doesn't use it much."

"Is that…roadworthy?"

"Yeah, I guess."

"I've got a Toyota 4-Runner that I don't even use. I drive the police vehicle nowadays. You can borrow the Toyota if you want. No strings attached."

"I don't know, Nick."

"No strings," he repeated. "Just as a friend."

"Yeah, maybe. Let me think about it."

He extended his right hand and held hers for a formal parting. "Okay, Miss Juliet Driscoll. I'm glad to know your real name."

7

Doris Blackwell punched in the lighter aboard her CL Class Mercedes and shook a white, paper-wrapped tube of unfiltered tobacco from a soft pack of Lucky Strike Classics. She wedged the cigarette into a corner of lips that were cracked and dry and untouched by cosmetics.

She waited on the lighter. The highway had been cleared during the overnight hours, but salt granules spitting against the undercarriage and lower body were prematurely aging her five-year-old vehicle. Dakota weather was hard on a car, and the time had come for a newer model, this time a BMW. Everyone had a Mercedes nowadays. Janitors drove them, along with busboys, truck drivers, you name it. The entire concept of an upper class system was becoming diluted. She'd have to add the car to the list of items for discussion.

The lighter popped from the receptacle. She fired up the smoke and drew in a scorching lungful of flavor that made her dizzy. One thing about Luckies: they gave it to you, like, *right now.*

She blew out a cloud and transferred the cigarette to her fingers on the steering wheel. There were other issues to be dealt with when she saw her brother. Cliffy had been given virtually a free ride concerning those kids. She'd done all the heavy lifting, and even provided the girl for his special enjoyment a time or two. Hell, he never did pay her back sufficiently for those interludes. She smiled. His pleasure days were over in that nursing home. That was a fact, Jack.

A Florida-bound Dodge Caravan loaded with bicycles, surfboards, and five or six members of a big, sloppy family hogged the left lane. The right side was clear, forcing her to blink the high beams five or six times until they finally wandered aimlessly back to the slow lane where they belonged.

Closing the Needle Nicely shop would be another good idea. She wasn't getting any younger, and the stifling boredom of the place drove her cross-eyed. The business never made any money, just gave her something to do in order to keep her wits. She glanced at the van in the rear view mirror. Maybe re-locating to Florida, lock, stock and barrel was not such a bad idea.

The road ahead was straight and clear and she pressed the accelerator. She'd be at her brother's house in time for Marietta to fix something for dinner. Cliffy wasn't going anywhere, and she could visit the nursing home in the morning.

Donald Rhinehart wore expensive suits, expensive shirts, and expensive watches. His platinum Rolex President peeked out from the cuff of an Eton, striped-blue poplin shirt. He pushed away from his mahogany desk, sank into the soft brown leather of his recliner, and crossed his legs in the effeminate manner of both gentlemen and women. He'd come a long way from a street-side lawyer doing divorces, wills, and the occasional real estate closing. Blond hardwoods from Sweden paneled his office in Bismarck. The floors were covered with a rich pile carpet so deep one could almost sleep on the thick wool. However, at fifty-five years of age he was not exactly where he wanted to be monetarily. The firm was too small to make him really wealthy. Fortunately, there were other avenues to that end.

He gazed at the legal documents comprising the Driscoll Trust piled on his desk. If growing the partnership promised a tedious, long term solution to riches, taking the Driscoll fortune away from Clifford, his obnoxious sister, and the worthless twins would take him there at light speed.

It was hard not to be pleased at the way things were developing. He had put up with Clifford—*Cliffy*—for more years that he could remember, from the time the Wolverine Mining

Company had been put up for sale. The man was an imbecile and vicious in the manner of a Russian soldier pillaging German women on the way to Berlin. He had to be pulled up by the balls the time Rhinehart found out he was raping the young Driscoll girl. The lawyer shook his head. That was trouble in the making. He knew it at the time, and sure enough, those buried incidents later emerged white hot when the girl, Juliet, turned eighteen. Out of the blue she filed a criminal complaint with the assistant state's attorney by herself. Just walked into the state attorney's office one day and slapped a charge of rape against Clifford, alleging the incidents occurred when she was eleven. Dakota law carried a seven-year statute of limitations for criminal offenses, so the charge had the punch of a body blow around the office.

Rhinehart blew a tuneless whistle. Fortunately, Harry Schwartzel was the state's assistant DA at the time, and after some intelligent bargaining—he was now a partner in Rhinehart's law firm—the charges went nowhere.

He looked up at the sound of a respectful knock on the door. His secretary poked her head halfway around the portal. "I'm going, Mr. Rhinehart. Anything you need?"

He retrieved his tumbler of scotch from the desktop. "Yeah, more lawyers in this goddamn firm, Billie. I want to be a Baker-McKenzie, maybe a K&L Gates. We've got to get bigger, a whole lot bigger."

She cleared her throat. "I've got my nephew, the one I told you about. He'll be starting law school in a couple of years."

Rhinehart laughed. "I won't hold my breath."

She drew back at the comment. "Yes sir. Anything else?"

"Nah. But you might check with Harry before you leave. And remind him to keep a sharp lookout for prospects in that night course he's teaching. Tell him I said so."

"Alright then," she replied as she closed the door quietly.

Rhinehart took a sip of J&B and soda. Billie wouldn't say shit to Schwartzel, but that was okay. If his partner didn't realize by now that Rhinehart was loading seventy percent of the workload onto his shoulders, well then, he deserved what he got.

Rhinehart helped himself to another long pull on his drink. He didn't tell anyone he drank J&B, but he actually preferred the brand to the more expensive labels on the market.

So, a couple of weekends playing golf and screwing teenage hookers in Colombia was all it took to become a trusted lawyer and friend with Clifford. The guy was an idiot, and Rhinehart's clever use of the *contingent beneficiary* clause was the path to his eventual takeover of the Driscoll estate. He was already listed as Clifford's successor trustee, the individual assigned to manage the trust at Clifford's death. But unknown to *Cliffy*, who signed anything put in front of him, Rhinehart had also inserted himself as the *contingent beneficiary,* the person who would inherit the entire worth of the trust upon the death of both Clifford and the twins. Cliffy was walking dead already, so that just left the twins. And who would ever give a shit about them?

Hopefully, he had also planted an important seed during his visit to the nursing home, one that stressed the imperative that Cliffy and his ugly sister had to somehow *do* the twins in the few months before they turned thirty years of age. Did the numbskull get that? Of course, the surprise would be that Rhinehart—and not Doris—would inherit the entire amount of the estate once Cliffy and the twins were out of the way.

He finished the slushy dregs of the alcohol and sucked on a particle of ice. Granted, there were *probabilities* involved. Doris had to believe that she would inherit everything with the death of the twins. It wouldn't be difficult to make the argument, given the fact that she was Clifford's sister.

So with proper handling and direction from his end, all that remained was for Doris to pull it off, since Cliffy was incapable and would never again leave the nursing home. He'd have to work on the woman, light a fire under her ass, encourage her to do the dirty work. People would do anything if they expected a big inheritance. Look at himself.

Clifford's house was a pile of bricks bunkered into the ground like a fort. From its foundation atop a small rise the brick and cement dwelling rose over two stories. Stupid-looking dormers curved outward from the roof, as if medieval archers were hidden behind the eyebrow windows. The monstrosity steamed Doris every time she arrived at her brother's subdivision east of Bismarck. His construction company had built five or six houses in the gated community, and he had moronically named the housing tract 'Chandelier Estates'. What? Every house had to have a chandelier? Added to that was the fact that Cliffy's house made her own place look like a hut. The by-God *unfairness* of it all was almost more than her blood pressure could take.

In the past, Marietta had typically answered the door as if Doris had open buboes from the plague ringing her neck. There were reasons aplenty for conflict, and almost all of them concerned money. The much younger woman obviously resented both her maid-like station in life and Doris' condescending intrusions. Tough shit. Marietta had never become more than a housekeeper, in spite of openly servicing Clifford's every deviant need. She obviously assumed Cliffy was going to marry her at some point. Well, that didn't happen.

For her part, Doris was continually pissed that her brother paid some cook-maid-hooker with the money from the Driscoll estate, instead of providing more to her. After all, she was raising the kids.

Now however, there seemed to be something of a truce in the works. Marietta opened the door with a thin smile, which made Doris immediately suspicious. Cliffy was obviously never returning to the house. Did the Cuban bitch think she owned the mansion in his absence?

Marietta leaned on the half-opened door and said to her, "It's been a while Doris, but I'm glad you could work in a visit. I've just come from the nursing home."

"And how is my brother?" Doris stepped past the woman and entered the foyer. She gazed upward into a pair of symmetrical, sweeping staircases that Clifford had not been able to climb for years. His last bedroom had been in the converted study on the ground floor.

Marietta closed the door and moved toward Doris. Her hands were clasped in a position of polite servitude, but her eyes were dark and direct. "He's…irritated at his condition. You remember he was always a very physical man."

Doris almost snorted. Marietta would certainly know.

"But mentally he's still as sharp as ever."

What did she mean by that? The statement had the ring of a legal angle.

"After you called I warmed up some things on the stove top," Marietta said. "That is, if you're hungry. I thought we could sit down and have a nice talk. I haven't eaten myself." She walked toward the kitchen and Doris followed, noting that Marietta still had the body and the looks. She had to give her that. The scent of jasmine rode air currents in her wake. Her flowered dress accentuated hips that swayed with a Latin-like movement as she walked. A fall of lustrous black hair was pinned up, baring her neck and shoulders. There was a possibility that her brother might go a little crazy over this woman in his final days. She would have to stay alert.

The kitchen was brightly lit. She had never been in one that wasn't, except her own.

Marietta nodded toward the table. "Have a seat, if you like." She seemed to take in Doris with a quick series of side-glances as she poured red wine without comment from a bottle.

Doris reached into her purse. "Do you have an ashtray?"

"You can use this coaster." Marietta placed a saucer and a large glass of wine in front of her. The view of her cleavage as she leaned over was something Cliffy boy would have appreciated. Under different circumstances maybe she might have been interested herself.

Marietta placed a hand demurely across the soft cotton fabric of her top. "I wore this for Cliff. Sorry, I just haven't had time to change."

Doris flicked her lighter and drew in a lungful of strong tobacco. She exhaled and helped herself to a full swallow of wine. A second followed the first, and she coughed lightly from the tag team of alcohol and tobacco. Now she was ready to talk. "Well, it's not like we've ever had much to say to each other, Marietta."

The woman clattered a pan or two on the range top. After a moment she picked up her glass and slid into a chair opposite Doris at the large table. "We haven't, but now perhaps there are a few things you should know." She sipped her wine, but her eyes stayed on Doris over the rim of the goblet. She wasn't quite the subservient maid that Doris had known in years past.

"Like?"

"Like your brother's an asshole. But you know that."

Her words carried a shock value so intensely unexpected that Doris felt her jaw drop. The cigarette clung to her lower lip for an instant, held only by the glue of her saliva. "I…" She lost the thought. Yes, she knew Clifford was an asshole, but the *nerve* of this servant to state the fact so plainly. "So what does that make you, Marietta? You've been screwing an asshole for what, seven, eight years?"

The woman rested both thumbs and forefingers against the stem of the wine glass and leaned toward her. "I've been sending money to my mother in Cuba for that long. I only slept with your brother for a few years. His emphysema cut into his…shall we say manhood? Not something he would want anyone—including his sister—to know, I would imagine." She took a breath and added, "His personality was lacking from the start, but sometimes we women are inclined to doubt our own judgment. We tend to give people second, even third chances."

Doris drew on the cigarette. She helped herself to another swallow of wine as she glanced around the room and took in various Latin-themed knickknacks. She returned to Marietta's face. "I don't…why are you telling me this?"

"Because I'm tired of being treated like Clifford's whore. I want you to understand that I've continued to live here for my mother and my relatives in Cuba. And I want you to know that your brother has added a codicil to his will giving me the house."

A red mist swam before Doris's eyes. She made a garbled sound and took a breath, then another. She felt hollow in the center, as if she couldn't get traction on the air coming in. Her gaze slid from Marietta, but she could feel the woman watching her reaction.

"I don't mean to be especially rude," Marietta said. "I just want to be up front about this before Clifford dies, and this seems like a good opportunity."

"He's not going to die anytime soon," Doris heard herself say. "The doctors say he could live a year, maybe longer."

"Six months to a year is the prognosis," Marietta corrected.

Doris sat for along moment. She could think of nothing to say, no jab, no acid comment to make in reply. She was blank. Finally, "If he's such as asshole, how come you got all dolled up for your visit with that cleavage and hair, all of that?"

"Because, believe it or not, I've always been a fair person, a nice person. Clifford has given me something of great value and I can start a new life somewhere else. He cannot. Showing him a little bit of my top is my way of saying thanks, even to an unpleasant individual."

Doris drank off the remaining wine and slapped the stem on the table. There was no fucking way miss pretty maid was going to get the house, regardless of her tits. Doris knew her brother and she was damn well going to correct this little screw-up. She had all the cards to play.

Marietta softened as a woman might when totally in control. "You can stay for the night if you wish. And I've made some *pollo asado*." She nodded behind her. "On the range top."

"*Pollo* what? No thanks. I'll find another place for the night." Doris crushed her cigarette and stood. There was no point in remaining any longer. Her work had to be done with Cliffy. "If I were you I'd remember one thing." She twisted her lips out of line. "Blood is thicker than—" She twirled her hand. "Any temporary living arrangements. You'd best keep that in mind." She moved with hard, impatient footsteps to the front entrance of the mansion. Marietta trailed behind. Doris pulled the heavy door latch open and turned to the woman. "I wouldn't get too used to this house, if I were you," she said. "And you'd better watch yourself."

"Is that a threat?"

"Take it any way you'd like." She stepped through the opening and slammed the door behind her.

Breakfast consisted of thinned orange juice that probably came from a Brazilian concentrate, along with bacon, and waffles that had been microwaved from a frozen package. Clifford could damn well tell the difference, even if the cooks figured most of the residents could not. The coffee was okay, which meant the staff members were drinking it also.

"Mr. Blackwell?"

A young girl he did not recognize materialized at his shoulder. The employee turnover in these places was incredible. He spoke around a mouthful of bacon and waffles. "What do you want?"

"A woman would like to visit with you. Here, over breakfast. She says she's your sister."

Clifford looked up and scanned the darkened entrance foyer adjoining the far end of the cafeteria. A woman in a light-colored dress extended a foot from a hippy stance and tapped the floor with impatience. That would be Doris. He nodded. "Okay. Let her come on in."

The girl moved away before Clifford realized he should have ordered another round of bacon. He dredged the last strip of crispy pork fat into the syrup and forked it into his mouth. Delicious. An extra serving would be nice, although it would undoubtedly necessitate a trip to the bathroom, and that was getting to be a hassle at this stage of the game.

His sister marched toward him like a Robocop. "Am I too late for breakfast?" she asked as she approached.

He shook his head as she took a seat in a huff. "It's fifteen dollars for guests. You got that on you?"

"You wouldn't pay for it?"

"No."

They exchanged looks. He assumed she was running a mortality calculation based on his color and general life force. He licked his lips, patted his belly, and smiled: the picture of health.

"You're growing a beard," she said.

"Makes me look more distinguished," he replied. She, on the other hand, looked like shit. His sister had started life with little in the way of natural beauty, a weed instead of a flower growing out of the soil. Now it seemed even the weed had died.

"Can I get coffee?"

"Coming right up." Clifford waved his hand in the air, a motion that led to a heavy bout of breathing. He adjusted the cannula.

Doris pushed aside a second place setting and set her purse on the table. "We need to talk, Cliffy."

"Oh, really. You out of money again?"

She plunked an elbow on the table and held up fingers. "Number one, I've been the one raising those kids, keeping them out of your hair. You've—" She lowered her voice as the coffee pot appeared. The waitress turned her cup right side up and poured. "Cream." Doris made the request an order.

"On the table, ma'am. Behind the vase."

Clifford weighed in a moment later. "I've given you plenty of money, Doris. You just throw it away on gambling. I can't help that." This was going to be the typical lengthy argument. He surveyed the room. Three semi-comatose individuals were still at their tables waiting for staff members to wheel them back to their apartments.

She plunged ahead. "Two, I offered to testify against those rape charges. That deposition thing kept your ass out of jail, Clifford. I never did get anything for that."

"Ancient history and incorrect on your part. If you remember, I treated you to a week in Vegas after that episode."

He let her run. Once she finished there would be more important things to discuss.

"Three, I stopped by the house last night, and Marietta tells me you're leaving the place to her." Then louder, "I'm your sister, Cliff."

That part was true, and his pulse quickened at the potential for trouble. He held up a hand. "Enough. Listen to me. I've been talking to my lawyer and we've got some serious shit to deal with. You especially, if you want to inherit everything after I'm gone."

She halted mid-breath, as though catching words on the verge of tumbling out. Her ears—it could be he was not imagining this—seemed to twist forward like a dog's to a whistle, and her eyes locked his.

He had her attention. "Have you bothered to read the trust agreement? You've got a copy."

"I'm no good with legal stuff. You know that. Besides, I've got other things to do."

He snorted into the cannula, "Like throwing your money away at the casinos?"

She pushed back. "What I do is my business."

He made a pained expression. God knows he could have done better in the sister department. "Doris," he enunciated slowly and with exasperation. "Juliet and Lenny turn thirty years old in a little over three months. That is the problem we have to discuss."

Doris waved for more coffee a short time later, but she didn't interrupt him again until he had finished. Clifford sat back, exhausted with the telling, and studied her expression for a sign. It was all there. The inflexible lines on her face detailed everything he needed to see.

She shifted a spoon on the tablecloth. "So, once you're…gone, and the twins, if they're not here anymore…"

"Then you inherit the entire amount of the estate. Rhinehart confirmed it the other day. 'Cause of how our beloved brother Jonas set the thing up. It's a huge amount, Doris. Millions. But everything goes to the twins if they reach thirty.

That can't be stopped. So you have to keep the time frame in mind."

It was plain she was making a mighty effort to keep a grin off her face. "Lenny is always fooling around the place. I'm surprised that he hasn't had some serious accident before now."

"You've got to be smart if you're thinking of all the...you know, possibilities. The girl's a lot brighter. And sneaky. The way she went behind us and filed those rape charges that time."

She frowned and jumped on the subject. " 'Cause you couldn't keep that weenie of yours in your pants? It still pisses me off that you've left the house to that Marietta whore. That's what she is and you know it."

He raised a hand again. "Okay, okay. That can be changed. Don't worry about it. Focus on what needs to be done to keep this estate. Do it for us. For me in my remaining time, then for you."

She pursed her lips. "I need a cigarette."

"You can't smoke in here."

"Then I'm leaving, Clifford. I've got stuff to work out."

"Be smart about things, Doris."

She nodded. "First I'll need a down payment, and I've been thinking about a new BMW."

8

Juliet had a car: Nick's loaner. He'd come by late the previous evening with his deputy and dropped the dark green Toyota in front of her apartment. He'd pushed it on her, really. Tossed the keys through the partially opened storm door and departed. Didn't give her a chance to say no, as if he knew she might. He was probably correct.

The higher driving position in the SUV was a treat. She put her hands on the wheel and adjusted the seat forward. Soft, tan leather that bore the worked-in creases of a man's frame cushioned her legs and back. She imagined Nick going about his huge spread in his flannel shirts, denim jeans, and muddy work boots. She inhaled deeply and caught a scent of perspiration mixed with the musky fragrance of an aftershave. The woody odor of dried topsoil and maybe last season's tomatoes lay lower down near the floorboards. She poked into the partitioned console between the seats. One compartment contained three small bullets covered by dust and loose change. Another held two yellow pencil stubs with teeth marks top to bottom. The third slot was designed for a cell phone, but instead held a red and white tin of Altoid mints. She fingered some scraps of paper and came away with two ticket stubs. They read: 'BSO, Row H, Seat 5 and 6.

She cranked the ignition and let the engine idle. There was no exhaust rattle, just a quiet, powerful sound that seemed like Nick in a way.

Overall, the car pleased her. There comfort, and maybe a sense of security in his vehicle, all of which were lacking in her old one. She peeked into the empty glove box. No one drove around with an empty glove compartment, and that told her something had been removed. She had a good idea what it was.

Juliet cushioned the heel of her left palm against the wheel and moved the shift lever into drive with her right. Pete had given her a few days break at the Crossroads because of her injury, and she was going to follow Nick's advice and look for her birth certificate. She'd pick up the rest of her things at Doris' house while she was there.

An hour later, her vehicle crunched over the snow and ice frozen onto the front yard of the run-down house. There was no driveway, just a depression worn by tire treads that led to the porch. Doris' car was not there.

The sun peeked through gray, low-hanging clouds, and Juliet shielded her eyes as she glanced to the east. The light diffused onto the snowy landscape and bounced back with a blinding whiteness. She honked the horn, then a second time. At ten o'clock in the morning her brother should be up. She opened the car door and climbed down. Time to start the search.

"Whataya making a racket for, Sis?" Lenny stuck his head outside.

"Thought I'd come out here and fix you breakfast. Hungry?"

He scratched his head. "Sure, but we don't have much in the house. Some bread, maybe some milk and baloney. Where'd you get the car?"

"It's a loaner." She reached for the brown, paper sack of groceries on the seat. "How about some eggs and bacon, toast and jelly, maybe some grits. They're kind of mushy and white. Ever had those?"

He shook his head. "They had grits at the R & J, but I never tried 'em."

She closed the car door and stepped to the porch with kind of a bounce. "Then we'll both try something new," she said.

"You okay, Sis? What's wrong with your hand? Truckers again?"

"I cut it on a water glass. Here, take this." She one-handed him the groceries.

"Looks like you've been to the hospital. Your face, and now your hand…"

"It's nothing, Lenny." She had an uptick in her voice. "Let's have a good breakfast. Then we've got a job to do."

Doris peered through the windshield of the Mercedes and watched the blur of asphalt disappear beneath the car. Highway 83 shot north of Bismarck, North Dakota as straight as a cannon ball for a distance of one hundred miles. The divided roadway dead-ended at Park City, uncoiled west as Highway 5, and passed the junction of State Road 28, which ran through Sherwood and directly to her place ten miles further on. She had maybe a twenty-minute drive remaining to the house, and damned if there wasn't a lot to put into motion.

She had Lenny in the bag. He was an idiot. She might just run over his ass. Back the car into him. Say it was an accident. She'd have to squash him good, though. Make sure she got him squarely the first time. The cops weren't going to swallow backing into a guy three or four times. If it came to that it wouldn't look like, well, an accident.

Juliet was a different problem, but she would figure out something. If she could trick the girl into going near the old well, then a shove at the appropriate time would do the trick. 'Course, she'd have to have the protective cover already removed. Cliffy had warned her, the girl was smart so Doris had to be smarter. And meaner. She was still pissed the little bitch tried to pull that fast one years ago with the state's attorney.

"Well? What do you think?" Juliet asked.

Lenny leaned back in his chair. The kitchen had warmed with the morning sun, and the smell of fried bacon was heavy. "About what?"

"The grits, silly. Do you like them?"

He shrugged. "Yeah, they're okay. They kind of fill you up, mixed with the eggs an' all."

"I think that's the concept." Juliet had made coffee, and she took a sip from a large mug with spider web cracks. "I came back to get the rest of my clothes, Lenny. And we've got to try and find our birth certificates. You got any idea where they might be?"

He cast his eyes toward the ceiling. "Lord, Sis. I haven't thought about them for years. Why do we need 'em now?"

"Because they're rightfully ours. They tell us who we are, who our parents were."

He shook his head with kind of a puzzled expression. "I've looked in most of her drawers before. Maybe they're hidden some place more secret."

"The attic, you think?"

"Maybe. Those pull-down stairs are pretty rickety. I've never much wanted to climb up."

"The witch probably knows that. That means it's time to take a look."

Doris had time for one more cigarette. She lit a Lucky Strike, nodded around the thick swirl of smoke, and thought back to her conversation with Cliffy. The time had come to stop living like white trash. Cliffy's house would suit her just fine. She could live there or sell it, she wasn't sure which, but the pleasure would come in booting his slut out of the front door. She'd have to reinforce the importance of family with her brother, make sure Cliffy didn't let a little bit of Latin pussy get in the way of her rightful due. Hell, he couldn't do anything with it anyway. And then a new BMW in the driveway. She'd lease one if she had to.

Juliet climbed the stairs as if she expected the wood to give way. She had been up once before when she was very young. Filthy boxes and old, dusty clothes didn't have much appeal.

"What's up there?" Lenny stood at the bottom rung.

She stooped to clear the beams. "Boxes and junk." she yelled back. "Let me look around for a few minutes." She pulled the lanyard on the single, naked light bulb and tried to ignore the stink of stale, burnt tobacco from Doris' old clothes. The smell of mothballs and mildewed cardboard actually helped dilute the odor. She brushed at a few wispy cobwebs between the rafters and scanned the small area. For a woman whose housekeeping skills were essentially zero, the place was oddly neat and organized. Cartons imprinted with the Needle Nicely logo were stacked to one side. Outdated clothes on hangers were suspended from bars fixed between the ceiling beams. The shoulders of the clothes were all showing layers of dust. Open boxes were stuffed with cast-off items: pots and pans, an old toaster, lamps, a set of blue glasses—she remembered those—an antique radio. In short, the attic contained all of the normal, discarded, meaningless trash one might expect to find. A locked safe did not exist, nor a sealed file cabinet, nor anything that looked like a hiding place for documents. In fact, there was no furniture whatsoever in the storage area.

"Sis?" Lenny's voice held alarm.

She turned to the stairwell and raised her voice. "What?"

"Doris's car is coming up the state road. I can see it from her bedroom window."

A creepy level of anxiety came over her. She was burglarizing the house, in a sense, but only for something that was rightfully hers. Doris wouldn't see it that way. She glanced about the space one more time and turned to the steps.

She hesitated. Something caught her attention. She turned back for a closer look.

"Sis?"

"*Okay*, Lenny. I heard you."

A pile of clothes lay at the foot of the knee wall behind the steps. They were the only items not on hangers. The image didn't fit. "Give me a minute, Lenny," she yelled.

"You'd better hustle," he replied with an urgent tone. "She's coming up the drive."

Juliet moved around the stairs and knelt at the bundle. A set of large, worn towels topped with old jeans and flannel shirts concealed something. She poked at a hard object underneath, then pulled the covering away and beheld a flat, leather portfolio brief open at the top like a purse. "Lenny?"

"She's sitting in the car smoking."

She withdrew documents from the side pouches, then unzipped the center pouch and grabbed what she could. She stuffed the case back under the towels. "All right, I'm coming!"

The sound of a car door closing reached her as she made her way down the stairs. "Close it," she said quickly. Her brother folded the ladder and slowly allowed the screeching, spring-loaded staircase to recess into the ceiling.

The front door opened and closed. A scratchy voice came from the first floor. "Who the hell owns that car in the yard?"

Juliet held the flutter of papers in her hand and looked around. "Lenny, we need to hide these somewhere!"

He threw a quick glance down the stairs. "I don't know, Sis. Where would we hide them?"

"Stuff them under your mattress for now. Can you do that? I mean way under, in the middle. I don't want Doris to find them."

"I hear voices up there. You got a girl with you, Lenny? I'm coming up."

"Hurry!" Juliet whispered.

Her brother grabbed the papers and disappeared into his room.

"It's just me, Doris," Juliet yelled back. "I was looking at some of my old clothes."

"You? You're not supposed to be here anymore, child." The toe of a stiff, leather shoe tapped the ground floor stair tread.

"We're coming down. Just hold your horses." Juliet brushed the dust from her hands and grinned at her brother behind her. "Let's go see the witch."

9

"Hey, Juliet. It's Nick."

"Nick?" Juliet could plainly read the caller ID tag on the handset base even if she couldn't recognize the voice, which she could. But in the middle of taking a burned, bubbling chicken pot pie from the oven she was feeling peevish.

"Nick Olsen," he said.

"Hold on a second." She squeezed the phone between her neck and shoulder, withdrew the entrée from the oven with a gloved pot holder, and kneed the oven door closed.

After a moment he said, "I hope I'm not calling at a bad time."

Four days had elapsed since the hand accident and her wound was still bandaged and sore. She thought back. Nick was a nice guy, maybe nicer than most, but she didn't want any romantic involvement. He was a man after all, and at some point like all men…hell, she didn't even want to think about it. There would be pressure at some point, the kind she was extremely familiar with. That's how guys were.

"Juliet?"

"Yeah, I'm…I'm here. I was just—"

"Look. Let me call back later. Would that be better?"

She took a seat, shucked her single mitten and pulled a strand of hair from her face. The pot pie obviously could wait for a while. "This about your car?" she asked. The words came out tight and annoyed. She added quickly, "I mean, I didn't mean that like it sounded. I've enjoyed driving it, and I haven't dinged it or anything."

"Not a problem," he replied. "In fact, that's what I was calling about. I've got a solution to your transportation problem if you'd like to hear it."

"Nick, I'm not a charity case. I can find a car. Besides, you've done enough already." She glanced at her bandage. "Especially with my hand."

"Is that sarcasm? As in, if I hadn't been at your place you wouldn't have cut yourself over a glass of water."

"I didn't mean it like that. I just…"

"Look," he said. "A couple of things. One, I talked to Pete about—"

"Why is everyone in this town so freaking nosey about my private life?"

"Take it easy, Ms. Driscoll. Allow me to finish." His words were delivered in a cop's voice, devoid of tone but weighted in an unfamiliar way. "One, I talked to Pete about the vandalism to your vehicle, what the chances were that I might find out specifically who did it. I'd like to make an arrest for willful destruction of property if I could. I'm the sheriff. That's my job. The conversation did not involve you in any personal way, except that he mentioned you'd be back at work tomorrow night. And…*and* he thanked me for fixing the cut on your hand. Mentioned that you were a popular fixture around the place and people were asking about you."

She lapsed into silence. She was in conflict again, with everything and with herself for no reason.

"Two," he said. "Tell me one thing. Have you shopped around for a replacement vehicle yet?"

With slight embarrassment she said, "No, not really. Look Nick, I know I'm coming over as a…as a bitch. I don't mean to."

"Not a problem."

"Not a problem I'm a bitch?"

He said nothing in response except that he cleared his throat. She wanted something more.

"That's supposed to be funny, Nick."

"You're not a bitch. Your problem is that you don't know how to accept a favor, and you think that if you *do* accept a favor then it puts you at a disadvantage, one that may result in an overture of sex down the road or something else that might generate a commitment. Is that about right?"

She closed her eyes and tried to keep any sentiment out of her voice. "I apologize for not knowing how to accept a favor. I was rude."

"Can we start over?"

"Yeah."

"Okay, my offer for the 4-Runner as a temporary loaner still stands, but here's the deal. I've got an aunt and uncle in their eighties who have a car they don't drive anymore. Uncle Buzzy occasionally drives his pickup, but Alice's sedan is an older-model Mercury of some kind, and it just sits in the barn. They'd love someone to take it off their hands."

"Does it work? I mean, how old is it?"

"Runs fine. It's maybe six, seven years old, but they'd like to get rid of it. They'll let it go to a friend of mine—you, of course—for half of the Bluebook price. You can pay them in installments, whatever."

"There's got to be a catch. No offense, Nick, but this sounds a little too good to be true."

"You're right. There's a catch."

She took a breath. "Why does that not surprise me?"

"The catch is that we, meaning you and me, have to stay for dinner with the old folks the day we pick it up."

"That's...kind of unusual. Are they, like, weird or something?"

"Of course. They're my relatives."

She went silent for a beat. Then, "You know, you're getting to be quite the comic."

"I'm a funny guy inside."

"Yeah, right."

"And I sense a little sarcasm again."

"It's...no, it's not. I'm just not used to anything given that freely."

"I gather that. But these folks don't get much company and they're nice people who are getting older and—"

"Okay, Nick. Okay. And thanks…really. I mean it."

"So how about this weekend? I know you're off Sunday and Monday at the Crossroads. They're just east of Grand Forks and it'll take an hour or so to get there."

"You're being too nice again."

"You think?"

"Now who's being sarcastic?" A little *tone* was in the reply, and she immediately regretted it. Now she was talking to dead air. She waited through a slow metronome of several breaths for his response. Finally, "Nick, you still there?"

"Yeah, I'm thinking."

"Don't…hang up or anything. Okay? I'm…I've got some rough edges, I know that."

He laughed. "No shit."

That made her feel better.

"So, who is this Uncle Buzzy?"

They were in his sheriff's Durango. The county could pay for the gas, at least to the county line. After that he'd fill up the tank on his own, keep his lifestyle principled. The drive was going to take a while, contrary to what he'd told Juliet. There was no easy way to get to his uncle's house between Devils Lake and Grand Forks. Route 5 had to become Route 1, which had to become Route 2 in a series of right angle turns that ran along county lines either north-south or west-east. The only straight shot to Grand Forks was Interstate 94, which was too far to the south. "He's my dad's older brother," he told her. "By at least ten years. They were not very close, you know as brothers, but Alice and Buzzy always had time for me, and a place to go sometimes, kind of like they were my extra parents. I guess it was because they never had kids of their own."

"That had to be hard, harder than you know."

"What?"

"Never having children."

He glanced over. Juliet had pulled her hair back, but there were strands that fell to the sides in kind of a pioneer look. She had thrown on an unzipped, fleece-lined vest for added warmth over a white cotton V-neck blouse and a cardigan sweater. The sweater he took to be purple. She said it was fuchsia heather, which reminded him how seldom he conversed with a woman, and how much he enjoyed doing so. He'd seen her designer jeans before, however the gold necklace was new. She looked fairly spectacular.

"So what's 'Buzzy' short for? Or is that a nickname?" she asked.

"It's a nickname."

"So?"

"I don't think he'd want you to know his given name, so I'm not going to tell you. But feel free to ask him yourself."

She sighed and stared off to a place in space. "God, Nick, if you aren't the most upright man I've ever met."

10

"Uncle Buzzy's got quite a driveway," Nick said to Juliet as he exited the asphalt pavement of the county road.

She peered ahead. Scarecrow trees outlined a hard-packed dirt lane with the look of frozen tundra. "I bet this gets muddy in the spring."

"And dusty later in the summer," he said. "But when the trees come out it's kind of a pleasant, shady drive. There's a nice creek over on the east side of the property. Grassy area, lots of trees. Great place for a picnic."

"And private, I bet. Is that where you take your girlfriends?" She sneaked a sideways peek. He was staring straight ahead.

"I would if I had any."

"So how much of this land is your uncle's?" She glanced left and right. A white, clapboard farmhouse surrounded by several red barns squatted in the distance. A tall structure towered close by. "Look! They've even got a windmill. Does it work?"

"No," he laughed. "I mean, the blades turn, but it doesn't pump anything anymore. The property was divided a long time ago, even before grandfather Olsen died. My dad got a thousand acres. Uncle Buzzy also took a thousand, but he received the best portion, according to my father.

" 'Cause he was the oldest? You said he was older than your father."

Nick gave a nod. "That's what my dad always thought, that Buzzy got the best portion because he was the first born. Probably why they were never really close as brothers."

"So what happens to all of this when they…you know, pass away. You said they were in their eighties."

He shrugged. "I think it all comes to me. Buzzy mentioned something to that effect years ago, but I'm not certain it's still set up that way. And anyway, what I'd really like to do is go back to med school." He waved a hand. "All of this would be a lot to maintain."

"You could always come back afterwards, be the local doc." She looked at her bandaged palm. "You did a good job on this, Nick. Thanks."

He smiled. "Wait till I pull those stitches."

After a moment she said, "It was about more than the stitches."

Nick's uncle had a thin covering of white, almost translucent hair making a last stand on a mostly bald scalp. A home-cut scrawl of light, facial growth passed for a beard on his square face. Twenty years earlier he might have posed as a Hemingway look-alike. Now his features were as gnarled as an old fence post. He held Juliet's right hand and eyed her with curiosity for a moment. "Well, come on inside then, you two, before we all catch cold. Nick, did you tell her about Alice's pecan pies?"

"I told her it was all in the pie crust. Isn't that what Alice always said?"

Buzzy winked over his shoulder as they marched up the porch steps. "Nick didn't tell you a thing, did he? He's only had about a hundred of her special desserts. One night he finished an entire pie by himself. Alice 'n I were a little worried that night, but he was hungry again the next morning." He gave a soft laugh.

"I was still a growing boy," said Nick. He appeared a little self-conscious.

The air inside the house contained heavy, almost tactile aromas. Juliet closed the door behind her and inhaled leaden molecules from beef drippings. She tried to separate the other components. The sweet scent of sugar and molasses had to be from Alice's pies on a cooling rack. A mouth-watering aroma of homemade bread reached her, along with the tang of orange cloves and the smoky musk of a wood stove radiating heat that she could feel from across the room.

Nick gave his aunt a warm hug and turned to her. "Aunt Alice, Juliet Driscoll."

Juliet was taken aback by the appearance of a once beautiful woman as she extended her hand. Alice wore gray hair pinned back from a face lined with a thousand wrinkles, but she carried herself as if each one was a badge of honor.

"You're lovely ma'am," Juliet said without thinking. "I'm pleased to meet you."

Buzzy chimed in, "I tell her that almost every day."

"He does not," Alice said with a pleased expression. "But you, my dear...where are you from? You're a beauty, but definitely not Norwegian." She lightly touched Juliet around her cheeks and brushed her chin with a feathery caress. Juliet had the sense that her touch was compensation for vision that no longer held sharpness or clarity. The older woman withdrew her hand abruptly and made apologetic noises. "My goodness. Pardon me for being a bit informal. Sometimes I forget my manners."

Juliet smiled. "That's okay. And as far as my background is concerned, I'm afraid it's getting to be a long story."

The woman's expression clouded. "I'm not sure what that means, but I'll accept it."

Buzzy interrupted. "Nick, ladies, why don't we all take a look at Alice's car before it gets too dark. Plenty of time for conversation around the table tonight."

Alice's eyes sparkled. "Kind of bossy, isn't he?"

Juliet had the impression that the vehicle was almost a gift, one that seemed to be of very little importance to Nick's aunt and uncle as they arranged themselves later at the dinner table. They were seated side by side as opposing couples across a large table crafted from aged wooden planks. Tall brass candlesticks buried in mountains of tallow held back the Dakota night.

She repeated her thanks, even though the brown mutt of a car was the last one she would ever have chosen for herself. Still, it ran like new and she was extremely grateful.

Buzzy shrugged as he cut into a thick wedge of prime rib. "We're just glad to have someone who will actually use it. When you get to our age...well, there's just pleasure in doing things like this." He chewed thoughtfully and swallowed. "Something else." He cleared his throat. "Nick was in college the last time he brought a woman out here. I believe it was college, right Nick? I know it was after you got back from Afghanistan, 'cause you had all those medals and the shrapnel still in your shoulder."

"College," Nick said.

"Yeah college. Anyway Juliet, that alone tells me that you're a good friend of his."

"And *I* was afraid that I might not be able to find a home for the car," Alice said. "It's a useless hunk of metal if you can't drive anymore. But now it's settled." Her voice carried an emphasis that signaled the end of the subject, and she turned her attention to the fluted crystal of her iced water glass. Beads of moisture condensed on the stemware as she helped herself to a sip. Then she said, "Please enjoy the wine. There are so many things I cannot do anymore. Drinking alcohol is one."

"Alice is from Connecticut originally," Nick said. "Her father ran an import-export business. Wine was one of the commodities."

"We have a cellar full," Buzzy added.

In the soft halo of flickering shadows Juliet beheld a meal she could not possibly finish. The generous cut of rare prime beef by itself might last her a week. Scalloped potatoes were shouldered up against pearl onions in a cream sauce, and on the same plate sat a huge mound of succotash. A platter of cornbread rested in the center of the table.

"I put that up last summer," Alice remarked, indicating the succotash. "And that's my mother's Connecticut-style cornbread. We Yankees used to make it with yellow cornmeal and we added a little more sugar."

"Alice, she won't have room for your pecan pies," Nick put in.

"Well then, she can just take one home with her. You can have the other one. The pleasure's all in the making."

Juliet flicked her eyes sideways and connected with Nick, who seemed to give her an encouraging nod. This was his family, and she tried to imagine herself as part of such an intimate group and could not. She had never experienced such generosity and immediate acceptance in her entire life. A wave of envy washed over her. If nothing else, this firmed her desire to discover her own identity and that of her parents.

Alice dabbed her lips with a napkin. "Juliet, you said your background was a long story. That, my dear, is one of the most intriguing introductions I've heard in a while."

Juliet took a bite of potatoes and prime rib. She was not delaying her response so much as formulating a suitable reply. If she omitted all of the bad parts she wouldn't have much to tell. She decided to leave out only the worst of the bad. And there was this thought: Nick had obviously been through a life threatening experience much worse than anything she had endured, so enough with her emotional shortcomings. She took wine in small sips and made the not-so-good parts of her life funny. The really bad stuff she left out.

At ten o'clock in the evening Juliet was so uncomfortably full she could barely walk, and the hour was much later than she would have imagined for older folks. Following a tight embrace and a kiss from Alice she was escorted down the porch steps to her new car by Nick and his uncle. The outside lights illuminated the brown shoe of a vehicle. She smiled anyway.

"I'll be behind you in the Durango until we get to Route 5," Nick said.

Buzzy pulled a toothpick from his mouth and said to Nick, "I guess you know your deputy Murphy and that ex-Sheriff Pritchard who you replaced are still around shooting ducks out of season. They're also baiting with corn. They don't seem to care about the rules for everyone else."

"Or the fact that it's against the law," Nick said. "Next time you hear about it tell me. I'll put a quick stop to that." He turned to Juliet, "George Murphy is—"

"I know who he is," she said. "And I don't like him. He comes into the Crossroads once in a while."

"That's why you're the sheriff now, Nick," Buzzy said. "No one can hide what goes on around here. People tend to know about these things, and they never liked Sheriff Pritchard once they got onto him." He reached for Juliet's hand. "Anyway, Juliet, if my nephew has a brain in his head he'll make sure you get back out here once in a while so Alice can put some meat on your bones. And tell Nick to take you out now and again. Alice and I used to like going to the movies."

Nick grinned. "Buzzy, they're making them in color nowadays."

"Oh really, Mr. Smart-aleck?"

Nick laughed. "Uh…Juliet, did you have a question for Uncle Buzzy? The one you asked me about in the car?"

She turned a questioning look to Nick's uncle. "I asked Nick what your real name was. He told me you never liked people knowing."

Buzzy ran a hand over his scalp and looked away. After a moment he leaned forward and planted a kiss below her ear. "It's Arf," he whispered.

"Like…" She tried not to laugh.

He laughed for her. "Like a dog, arf, arf. Why do you think I like the name Buzzy?"

"But…?"

He raised a hand. "My name was supposed to be Alf. However when my Norwegian father—Nick's grandfather—gave the name to the recording nurse his English was so poor it must've sounded to her like 'Arf'. So it became official, and everyone's had their fun over the years."

She fought a smile and returned a kiss to his cheek. "You've got a nice family, Alf. And this has been just a perfect dinner. Please tell Alice how much this has meant to me."

"She knows. I believe she already knows."

11

The kitchen window offered an excellent, running view of the wide-open slope of the hill, past the well, all the way to the barn. Doris observed Lenny screwing around with his pickup truck when the phone rang. She plucked the remote handset from the opposite wall and returned to her station over the sink. She let it ring a few times as she watched Lenny. He was probably changing the oil in his truck. That's about all he was capable of.

She punched the green talk button. "Hello."

"Doris Blackwell?"

"Who's this?"

"Mrs. Blackwell, could I call you Doris? This is Donald Rhinehart, your brother's lawyer and his close friend. I recall that you and I met briefly during your deposition regarding Clifford years ago."

"Wait, I—yeah, I remember you."

"Um, have you got a minute? I can call later if I'm interrupting."

"I guess this is as good a time as any. This about Clifford?"

"And you. But yes, I am actually calling for Cliff. He knows...well, we all know what his prognosis is. And since you are his only blood relative left in the world, he wants me to touch base and clear up any questions you might have regarding his final wishes, especially since his position as successor trustee of the Driscoll fortune makes things a little involved. These legal documents are more complicated than they should be. Sometimes we lawyers just can't get out of our own way." He put out a self-deprecating laugh.

Did he use the word 'fortune'? She took a breath. "I…Cliffy wants me to have everything. That's what he said."

"That's correct, as far as it goes, and the possibility does exist that you will inherit the entire fortune."

There it was again. So Cliffy was telling the truth. She gazed unfocused through windowpanes layered with a brown coating of grime around the edges. The sun was out for a change, but the day was still cold. Maybe the North Dakota weather wouldn't matter for much longer. She'd be in—pick a state: Florida, Arizona? But first she'd sell Cliffy's pile of bricks out from under that Marietta bitch.

She coughed back a bit of respiratory mucous and reached for her cigarettes. "So, do I need to sign anything, or you know, fill out something?"

"Actually, yes. Frankly, if the proceeds from the trust go to you, I'd like some idea of how you'd like me to manage the funds. We're talking millions of dollars here, and it's not too early to set up an investment plan. It would be best to work with a financial advisor. I can help with that."

Her heart thumped in a series of hard, fast beats, a runaway freight train with the hammer down. This was real. *This was damn near going to happen!* Why else would Rhinehart be calling? *A financial advisor?* Holy shit! Doris tucked the handset between her shoulder and neck, mumbled a few incoherent words, and pulled a Lucky from the pack. Her hands were shaking as she flared a paper match. She pulled in a deep drag from the unfiltered tobacco, held the smoke in her lungs for a half-second—she needed the full hit—and expelled the cloudy vapor like a jet exhaust from her nasal passages. The match and a reflexive tap of the ash went into the sink.

He went on. "I can send you some brochures to look over. These are the special ones that typically go to our high net worth individuals."

"Ah…" A freeway of blood was pouring into her brain. Synapses were popping in her head like oil dropped on a red-hot skillet.

After a suitable pause he said, "Of course, your official designation as the contingent beneficiary would be subject to several—let's call them 'conditions of fate'."

She noted a tiny apology in his voice. "Like what?"

"Actually, the Driscoll twins, Lenny and Juliet, would stand in line ahead of you, that is, if they're still…present."

Stand in line? Like outside a fucking movie theater?

"They've got an important birthday coming up. Perhaps Cliff mentioned it."

"They get the trust when they reach thirty." Her voice was shaking. "Yeah, he said that."

"That's…" He paused as if checking his wristwatch. "That's about three months away. Their birthday's on the fifteenth of May."

"I got that."

"So when we get closer to that date, I'll be sending them the same brochures, if they're in good health and…available."

"And if they're not, like available?"

"Then you are going to be extremely wealthy. And trust me, you'll need help managing the investment of all those millions."

She swallowed and croaked a few dry words. "I'll be interested in seeing the brochures."

"Yes ma'am. I'll put them in the mail today." he said.

She took the final nicotine charged puff from her cigarette and flicked the remains onto the cracked linoleum floor. She wedged a shoe over the butt and mashed it into the dingy gray surface. Fuck it. She wasn't going to be living in this dump much longer.

She had to settle down, get some air, and put a weather eye out on her course of action for the twins. Rhinehart's call made her head spin. She'd already found flaws that a simpleton could have anticipated. She wouldn't call herself *stupid*. She was simply *ignorant* of the ramifications. The two words were similar. However, the meanings were completely different. For instance, plenty of smart women had come to her needlepoint workshops a few years back. They were ignorant in their knowledge of yarns and stitches and mesh counts, but they were not stupid. No more than she was in the application of her plan for the twins. She just hadn't seriously thought it through.

Lenny, however, was stupid in the truest sense of the word. Her plan was therefore backward. He, and not his sister, would be going into the well. Juliet would see through the thing in a second. The bitch was too smart. Lenny, on the other hand, could damn near be tricked with a Hershey Bar just inside the rim. She just hadn't fully considered the situation.

And frankly, ever since Juliet had gone and filed the criminal complaint against Cliffy she hadn't trusted her. The slut had been around the other day in a nice looking car—probably screwing some guy for it—and talking to Lenny in a way that made her uneasy. When they came down the stairs Juliet had a sneaky smile, and her stupid brother looked as if he'd just been told about the tooth fairy. It was time to move ahead with her agenda, big time.

Working the old water well into the plan was not going to be that easy. The problem was not in getting Lenny to the rim of the old structure. The problem was making the mishap look reasonable in the eyes of the law. There was a way, however.

For years, hell, almost as long as she could remember, their water had come from a submersible pump buried deeply in the guts of the shaft. The quality of their water had never been good. It stained the showerheads, the sinks, the tubs, and the toilets. Not only that, but the taste was off. She'd gotten used to it, but only because she'd never thought about replacing the pump, maybe having a crew place it deeper into the bottom of the well. They could hit a different aquifer or something. Of course, for the day or two that they'd be working, the well cap would have to be off. Plenty of leeway in there for what she had in mind.

Juliet would have to be the one squashed beneath the car. The accident would be quick and deadly. Hit her once and go back and help things along if that's what it took. Put a gentle hand over her mouth, nothing more.

She lit another Lucky with a second paper match from the casino stash. She had two dozen booklets with black enameled covers imprinted with an Indian's profile in full headdress. Damned if she was going to leave them lying around in that shitty room they gave her. She dropped the spent match in the tea-stained porcelain sink and took a deep breath. She had a lot to think about. Holy Mother of God.

12

Juliet caught her breath as she peered at a likeness of her mother, Lyra Driscoll, for the first time. Her kitchen table held a clutter of pictures, documents, and clippings that she had brought down from Doris' attic.

Earlier, rather than placing a call to her brother, which was problematic in the best of times, she had driven by the house on the chance that Doris was out. She got lucky on the first try and retrieved the papers from under Lenny's bed.

Her mother's photo was still clearly discernible on a yellowed page of old newspaper print. She had carried a slight grin as she looked directly at the camera, as if she knew and liked the photographer. Juliet's father stood beside her. His expression appeared faraway and serious, a man caught in the act of scanning the far mountains for the mineral deposits he knew were there.

The article profiled her father, a young geologist named Walter Driscoll, who seemed to have a knack for unearthing the richest ore deposits. Her mother generated the magnetism in the photo, however. She was younger at the time than Juliet was at this moment, and the resemblance was startling. Juliet traced her own facial features with the fingertips of her right hand. Her eyebrows, straight nose, and the curve of her lips duplicated her mom's. Yet the woman in the photo had a look of contentment, and Juliet knew why; her mother was pregnant at the time, but only just. The newspaper was dated seven months before the date on their birth certificates. Did her mother know? Of course she did. And the camera captured the secret exhilaration that even her husband might have missed. The photo brought forth a twist of sorrow that Juliet had never experienced. Her mother could not have been aware that she would never really know the children she would bring into the world.

Other documents littered the table. She separated the birth certificates from the pile.

She and her brother had been born in Lewiston, Idaho, county of Nez Perce, on the 15th of May. She had been first at 7:10 am. Lenny was a full thirty minutes later at 7:40am. Was that normal?

The certificate listed her father as a mining engineer, her mother as a lawyer. Juliet blew a soft breath through her teeth. That would explain her ease with academic concepts. But then, what had gone wrong with Lenny? They should have the same abilities, but did not. Unfortunately, whatever might have happened would never be known.

She slid the birth certificates to the side and retrieved a second page of newsprint. The same gray-toned snapshot from before had been reprinted under a different article dated two years and seven months later. This one was reduced in size in order to fit on the bottom, front page of the Idaho Star-News. A prickle of apprehension gave her goose bumps. She took a deep breath and release it slowly.

Her parents had been killed in a small plane crash, not in a car accident as she and Lenny had always been told. According to the flight plan on file, their route had taken them over the rugged Bitterroot Range. They were never heard from again. A search was underway, the article stated. However, the responders were quoted as not being optimistic that the crash site could be found.

So there it was. A wistful sadness settled over her, but no tears fell. Her parents had departed life too many years before, had spun away their offspring as if they were already fated to die.

There was more in the obituary: references to a mining corporation, her parent's home in Coeur d'Alene, their surviving children. She had never before seen her name in print, and now on the faded page of her parents' final notice the mention gave her an eerie sensation of a split dimension, something forever left behind in time and space.

She shoved the remainder of the paperwork to the side and pushed away from the table. She had seen enough, at least for the time being. The wall clock showed three o'clock in the afternoon. She needed to talk. Darlene would be starting her shift at the Crossroads. Her spa girlfriends from the Zumba group were always available for gossipy phone calls, but that was the problem. As much as she enjoyed their company, they had their own troubles with kids and divorces and late alimony checks, not to mention the walk-through lovers. That left Lenny, but the facts would disturb him for no reason. He didn't have to know, maybe ever. She knew who she wanted to talk with, but her throat went dry at the thought.

She made coffee, sat at her computer, and worked listlessly on her physics problems. The elegant equations for flow and kinetic energy were blocked by a restlessness within. The sequential derivations that came so easily before seemed impossible to solve.

She gave up, took a deep breath, and picked up the phone. She punched in the number for the Sheriff's Department in Sherwood. A guy picked up on the second ring and gave his name as Murphy. She knew who he was.

She cleared her throat and held back the nervousness in her voice. "Yes, I'm calling for Sheriff Olsen if he's in."

"Name?"

"Driscoll." She answered with the same clipped cadence Murphy used.

"Is this an emergency?"

"No. It's personal."

"Hold on."

She waited through a short delay. A door slammed somewhere. She heard the rumble of male voices. The guy had evidently dropped the phone on the table. Didn't they have a hold button on the console?

"Olsen here." Nick's voice came through the line, maybe with a question mark in the tone. A thought poked her: Did guys walk around all day calling each other by their last names? 'How you doing, Jones? I'm okay, Smith.'

"Would that be Nick Olsen?" she asked.

"You are correct. And you would be Juliet. Nice to hear from you, Ms. Driscoll. My Toyota hasn't broken down, I hope." His voice held warmth and concern.

"No-no. Actually I used it this morning to run up to Doris' house. A little sleet was on the road, but the fact is I just enjoy driving it. Hope you don't mind."

"I wanted you to use it. Otherwise it just sits in my carport."

"You can pick it up anytime, now that I've got the Mercury. And thanks again for all your help, especially for the evening at your aunt and uncle's. You've got a nice family, extended family I guess."

"They're all I've got left. We Olsens don't seem to produce much in the way of offspring."

He left a slight pause on the end of the line. Juliet took a breath. "I took your advice about my birth certificate, Nick. I found it, along with some other papers that I've never seen before. I know who my parents are, and I know what happened, and I... " Stop. She was rushing the conversation like a schoolgirl. She held her breath for several seconds. Sometimes that calmed her.

"What? I missed that, Juliet."

She spoke slowly. "I was going to say that I know who my parents are, or were I should say, and how they died."

He seemed hung up in thought on the other end. "Good news. And I mean it. You've got a family now. You've always had a family, of course, but you never knew who they were. And what do you mean 'other papers'?"

"I'm not sure. I haven't gone through everything. All this stuff was hidden in Doris' attic all these years."

There was a silence. She sensed he was making a cop-like assessment.

"Nick?"

"I'm just thinking that the woman is beginning to fit a profile."

"What do you mean?"

"Nothing maybe. I ramble sometimes. Hold on for a second."

He held the receiver to his chest. She could hear an indistinct, guttural flutter that moved with the stops and starts of a conversation.

He came back. "I can help you sort through everything. I mean, if you want. I'd like to know a little more about the mysterious Driscoll family."

Her blood pressure took a leap. She could feel it in her temples. "I don't know if that would be…you know, necessary."

"I can take a look at your hand while I'm at it. Stitches have gotta be about ready to come out."

She inspected her left hand, turned it back to front, as if making a determination. "There's no blood showing through the gauze. But it's starting to itch."

"That's a good sign, and it may indicate they're ready to come out. I can change your bandage, at least. You can't do that as easily with only one hand."

She stared at her dressing as though waiting for a sign. She had done a sloppy job when she changed it earlier. "Just you and me? What would we…I mean, when would we get together?"

"How about tonight. Murphy said he'd cover for me. We could discuss everything while I fix you dinner."

Her heart skipped a beat, then another. She pressed her bandaged hand against her chest to steady the rhythm. "Wouldn't that be like a date?"

"Maybe. But we could call it a discussion session if you like."

"Nick, remember we already had a date years ago in high school. It didn't work out so well."

His voice changed. "That was a long time ago. Besides, I wanted to ask you out again at the time, I just never did. I was just a teenager myself and kind of nervous. This could be our second date."

She expected him to continue. He seemed content to wait on her response. She said, "I… So you're not nervous anymore?"

"Not as."

"Okay, then. A date would be nice."

"I've seen your kitchen layout. Pretty simple. How about steaks?"

"Steaks would be fine."

Nick arrived as the winter darkness bore down on the northern plains. He stomped his feet at the door and took her hand in a formal greeting. A sack of groceries wedged itself under the other arm. "Like I said, we can call this a discussion period, if you like." He stood over the threshold, half in and half out of the door. "It doesn't have to be an official date."

She had to remind herself she was not in high school anymore. "Nick, for crying out loud, would you come on in? Don't tell me you're still nervous. We've already had dinner together at your aunt and uncle's."

He lurched through the entrance with a puff of cold air. "Yeah, but that was neutral territory. Your place is a little different."

She closed the door behind him. "When a man treats a woman to dinner, especially a woman he's not married to, it's usually called a date. I'm fine with that."

"You took your bandage off," he remarked in surprised.

"It just felt like everything was almost back to normal." She had showered and changed earlier, and that involved unwrapping the dressing on her wound. A spot of red had welled up as she flexed her fingers and put tension in her fist, but the water had quickly washed the blood away.

"Okay," he said with doubt in his voice. "You look nice by the way."

Juliet had pulled her hair back, fastened a turtle shell clasp in the back, and allowed her longer locks to drape her shoulders. A pair of black denim jeans, topped with a cream-colored turtleneck completed her outfit. "What's in the bag?" she asked. "Looks like more than a few steaks."

Nick moved to her small kitchen and deposited the brown paper bag on the counter. He took off his heavy parka and looked around.

"Here, let me take it." She reached for his jacket and tossed it on the sofa.

"I've got a bottle of wine, frozen French fries, fresh broccoli. Not sure what you had in the fridge." And then, "Your cut is bleeding again."

She turned her hand palm side up. "Damn. I grabbed your parka with my left hand. Just forgot."

He shrugged. "It's got to be healed by now. You just pulled something. I was going to examine the stitches anyway."

"Can I can get you a bottle of beer first?"

"How about I open the wine?"

"That would be nice." Juliet sipped the delightful red wine a few minutes later and watched while he re-applied a dressing to her hand.

"I'm going to leave the sutures in for another day or two," he said. "I can see where you pulled apart a tiny corner of my repair job." He nudged back her sleeve until more of her arm was exposed. The ugly tracks left by the razor years before were once again plainly visible. Well, he'd seen them before, she reasoned. She tried to ignore them, and hoped that he would too.

They were seated at her kitchen table. Nick had produced a pair of rimless glasses, and his longish, white-blond strands fell over his forehead despite his repeated attempts to brush them away. The cuffs of his blue, oxford cloth dress shirt were rolled back exposing light hair on his arms. He wore no jewelry: no gaudy macho ring, no oversized wristwatch with heavy, dangling links. His hands were not rough or brutish looking, and she wondered how he could have taken down a man like the Kellam thug so easily. His fingers had a graceful, curved appearance, and she imagined him moving a T-square on a drafting board, or tying sutures over a patient on an operating table. Almost invisible filaments of fine, blond hair sprouted between his knuckles. His total absorption with regard to her person struck her in amazement. She had scarcely in her life been the focus of anyone's complete, undivided concentration unless the possibility of sex was involved. Yet here was a man who seemed to take interest in a very small part of her body for no other reason than to help make her better. A vague sense of something nice took hold, as if she might be drifting with the current for a change and not fighting against it.

Nick's eyes flicked to her face. "You okay?"

Juliet nodded and hid behind another sip of wine. Her thoughts slid around, moving with the ebb and flow of his gentle ministrations. "Nick?" she said in a sudden realization, "Ever since Buzzy made that remark at the table I've wanted to ask you about Afghanistan, the terrible danger you were in, your wounds. Can you...are you willing to talk about anything?"

He raised his head and took off his glasses. For an instant his gaze remained unfocused, as if a thousand images were downloading onto his retina. "It's not something that's easy to discuss," he said slowly. "Simply because so much happened. Perhaps later. If we end up close to each other, maybe as friends, then I'll want you to know."

"And if we don't end up close to each other?"

"Then I won't care." He replaced his glasses and ripped a section of surgical tape with his teeth. He folded a square of gauze to match the size of her palm. If he was upset he didn't show it.

She tried again. "What was your wife like? Can you answer that?"

That brought a smile, and he thought for a moment. "That's a good question."

"And?" she said after at least thirty seconds of silence.

"You have to remember I was younger. However, I never did know who she really was. It's possible she didn't know herself, or didn't care."

"That's kind of general."

He brought his eyes up to hers. "She was calculating. By that I mean she made herself into whatever she needed to be in order to get what she wanted. I kind of screwed up her plan when I didn't finish med school."

"Where did she end up? Any idea?"

He shook his head. "Probably went looking for another doctor."

"Was she pretty?"

He exhaled thoughtfully. "Yeah, I guess. She had a cheerleader's face and figure. One that won't last."

Juliet laughed. "You don't know that. She might be a total gym rat."

He shook his head again and smiled.

A short time later Nick lightly placed his thumb on her scars. "Do you want to talk about these?"

"No." She put her glass on the table and eased her hand from his grip. He tightened in response.

"Juliet?"

"No!" She withdrew her hand sharply. Her smile—she realized she'd been sitting there like a stooge—vanished. Everything inside her began to tighten. God, to go through those terrible days again... She'd cramp if she had to talk about it, an acid knot would take hold and twist her insides for hours.

"Juliet?"

"Stop pressuring me." Her voice went shaky and she brought her left hand tightly into her lap and protected it with the right.

"I'm not going to hurt you, Juliet. I'm not going to hurt you..." He repeated the phrase over and over in a soft voice. Was he trying to hypnotize her? She couldn't focus. Clifford Blackwell was bearing down on her, his sweaty lips crawling over her skin leaving the slimy, mucous trail of a leech. She felt nauseous. The razor blade she had used days afterward floated in her mind's eye.

He continued speaking in a hushed monotone of windless calm, a gentle drizzle after the burst of her storm. The words fell away without meaning, but she rode the up and down inflections in his voice for a while, like an infant being rocked to sleep. The ugly images dissolved at length, although she couldn't determine the exact measurement of time. His face came into focus, and she concentrated on his words.

"...and so you've got to understand that," he said.

"What?"

"I said..." He handed her a tissue. "Here. Take this."

Her eyes were wet, and she dabbed her face. After a moment she surfaced. "Sorry," she said, trying to keep her voice even. "I have trouble with some of the things in my past. I blank them out, or try to." She made a thin, apologetic smile. "You might have guessed that."

He held his open palm out for hers. "Here."

"Here, what?"

"Here, take my hand again with your left."

She shook her head sharply. "Why would I do that?"

"It's for me, not for you."

"Why for you? You want to humiliate me or something? I'm already there, Nick." She felt renewed wetness in her eyes.

"I want you to become comfortable with me touching you, especially in a place that's sensitive and private."

She couldn't speak for a minute. She studied the creases and folds in his blue shirt. The cotton had a soft, supple look, like he never ironed it or anything, just hung it up straight out of the dryer. He'd left the top button undone and a wisp of blond hair curled underneath the fabric. He was covered in blond. Would he someday father all blond-headed kids?

"Please, Juliet. Your hand."

She sighed. "Wouldn't this be kind of like getting back on the horse that just threw me?"

He nodded. "You could say that. But keep in mind this is for me, not for you."

"That's just bullshit, Nick. Some kind of psychotherapy crap. What, now you're a shrink? What happened to the sheriff?"

His smile seemed a trifle self-conscious. "I like touching you, Miss Driscoll. And I have to play doctor to do it. That's really what it's all about."

"Well, you could've said so." Her hand moved slowly toward his without conscious intent. She watched him wrap both of his large palms around her newly bandaged wound, then move his fingers very carefully over her scars. She flinched but did not pull away.

"Just relax and feel the warmth of my hands. It's freezing cold outside and it's even cool in here, so this ought to feel good." He slowly began to massage her tendons and muscles.

"It's only cold in here because you were standing in the doorway for so long," she said. "Like a dope." Her normal tone of voice had to be returning, because he smiled again. "You were nervous," she added for good measure. "You admitted that."

"Yes, I was a little."

"Me too," she said, surprised at herself. She couldn't think of anything else to say, so she decided to relax, despite the sheer lunacy of his pop therapy. She picked up her glass of wine, helped herself to a large swallow, and reclined comfortably in the chair. His touch did feel soothing, and after a minute or two she said, "I suppose you took some type of psychology course in med school?" The words seemed to drift away from her.

"Some. But I also picked up a little knowledge of massage: neck and back, hands and feet. Those are the most stressful areas for most people, especially for women. The human foot has twenty different muscles attached to ligaments and tendons."

Juliet had never had a foot massage, and she couldn't get there in her mind with Nick. The concept seemed too intimate, something she associated with lovers, or maybe a husband and wife on a couch late at night watching TV. Instead, she concentrated on her wine, tucked the glass to her lap. Her left arm seemed to know where it wanted to be. Who was she to interfere?

He went on. "Ever had a neck or back massage?"

She shook her head and brought her glass to her lips. The wine was good.

"Would you like one? We could call it a doctor's prescription."

"Nick, why are you being so nice to me?"

He slowed the gentle manipulation. "I'm not going to tell you all the reasons. I will say that I've always liked you, even from the first day of high school. I'm talking years ago, Juliet. Besides that, you're a smart, good-looking woman."

"Be careful, or you'll start sounding like some of the guys at the Crossroads when they're drunk."

"And you're complicated. That appeals to me. You've got walls, but you've also got direction. No one's going to tell you who you are."

"Maybe I'm unsure of that myself."

"Nope. You're definitely not trying to be anyone else. The whole world couldn't make you do that. Unlike my ex-wife."

A thought struck her. "How come you never called for another date back in high school? Did I scare you off that badly?"

"I did call a couple of times. I got Doris. She didn't tell you?"

Juliet shook her head. "Jeez. Why didn't I expect that? She's worse than mean. I should have known better. But how come you never talked to me at school?"

"I guess I was a little embarrassed. I tried to accidently bump into you a couple of times, but you were always with two or three other girlfriends. I even thought about just walking over to the freshman wing, but I chickened out. Besides, I wasn't that positive that you wanted to go out with me. You seemed pretty uptight the first time."

She sat up straight. "Well that's flattering. I guess. It'll give me something to think about."

The bottle of wine was almost empty and they had yet to start on the steaks. Her cramps and nausea from earlier never took hold in a big way and she was hungry.

Nick's focus was intense as he sat at the kitchen table and worked through the documents and newspaper clippings. "Have you read through all of this," he asked.

"Most of it. I never knew my parents were so smart," she said. "Now I understand where my math aptitude comes from."

"They were definitely accomplished individuals."

She smiled. "Can you believe it? A mining engineer and a lawyer?"

"You should have been the one going to med school. And by the way, you've got your mom's good looks."

"Thanks." Juliet couldn't help herself. "And you may not believe this, but for the past two years I've been working problems in physics on-line with the university. Things like thermal dynamics, kinetic energy, equations of flow dynamics. If I keep at it I'll end up with a degree."

"What?"

"Physics. It's—"

"I know what the science of physics is. I took enough of it in college. Some in med school." He reached for his wine and drained the glass. "Ever heard of Avogadro's Number?"

"What?" She laughed. "You don't believe me?" She divided the remainder of the bottle and plunked it on the table. "Dead soldier."

"I believe you're smarter than me. Really smart, but I'm not sure how much you've been able to learn on your own. It has to do with—"

"Don't tell me! I know what Avogadro's Number is."

"So?"

"It's a constant value referring to the number of molecules or atoms in one *mole* of a substance. Commonly referred to by a capital 'N', smaller capital 'A'." She right-handed a pencil and scribbled 'N_A' on a sheet of paper.

He shook his head, a light in his eyes. "Lord, woman."

"Impressed?" She grinned.

"I've always been. I told you that."

"Nick," she replied a little uncertainly, "You're making me feel…I don't know, indebted, like you've always felt this way, so I've got to return the emotion. I don't know what I feel."

"You don't have to return anything. I'm a big guy, all grown up. I've been married, had relationships. If something develops it develops. I think I can handle your attitude, whatever it is. I had a high school crush. You're not that person anymore. Neither am I."

"It's not that. It's…guys I've been with, they don't want a relationship or anything. It's comforting in a way. You can keep yourself locked up inside, just do the superficial stuff. With you it's different. You want me to open up, let you see who I am, and as I mentioned, sometimes I don't think I even know who I am."

"Then let's call a truce. There's enough mystery spread out on this table to keep us occupied for tonight."

"Yeah." She smiled just a little. "Okay. Then we can go on?"

"Please."

"Okay." She breathed a sigh and extracted a manila folder from the pile. "I wanted your opinion on this. I just glanced through it. There's a lot of stuff that looks like corporate legalese. Thought you could take a look at that."

He pulled out the first several pages. "It's a document of incorporation, dated about the time you were born."

She nodded. "I got that much. Something about the Wolverine Mining Corporation."

Nick had pocketed his glasses. Now he brought them out again. "It appears that your parents set up this corporation. Their names and signatures are right here at the bottom."

"So this was their company?"

"Yeah, hold on. Let me read this." He pursed his lips and mumbled a couple of syllables with his head down. "This was set up by a Jonas Blackwell, evidently their lawyer." He looked up. "Ever heard of him?"

"I think he was Doris' brother. There was one who died years ago."

"Aha. I'm beginning to see something here. Maybe that explains how you and Lenny ended up with his sister Doris. There must have been some type of agreement in the event of the death of your parents."

"But they wouldn't have just shoved us onto their lawyer's sister? Why would they do that?"

"Maybe they didn't. It could be that this Jonas fellow agreed to raise you as his own, but then he died too. And it had to have been very shortly after your parents were killed. You wouldn't even remember, given your age at the time. What were you, two, almost three?"

"So we went to live with his sister? But wait, Nick. I do remember living in a big house. I think we actually stayed with Clifford for a while." A shiver passed through her at his name.

"And he was…"

"*Is* Doris and Jonas's brother."

"Okay. The guy from Bismarck. He came around once in a while. Helped out."

"That's him."

"We should have thought of that. He would have been the natural, first choice, especially if he was married."

"I don't know. Maybe he was at the time." She released her tortoise shell clasp, tipped her head backward, and combed her fingers through her hair. After a series of readjustments she refastened the clip.

"Very few guys are lifelong bachelors," he said. "We'll assume at some point he was married and inherited the responsibility of you both. But…" He picked up the pencil, stuck it between his teeth, and cracked the glossy, yellow surface.

"What?"

"I think there's something missing. Was this all you could find?"

"Doris was coming in the house. I had to grab what I could. What are you looking for? And you've got a fleck of yellow paint on your tongue."

He put the pencil on the table and pinched away the particle. "I'm almost positive your parents would have taken care to guarantee that a trust of some kind followed you and your brother. You know, to pay for college, all the stuff that parents do for their kids." He leafed through the pages. "What happened to that?"

"There was some other stuff in the attic. I could feel more in the satchel, but Lenny kept yelling that Doris was coming, and I had to get down that rickety ladder in a hurry. There's more here anyway, stuff that I haven't looked at real closely."

He slid a sepia-toned photocopy from the envelope. "Your birth certificate. You'll be...holy shit, you'll be thirty in a few months!"

A single eyebrow went up. "Are you trying to be funny again?"

"Yeah."

"Why don't I cook the steaks and let you alone for a few minutes? You can learn even more about me."

"That'd be nice, Juliet The Engineer."

Nick realized immediately that Juliet was telling the truth. She had not waded through all nine or ten pages of the legalese. He scanned the letter-sized sheets stuck behind the corporate filings in disbelief. A soft whistle of air escaped from his lips. He had before him something so private, so personal that he questioned reading further. The cop part of him put the misgivings aside and he plowed ahead.

"How do you like your steak?" Juliet asked. "And please don't say well done."

He looked up. "Rare. Maybe medium rare."

"How about blackened? I can do that too."

"What?"

"Blackened. I help the guys cook once in a while at the Crossroads. I've got all the spices."

Her voice had a nice, relaxed quality, and he made an effort to match it. "You're a chef also?"

"I'm a little bit of everything, and more of everything as I get older."

"Yeah, an old woman. I can see that."

She turned with a rapid movement and flicked water in his face. He blinked and tucked his head sideways. "Okay, okay. I take it back."

"It's my bar training," she said. "And blackened it is."

He watched Juliet light the propane with a *whoosh*, but his mind was on the three pages of a legal deposition that he had uncovered. The testimony signed by Doris Blackwell and a lawyer named Rhinehart referenced a criminal complaint entitled *USA vs Clifford Blackwell*. Doris' testimony refuted allegations that Clifford Blackwell had subjected one Juliet Driscoll to forced sexual assault. Nick read to the end, pushed back from the table, and thumbed quickly through the entire handful of pages in his lap. Somewhere in the stack there probably existed the actual criminal complaint of rape that Juliet lodged against Clifford Blackwell. He needed a few minutes, but she looked over with a faint crease in her brow. "You find something in there?"

He tossed the documents on the table and spoke over the sizzle of the steaks. "There's a lot here and I'd rather watch you cook."

She turned her profile in his direction, and her form-fitting jeans and turtleneck centered his focus. "What, Nick? Say something." The half-smile that she'd been carrying disappeared.

"How's the car working out?" he said for lack of anything else.

"Which one? I still like driving your 4-Runner, even though your aunt and uncle were incredibly generous with the Mercury. You want yours back?" She motioned with her head. "It's out there on the lot."

"Whenever. If you like driving it just keep it for a few more days."

She turned off the burners, killed the microwave, and pulled out a chair opposite him at the table. "The steaks'll keep for a few minutes. Everything else is ready." She brought her eyes to his. "I may be getting a little woozy or something, but when you came in you were…I don't know, more lighthearted, funny. Now you're acting weird. What happened? And this doesn't have anything to do with the cars."

The problem was he knew her inner secret now. The moment she discovered Doris' deposition in the pile her attitude toward him would change. She would accept that he'd read enough about the rapes to see her in a different light, and that he'd try to open doors inside her that she wanted closed forever. She'd lock the gates and raise the drawbridge even further. Her layers of emotional armor were already as tough to penetrate as a hardened missile silo. Was it even worth it? That was the question.

"Say something, Nick. You're still freaked over my meltdown. Is that right?" She leaned sideways in her chair and stretched a hand to the fridge. She produced two bottles of dark beer and popped the caps with an opener. "I don't usually drink beer on top of wine, but the wine's gone."

He slid his empty wine glass to the side. Out with the old, in with the new. "We've got to get something to eat," he said.

"You're being evasive."

"I know."

"This is delicious," Nick stated a short time later between bites. With the steaks and fries looking at them he'd avoided further cross-examination.

"Thanks."

"No broccoli? I know I brought some."

"I don't eat broccoli," she said, and then added, "I take vitamins."

They'd walked through the meal at a leisurely pace while saying little to each other. He watched her. She watched him with the hooded expression usually reserved for a husband arriving home late from the office once too often. Scattered flecks of green appeared now and then in her irises. He decided her lips were becoming his favorite feature. They were formed with appealing arcs that intersected along the top, creating a sultry mouth that he doubted she was even aware of. Her bottom lip was bare along the inner edge where her lipstick had worn away. She was completely kissable right then and there, and he had an insane desire to do so.

"You're doing it again," she said.

"What?"

"Hiding things."

They were talking in monosyllables. Did this mean that they were connecting too well, or too poorly? "I'm beginning to believe you can read my mind," he said.

"I read a secretive thought. That's what I read. Probably sneaky too."

"It wasn't secretive or sneaky."

She waited through a long silence, a priest anticipating a guilty parishioner's confession.

He said, "I was fantasizing about leaning over the table and kissing you on your incredibly appealing lips. I thought it was funny because of the shock value it would probably create."

Juliet said nothing for a long moment. He watched her pick at the remains of her plate. When she spoke her voice was tight. "I don't seem to be able to kiss anyone on the mouth, Nick." She shrugged. "Just something else quirky about me."

After dinner he stood in the doorway, coat in hand. There was something he had to say. "Juliet, that night we came back from the basketball game. I couldn't figure out why you were so nervous, on edge."

"You wanted to kiss me. Remember?"

He nodded. "Only you were too tense. Like now." He bent toward her. "I'm going to kiss you on the cheek. Okay? Just the cheek."

She closed to him imperceptibly, rested her hands loosely around his waist. He touched his cheek to hers, brushed the soft indentation below her ear with his lips, and exhaled a warm breath alongside hers.

"That okay?" His heart rate accelerated. He was almost certain hers did the same.

"Nick, I'm not…you know, frigid. If you recall, you went so far as to caution me about staying out of trashy motels, or something to that effect. And anyway, I'm not really like that."

"I didn't mean it the way it came out. I apologize, Juliet. It doesn't take much to get things blown out of proportion in a small town. Besides, I'm beginning to understand you a little better."

"That's a nice way of saying I've got a lot of problems."

He took a breath. This had to be said. "Juliet, there's a legal deposition from Doris Blackwell mixed in with the stuff on your parent's corporation."

"What legal deposition? I've never heard of anything like that."

He held up a hand. "It's a reference to a sexual assault in a criminal complaint filed with the state attorney's office in Bismarck. The statements from Doris deny anything ever took place."

Her lips moved, formed words that had no voice. A choked-off sound registered in her throat.

"Juliet, whatever it is—"

"Let's say goodnight, Nick. You're…maybe you'd better let me live my own life and stop interfering. I'm not ready for all this intimacy, and that's what you want. I'm not ready for it." She ran a hand over her eyes. "Maybe it's best if you leave me alone. I'll get your car back to you."

"Juliet—"

"Goodnight, Nick."

13

Juliet's second night back at work was slow. Fridays were usually crowded at the Crossroads, but tonight was the exception. Business was off and Pete Haskett blamed it on the cold weather. An artic front was making its way down from Canada.

"Weather's gotta be the reason." Darlene nodded at Juliet. They were sitting at a half-sized corner table next to the bar. "Because last night we were slammed."

They were keeping an eye on things, but nothing much was moving. Juliet counted a four-top of local boys at one table and the off duty EMT crew at another. The EMTs were having trouble finishing a single bucket.

Her hand was finally healed and the wraps and stitches were gone. She flexed her fingers and considered the past week. The episode with Nick remained fixed in her mind, a pleasurable, dreamlike fog that drifted in and out but never completely dissipated. In a way, she had the sense that at least a part of her left hand now belonged to him, a notion that made no sense whatever.

"Where you off to, girlfriend?" Darlene had a grin.

Juliet blinked and looked over. "A lot's been going on in the last few days. Almost too much to explain. I was going to catch you up last night."

"Not like we had a moment's break."

"I cut my hand," she said lamely.

Darlene laughed. "Pete told me that much."

"I feel like I've got tons of stuff to do, to catch up on. I found out about my parents, who I am. I saw a picture of my mom for the first time. My dad, too. They were lawyers, scientists. Educated people. Nick Olsen's been helping me out."

Darlene placed her hand over Juliet's. "So you can finally sweep all of that shit away, your foster upbringing you told me about."

"Yeah. Maybe. Some things I've never said, though."

Darlene squeezed her hand and sat back. "Honey, you didn't have to tell me everything. I'm pretty sure I've always known what you've been hiding."

For a few minutes neither woman spoke. *The Wichita Lineman* was on the speakers. Pete Haskett popped Glenn Campbell up on the sound system anytime business was slow, and Juliet caught Darlene's headshake. "Gotta get Pete away from that old stuff," she said. "I have to say it's got a nice, easy rhythm, though."

"What do you think I've been hiding?" Juliet asked.

Darlene reshuffled her expression, went serious. "My sister—you know, the one I've told you about in Tennessee. She's a high school counselor in Nashville. Got diplomas and degrees in psychology and developmental stuff with kids. She specializes in childhood abuse, and we've talked a lot about that. I've always thought you kinda had the signs."

Juliet felt her lungs deflate. Was she that easy to read? "Like what?" she said. "What are the signs?"

"Talking like this is gonna be a little painful, even if it's just us, Julie."

She forced a thin laugh. "I don't guess it makes any difference now. Apparently, the whole world is finding out about me."

Darlene moved her hands to her lap. "Well for starters, your left wrist. I've never said anything, but I've noticed. It's a very common signature of abused kids. You were what, eleven, twelve when you did that?"

Juliet nodded slowly. "Maybe. About that, I guess. What else?"

"Your emotional distance. You keep about a mile of separation between yourself and guys. Sometimes you're even a little closed up around me. I understand it though, like I say."

"I take it you had a word with Pete. We had a similar conversation the other night when he took me home."

Darlene nodded. "We talk. You know, pillow talk. But it's not something I couldn't see before."

Juliet could feel tears begin to form. She fought them back. "You're right. This is painful. I've wanted to tell someone for so long but...and here we are in a bar. I thought I'd be talking to a shrink one day."

Darlene shifted forward. "When the time is right, when you feel comfortable talking, let it come out. Sometimes good friends are better than shrinks. Besides, I already feel as if I know. You don't have to say anything if you aren't ready."

The words were ugly. Juliet choked them into a sentence. "The slimy asshole held me down. Twice. Two separate occasions."

"An uncle. Right? Or some family friend?"

"He was called 'uncle', but he wasn't any relation." She dug in her jeans pocket and retrieved a crumpled tissue imprinted with lipstick. "The last time he tried coming after me I kicked the shit out of him."

"Hit him in the nuts?"

"Right at 'em. He was limping after that, I have to tell you."

Darlene grinned. "You shoulda killed him. Would have been total justice."

"He's dying anyway now, or so I've heard. Some nursing home in Bismarck."

"Good. Let's hope he's peeing all over himself in a wheelchair."

Juliet scanned the tables for empty bottles and thirsty looks and found none. She cleared her nose and dabbed at the corners of her eyes trying not to make a huge mess of her mascara. "Well, that feels a little better."

"It's always better to talk it out, girlfriend. We're women, and no one said it'd be easy carrying around the weight of the entire human race."

She laughed. "I've got one more thing to run by you."

Darlene rose. "Hold on a sec. Let me walk by the tables. Be right back."

Juliet sat for a minute as the *Lineman* wound down. She'd heard somewhere that Glenn Campbell had died.

Darlene returned and released a few breaths as she took her seat. "The EMTs can't even finish. They're taking the last few bottles with 'em. It's against the rules, but what the hell." She pulled back a stray lock of hair. "So spill it. You've got something else, and I'm listening."

"You think I'm…that I go with guys too much? Word can get pretty negative in a small place like Sherwood."

Darlene puckered her lips. "Now why did I know that was coming? This have something to do with Nick?"

Juliet shrugged. "Maybe. I don't know. I'm not sure what's going on, really. He's got me totally confused."

Darlene laughed. "Anybody ever tell you that's how it all starts? And Julie, you probably get less sex than any girl I know. I know this is personal, but I bet it's been six, eight months?"

"I guess. Seems like a lot longer than that."

"I'm not sure I could make it with as little cuddling as you get."

"You and Pete are steady though. It makes a difference."

Darlene nodded. "True. So what about Nick? He say something?"

"He was just repeating what he had heard. He apologized."

"You starting to see each other?"

"I fixed him dinner the other night." Juliet grinned. "We kind of had a date."

"*And?*"

"And he gave me a kiss on the cheek when he said goodnight."

Darlene gave her a considered look. "Lord, girl. Your life is so full of super-charged sex I'm about to wet my pants."

"There's something else. I think Nick's found out about the abuse. I filed a criminal complaint about the…well, about the rapes with the state attorney's office years ago when I turned eighteen. Over dinner Nick and I went through a lot of old papers that I discovered in Aunt Doris' attic, in the old house outside town where I used to live. There was a deposition that I think he read."

Darlene shook her head. "You've got to stop thinking you're soiled, and that Nick may think you're soiled, because none of it is true. I've known Nick for a good many years, and I know he's a guy who wouldn't think anything of the sort. Trust me on that."

The entrance door banged open and then closed with a thump. A blast of cold air drifted in behind the noise. Darlene's focus shifted to the door along with her own. "And speak of the devil. Here comes that good-looking sheriff now," her friend said.

Juliet's eyebrows shot up. Nick was standing inside the foyer area, his eyes screwed up adjusting to the dim light. As he moved toward them her heart rate increased. She squirmed in the seat. Nick sidestepped around tables and chairs, and got caught by the EMT's on their way out.

Darlene smiled. "Looks like you've got a minute to compose yourself before he comes over and scoops you up, takes you back to his castle, and ravishes you all night."

"Darlene," she blurted. A quivery excitement filled her. "I'm not sure he's here to see me. I was rude to him last time."

She laughed. "Are you kidding? Guys don't take that shit to heart like we do."

Pete Haskett stepped out from behind the bar and walked over to the group. There were handshakes, laughter.

"He draws a crowd, doesn't he, Julie?"

"You're loving this."

She laughed. "Yeah. I think I'm going to go say hi, maybe get my own kiss on the cheek. Then I'm going to tend to the customers, such as we've got." She came to her feet. "And Julie, the table over in the far corner is just for you guys." Darlene winked. "Nice and private."

Juliet was left high and dry, like a boat stuck on a sand bar as the tide receded. Should she stand and walk over with the rest of the crew, or remain seated like some prom queen? She grabbed a basket of peanuts from the bar and made her way to the table full of guys in ball caps. She plunked the basket down in the center of the group and tried to strike up a conversation. For once, no one seemed interested in talking and she stood there feeling ridiculous.

Nick pronounced her name in a firm voice as he came up behind her. She swiveled full face toward him at the same moment he placed a hand on her waist. The turn resulted in a natural, close-in dance position if only Charlie Rich had been crooning on the speakers.

"Nick. Jesus," she said. Her heart thumped like a spinning clothes dryer full of tennis shoes.

"I told Pete I'd come by for a visit sometime," he said. "I didn't tell him I'm really here to see you."

"I'm…uh, I saw you come in. Look, my hand is better. Got the bandages off. See?"

He stepped back and examined her palm, but did not release it. "Darlene ordered me to the booth over in the corner. Said you had to accompany me."

"She thinks she's in charge tonight. I guess we can sit there." She took her hand back and walked him to the table. He slid in the booth facing the door, she with her back to the bar. "I can't see the customers this way, Nick."

"I'm a customer. Besides, Darlene said she would cover."

"I heard that," Darlene said as she appeared with two beers. "You both are my customers now." She plopped the bottles on thin, cork coasters and swirled away.

Nick was wearing another one of his Oxford shirts, maybe sea-foam green this time. She couldn't tell for sure in the light.

He wore a beige parka-style vest over top. A thin sandpaper layer of blond stubble covered his jaw line.

He helped himself to a full swallow of Corona and released a fizz of muffled carbonation into his closed fist. "The 4-Runner still working okay?"

"Yeah, look, about the other night…"

He held up a hand. "Don't worry about it." He lowered his beer to the table and centered the bottle over a coaster with a green and red Becks logo. "You've got enough complications in your life, and all kinds of stuff from your past. Baggage, issues, whatever women call all these things. But you've got a nice place inside you, once I get to it, and don't take that sexually. You're not mean. You're not vindictive in the slightest. You're not conniving. You're a good person, Juliet, and you're giving me who you are right now. Nothing that's fake. Hell, I don't even think you'd know how to fake it if you tried."

She lapsed into silence and finally replied, "I don't know what to say. How come you can see all this?"

"Because I had a good, close look at someone who wasn't like you. She was dead opposite, in fact."

"Your ex-wife?"

He nodded, tipped the beer to his lips, and cleared away a couple of quick swallows. "Plus," he said, "I've known you since high school, and maybe I sensed the difficulties you went through. I sure as hell don't trust Doris Blackwell. Never have."

She glanced away. Over her shoulder she took in Darlene talking to the group of guys at the sole remaining occupied table. She refocused on Nick. "Well, everyone's certainly learning about me now."

"Not a bad thing, unless you're a criminal, which you're not."

"A crime…" She struggled for the right words and felt her voice go small. This was the time, and this was the place. If he was so intent on unlocking doors inside her, she was going to hand him the key to one right now. "A crime *was* committed, Nick. My supposed 'uncle', Clifford Blackwell, assaulted me—sexually assaulted me—when I was a kid. You're a cop. I'll use the ugly word. He raped me. That's what that deposition that you saw was all about." There. It was out. She was over the waterfall now and headed for the rocks below.

His eyes did not leave hers, but his expression varied from neutral to sympathetic to neutral again. He said, "Juliet, you do not have to talk about this. I read enough of the deposition to put the pieces together."

"Yes, I do need to talk about this." She tried to keep her voice even, a matter-of-fact chronology. "I waited until I reached my eighteenth birthday to file the criminal complaint. Did it all on my own. Just walked in to the State Attorney's office in Bismarck."

"But the deposition—"

"Was attesting to the fact that *nothing* happened, that I made everything up. Doris was protecting her brother."

"So what became of the whole matter? Have you got a copy of the criminal complaint? I didn't see it in your stack of papers."

Juliet shook her head. "I never saw one after I signed the documents. They kept telling me everything was going through all the legal channels, but nothing ever happened."

"You should have heard back from the DA. A criminal complaint can't just be swept away. Someone with legal authority sat on it. But why?"

She tasted a slow sip of beer. "Who knows? Someone didn't like my accusations. Pretty obvious, but what could I do? At eighteen you're still just a kid. It's not like I could have run out and hired a lawyer with money from my babysitting."

"Clifford and Doris. God, what an evil pair."

Juliet nodded slowly. "Okay, so now you know. It's water under the bridge. Do you mind if we get off this subject?"

Darlene turned toward them as if she was dialing in their conversational breaks from across the room. She walked over. "Who's ready for another one? Nick?"

"I guess one more." He drained the Corona in a single, full swallow.

"Julie, you've got to drink up girl. I can see who's been doing all the talking. I'll bring a fresh one out for you anyway. Pete says they're on the house."

Juliet nodded and watched as her friend retreated to the bar. A short silence intervened that was not uncomfortable. Nick had his hands on the table as if he wanted to reach forward to hers. She wouldn't mind.

"I'm still intrigued by that mining company your parents founded," Nick said.

"The Wolverine Mining Company," she said. "I've been doing some checking on the internet. The company still exists."

"And?"

"It's a company in Idaho. They mine silver, lead and zinc from ore. But I couldn't find any references to my parents."

He angled his head and frowned.

"What?"

"Is it a publicly traded corporation? Do they sell stock?"

She shook her head. "I don't think so. I didn't see any reference to a listing abbreviation, any kind of stock quote."

"There is something about this process, this *investigative* business that reminds me of figuring out a disease. You take the symptoms—in this case, clues about your past—and run everything through what you know or what you suspect, and see where the path takes you. In your case, I think people are hiding things in the same way a little bacterium or virus acts when it doesn't want to be found, but there are always markers that they leave behind."

"Like?"

"Like that bundle of papers that was hidden in the attic. You've *got* to get the rest of those papers, Juliet. Look, your parents were really, *really* smart people. You think they would have cast their children off without a life raft? No way. And what happened to their company? Where did the money go? They founded it, and it still exists. That means it was sold to someone after your parents' deaths."

"I'm not sure where else to go."

"Not everything was computerized, especially years ago. There are volumes of Standard and Poor's corporate filings still stuck away on reference shelves in libraries. They've got dust on 'em, because no one ever uses them anymore."

"So you're saying I should start there?"

The beer arrived, ice cold and frosted with beads of moisture. The caps were cracked open and lying loose on the tops trapping curls of condensation in the necks.

"Darlene's a sweetie," Nick remarked as she marched away with a backhanded wave. He took a bottle in hand and flicked off the cap. "They wouldn't have anything at the library here, maybe not even in Minot. It'd have to be in Bismarck."

"I can do that. Shouldn't be too hard for a mathematician-engineer like myself."

"That-a-way. And I'd like to help if you'll let me."

"Don't need it. Like you said, I'm smarter than you." She gave a little hollow-sounding laugh

He nodded. "Okay. But let's keep in mind that there's an evil, nasty virus here, and it's been around for a while. I think it's time we found out about this thing and wiped it out."

Later Nick escorted Juliet to her car. He extended an arm lightly around her waist, and she allowed herself to be drawn close enough to feel the hard muscle of his torso. She shivered reflexively under her parka, as much from the cold as his touch. "Another freezing night in North Dakota," she said, mainly to break the quiet. Then a thought emerged. "Nick, Pete said that there's a bad storm coming in. That's why no one's here tonight. Is that true?"

"Yeah, but it won't be here for a few days. A typical March blizzard, and just when Spring is right around the corner. These things really foul up the county roads."

"Could I keep the Toyota for a couple more days? The four-wheel drive would be kinda nice to have, and I don't think Brownie—that's my name for Alice's car—is meant for heavy-duty snow."

"Yes."

"Yes, what? No conditions this time?"

He shook his head. "Nope. You may keep it without a dinner requirement."

"How about I owe *you* dinner. Why don't I bring out something to your place this weekend? At least return your favor from the other night. And then I can tell you what I find out about my parents' mining company."

He pursed his lips with a look that appeared way too thoughtful. "We'd have to watch the weather. My place is just as isolated as Buzzy's. And…would we call this a date?"

"Yeah."

14

Clifford was dying. Everyone knew that. Marietta visited anyway. She parked at her usual spot in front of 'G' Wing at the nursing home. That way she didn't have to enter through the front entrance, troop down two hallways, and eventually wait for an elevator that moved at the same snail's pace as the residents. She climbed the outside stairs at the end of the wing and entered via a door that was unlocked for maintenance during daylight hours. Cliff could always be found asleep in his apartment at three in the afternoon.

There were issues on her mind. She had begun to worry in the days following Doris' brief and angry visit. Was the house actually going to become her property after Cliff's passing? His sister's parting words kept popping up time and again, something to the effect that 'blood was thicker than temporary living situations'.

Granted, Clifford could do as he pleased with the house, especially if he still viewed her as simply a live-in housekeeper. However, he did explicitly promise the place to her. But there she went again, always believing the best in people, and neither Cliff nor his obnoxious sister deserved such consideration. If nothing else she'd just settle for a straight answer.

She did have a plan, and that was to read the will herself. A tacky, swing-out painting covered a wall safe, and that's where she assumed he kept his important documents. Toward the end of Cliff's time in the house he occasionally leaned against the small steel vault and retrieved the combination from his cell phone. She was subsequently excused, but not before she glimpsed his index finger sliding over the 'Contacts' icon.

The door to his apartment lay open a foot from the jamb, and she peeked in on a sleeping man fuzzy with white, facial hair. He was sitting upright in a patterned wing chair, slack jawed with his head cocked against the high back. She drew out a soft voice full of honey. "Cliff? Cliffy?"

A reflexive hand went to his face as if to swipe away an insect. He snorted.

She spoke louder, "Cliffy. Marietta is here!"

His eyelids parted and his pupils tracked a phantom back and forth across the room for a moment. He settled on her face with a smile. "Marietta."

"I've got on your favorite dress, Cliff." She posed with a little side step as an alternative to an embrace. She wore the same flowered dress with the scoop neck, but this time she had changed to a push-up bra that put everything front and center.

He coughed in a slurry of noise that crackled the phlegm in his chest but didn't appear to dislodge anything. "What time is it?" he asked when he settled back.

"Not time for cocktails yet. I had the afternoon free so I thought I'd come by and see how you're doing."

He nodded. "Can you get me a glass of water? There's a Brita in the fridge."

She poured water from the cold container and brought up a chair opposite his. "Cliff, your sister dropped by the house the other day. Did she mention her visit?"

He shook his head and took a long drink. Then in a wet, sloppy voice he said, "Must've been the same day she came by here."

She crossed her legs and allowed her hem to rise mid-thigh. He had seen everything before, back in the day when he was more interested and she was more naïve. But now he was a dying man, and it didn't bother her in the slightest to show a little bare skin. "She said some things that upset me Cliff. I don't mean to bother you with this, but I have some concerns."

"Was it about the house?" His focus seemed to drift in and out as he readjusted the cannula.

She nodded. "She swears that what you promised to me doesn't matter. I told her you wouldn't go back on your word. You did promise me, Cliff. You promised me the house."

A calculating grin replaced the look of empty puzzlement on his face. "Does it really matter whether you have the house or something else from the estate?"

Yes, it did, because he had given his word. Were the men in America no different than in Cuba? In any case, there it was. He'd obviously lied to her again. His deceit made things easier in a way, a fraud that fortified her resolve. There had to be other things in the safe equal to the value of the house, and only the value of the house, if that's how he wanted to play it. Now she simply had to find his phone. She leaned forward. "It's just that I've been responsible for the upkeep and maintenance, and did I tell you the hot water is out in the upstairs bathroom?"

A glimmer of interest enlivened the expression of the ex-builder. "Got to be the water heater, the eighty-gallon one. You should have it replaced."

"What company do I call? And could I call from here, in case they ask me something?"

He glanced around uneasily, as though the weight of the world was suddenly on his shoulders. "I suppose."

Thirty minutes later she left with his cell phone in her pocketbook. Forty-five minutes after that she arrived back at the house. She poured a glass of cold white wine from the Albariño area of Spain and sat down at the kitchen table.

First and foremost, she did not want to screw things up. The steel door of the vault was inset with a combination keypad much like a cell phone. She had never played the lottery, but at least here she could make a reasonable guess, perhaps even discover the correct combination from Clifford's call list.

She sipped her wine and retrieved the mobile phone from her handbag. She touched the 'Contacts' icon on the small screen, and that brought forth three entries. She needed something with ten numbers or characters, and all of the phone numbers held ten digits if one counted the area codes.

She sat back. She had known Cliff for nine years, and become more of a housekeeper and less of an intimate companion for the last eight. Back then, she'd only recently come from Cuba via Canada and needed a lifeline. She spoke almost no English and Clifford had given her a job. At the outset she bossed a crew that cleaned the interior of newly built houses, and a short time later she became his personal housekeeper. Yes, she offered more than the typical housekeeping services at first, but Cliff was working on securing her Green Card. And though the matter was never successfully completed—a problem with her resident alien status, he had often told her—she rationalized that portion of her life as a bad dream that lasted no time at all. She didn't blame herself. Life was not always a 'bed of roses', as Americans were fond of saying, and sometimes one had to do what one had to do. In any case, an understanding with Clifford had been eventually reached which created the present arrangement, and she became comfortable with that.

Clifford was an abrasive, unhappy man, shunned by an ex-wife and just about everyone else except for a lawyer and an equally hateful sister. The fact that he had three entries on his cell phone actually surprised her. As far as she knew he had no friends. Therefore, one number had to be his sister's, one had to belong to the lawyer, and the remaining number had to be the combination to the safe.

She dialed the first entry and got a lawyer's receptionist. That made sense. The second number rang repeatedly with no answer and no message prompt. His sister's? Marietta had a hunch that it was. That left the remaining number, and she finished her wine and decided it was time to try the combination.

She donned a pair of half-glasses and stationed herself in front of the safe. Methodically she punched nine digits and watched as the numbers illuminated with accompanying beeps in the digital boxes. She hesitated and touched the last numeral. A longer beep sounded, then silence, as if the contraption was having trouble with a difficult decision. Suddenly the whirring gears of a servo could be heard as the locks retracted. Released

from the tension of the holding latches, the door relaxed on its hinges and opened a tiny fraction of an inch. *¡Caramba!*
A short time later Marietta inventoried the contents. She stacked handfuls of one-hundred dollar bills on the kitchen table, still unused and banded in their crisp paper wrappers. A heavy sack of coins weighted the center of the table. She plunged a hand inside and fingered hundreds of solid gold Krugerrands, Maple Leafs, and others that carried beautiful crests of American Eagles. Several official-looking document bundles wrapped in heavy, blue paper and tied with worn, red ribbons were arranged on the table. She'd get to those in due time.

Finally, she inspected a thin leather fold, hardly larger than a credit card case. She palmed the tanned animal hide and flicked the wallet open. A photo of herself was imbedded onto a plastic card below the words 'United States of America, Permanent Resident'. She blinked hard in disbelief and lowered her head, overcome with the reality of the pointless waste of years gone by. She folded her arms on the table, buried her head in her arms, and began to sob. After all this time she was staring at the Green Card that Clifford had hidden away.

15

George Murphy slouched in a lecture chair bolted to a row of other chairs in the William L. Guy Federal Building in Bismarck. His normal Monday-Wednesday-Friday class routine had been changed to a longer Tuesday-Thursday period to accommodate a new professor, Harry M. Schwartzel.

Schwartzel's presence at the lectern was a welcome departure from the stuffy *Juris Doctorates* attached to the university. He brought a wealth of practical knowledge to the subject of Contracts from his brief tenure as a district court judge. Prior to that, he held the position as Assistant State's Attorney for Burleigh County. Presently, the somewhat overfed lawyer was the back half of the Rhinehart & Schwartzel law firm.

Schwartzel approached the podium and eyed the crowd. "I see we've got a small group tonight." The electronic pickup returned a feedback squeal, and he collared the gooseneck with two fleshy fingers and moved the microphone to the side of his mouth. His voice now held a reverb. "Seven prospective lawyers? What happened to everyone? We're a dozen or so short tonight."

Murphy volunteered. "Cold night in North Dakota. Gonna get colder by morning, they say."

Schwartzel squinted in his direction. "Murphy?"

"Speaking, sir."

"Sheriff's Department. Deputy. Right?"

"That's right."

Schwartzel smiled. Pockmarked skin surrounded thick lips. "Well, I liked your explanation of the *preexisting duty rule* last session. You want to start us off tonight?"

Murphy took in his fellow students as they turned their attention toward him. He was by far the oldest in the group. Most of the kids appeared barely out of college. The solitary woman was somewhere in her late twenties, maybe a real estate agent caught high and dry in the downturn. He came to his feet and addressed the podium. "All right, shoot."

Schwartzel raised a good-humored eyebrow. "Not sure I want to hear that word from a deputy sheriff." His chuckle drew out the others. "And you don't have to stand. I thought I made that clear last week."

"I'm used to being on my feet in my line of work," Murphy replied. "My height helps me intimidate drunks and dope dealers."

Schwartzel nodded in a more serious vein. "I keep forgetting that you grownups are a little different to deal with than these younger folks—no offence intended gentlemen…and ladies. Okay. See if you can intimidate me with the doctrine of *unconscionability*. Explain how it relates to *Williams v. Walker-Thomas Furniture Company*."

Murphy rambled, but only a little. He knew the subject, and he was used to making pronouncements. He had held both the Kiwanis Club and the Rotaries at bay in the past, making it up as he went along. It wasn't that difficult for a cop.

Fifteen minutes later he took his seat and listened with half an ear as Schwartzel and the other students dredged through the pile of legal tailings pertinent to the doctrine.

"…or maybe a beer. Whataya say, George? We'll cut it short tonight."

Murphy jerked his head upward and refocused on the podium.

Schwartzel laughed. "Caught you napping, deputy. I said, let's cut it short tonight—cold weather and all—and I'll buy you a drink. We'll let these other tired students go home."

Murphy moved his head in an irregular movement halfway between a nod and a shake. He couldn't decide. Marge would be expecting him home, but a beer would be better.

Schwartzel cut in, "Someday you'll be running for sheriff yourself, or maybe Assistant DA. Now is a good time to start making the necessary contacts."

After a quick consideration Murphy tipped his head in the affirmative. "You make a solid argument for a beer, sir," he said.

Webster's Tavern occupied a windy corner one block from the Federal Building. Lengths of polished bronze piping ran along the upscale brick façade cornering the street-side windows. Silver cutlery on white tablecloths reflected the glow from brass candle sconces inside. An oversized, comfortable bar inside the restaurant made a popular watering hole for prosecutors, defense attorneys, and practically everyone associated with the legal profession, Schwartzel informed him as they walked over. "It's been my home away from home for years," he said, as he moved with a rolling gait. "I'm surprised you're not familiar with the place."

"I don't come into the city much," Murphy answered. Schwartzel was a large man, flat-footed and out of shape. A step to the side was required as the lawyer swung into the entry portal. Inside, the tavern had the feel of a warm hearth, of bread in the oven.

"Noah Webster—you know, the dictionary fellow—supposedly stopped by here way back in history," Schwartzel stated. "But no one I know ever thought he got this far west. Anyway, the tavern's named after him."

"I thought the dictionary guy was Merriam."

The lawyer shrugged as he caught the eye of a hostess. "Noah. Merriam. Who knows?"

An attractive woman approached with music in her voice. "Well, if it isn't *Mr.* Harry Schwartzel. We've missed you for a few days."

"You know how it is, Lila. Busy sometimes. How 'bout a booth tonight? Too late for dinner."

Schwartzel greeted several lingering diners as Murphy followed the man in the direction of the large, darkly paneled bar that swept toward them like the bow of a clipper ship. Florid-faced patrons in loosened ties and unbuttoned suit vests reshaped their expressions into wooden glances as they catalogued his cheap attire and rubber watch. The woman ushered them into the gentle scoops of what Murphy assumed were full-board mahogany pews polished by thousands of worsted wool slacks over the years. His quilted vest and khaki Dockers were clearly downscale for a place that probably served six-dollar beers and even pricier cocktails. He shucked the vest and unrolled his cuffs over his watch.

"That's the style," Schwartzel said. "Got to be comfortable. So what'll it be, Murphy? I could call you by your first name, if you like."

"Okay. George'll do, or just Murph if you like."

Schwartzel nodded. "Call me Harry." He glanced sideways as the waitress approached. "You want a beer or a mixed drink?"

"I'd better make it a light beer. I've got to drive back to Sherwood."

"Two light beers, Lila," Schwartzel ordered, as the woman parked herself beside their booth.

"No double martini tonight?" She looked down in a manner that seemed half a notch too familiar.

The lawyer laughed. "Okay. Make it my usual, sweetheart. You know me too well." He fixed his gaze briefly on her backside as she departed. Then to Murphy, "I've got mornings off after I do a night class. I get to sleep in."

"Wish I could say the same," he said.

"Aha. A man with a family."

"Yeah, a wife and a couple of rug rats. You know how it is."

"Actually I don't. I've been divorced twice. No children. I want it to stay that way."

"Sounds like you had it figured out early," Murphy said.

Schwartzel nodded, then after a pause, "So how are things in...Sherwood you said? Now that rings a bell." He creased his brow. "Not sure why. I haven't come across that town's name for years."

Murphy reclined against the backboard. A soft, drifting sound from a female vocalist accompanied by single piano reached him over the clink of glasses and subdued voices. "Sherwood's okay. Small place. Not much trouble keeping up with things."

"Ever thought about moving to Bismarck? I mean, once you pass the Bar. You're getting close now, and my partner and I might like to take a closer look at you. We need lawyers, but we'd like 'em a little more grown up than these kids in class, if you know what I mean."

Murphy's heart rate flared at the compliment but he dialed it back and tried to stay calm. Nothing had been offered, not by a long shot. Yet, it was hard not to project himself as one of the regulars in a place like this, maybe wearing a three-piece suit and a gold Rolex.

Schwartzel added, "I like your law enforcement background, and you've obviously got a good grasp of the law."

Lila appeared at the lawyer's side and served a martini spiked with two olives. "I've got some oysters on the half if you guys are interested," she said. Her glance took in Murphy, although it was clear she was asking Schwartzel. She placed the beer on the table almost as an afterthought: a tall, fluted vase containing a golden liquid full of bubbly effervescence.

Schwartzel shook his head. "We're fine, Lila. No oysters tonight."

She nodded, and once again Schwartzel concentrated on her figure as she departed. "So that's my pitch," he said. "All this." He waved his hands to indicate the tavern, the city, and it seemed the good life in general. "It's normal at the higher income levels you'd be reaching. Let the sheriff handle the kind of trailer trash you have around Sherwood."

Murphy took a cold, fizzy swallow of beer and groaned inwardly at the contrast he represented in this setting: his clothes, his background, his...well, his paltry savings account that in all probability couldn't handle a couple of nights' dinners at this place.

Schwartzel sucked down an olive and smacked his lips. "You might even end up as an Assistant DA like I was."

Murphy had a thought. "Speaking of that, I was discussing a legal twist a day or two ago with the sheriff back in Sherwood. He thought I'd have the answer and I didn't. Maybe you can help me out."

"Shoot," Schwartzel said. "To use your own expression."

Murphy steepled his fingers around the beer. "Olsen— he's the sheriff—was asking about a criminal complaint, wondering what happens when one is filed with the DA, where it goes, how it's finally resolved. He claims to know of a case where a complaint of sexual abuse, and I assume we're talking rape, was somehow just shelved, kind of forgotten. Can that happen?"

Schwartzel unbent slowly from his relaxed position and sharpened his focus. He formed a slight smile that held no humor. "This sheriff of yours, is he kind of a dullard?"

"Actually, he's a pretty bright guy. He finished three years of med school."

"A wannabe doc who flunked out? Doesn't sound that bright."

"Yeah, well he left for other reasons. But what about the complaint? The sheriff believes something improper might have taken place."

Schwartzel took a full sip of his martini and sucked the remaining olive from the swizzle. He shook his head. "Impossible. Normally criminal complaints are given a docket number by the clerk of courts. We're talking felonies here, as you probably know. Then they're scheduled for further processing via a conference, a motion hearing, or straight off to an arraignment."

"So what the sheriff says can't happen?"

"I'd have to know more about the case. When this supposedly occurred, who the plaintiff was, that sort of thing."

"He won't say, but I think I know who he's talking about. A girl by the name of Juliet Blackwell or Driscoll. I'm not sure which, actually. She's..." He opened his hands. "The woman's been in trouble ever since she was a young girl, if that's who it is, so I wouldn't put too much stake in her claim."

Schwartzel stiffened as if he'd been hit with a cattle prod. His voice came out low. "When did this happen, allegedly?" The words were enunciated slowly, as if he might be reading fine print.

Murphy blew air through his lips and shot a glance at the ceiling. "Maybe ten, twelve years ago. I'm not certain, but it seems like Olsen mentioned the time frame being about then."

"That's a long time in this line of business."

Murphy helped himself to a swallow and shrugged. "I just thought 'cause you were in the DA's office back then, you might, you know, have heard something."

"Sorry. Nothing's coming to me. Believe me, if you knew how many cases and briefs I was involved in during those years, hell, sometimes I'm surprised I remember my own name."

"I understand."

"What's this sheriff trying to do, anyway?"

"Nick's pretty closed up about it, but I think he feels he's on to some deep, dark conspiracy."

Schwartzel twisted a grin. "It could be this woman is giving him something on the side to make him feel that way. I'm assuming from what you say she's kind of a slut."

"You got it exactly, Mr. Schwartzel."

"Harry."

"Okay, Harry." He thumbed a cuff away from his wristwatch. "Look, I've gotta go. My wife'll be wondering where I am."

"Give her a call on your cell."

"I'd rather not."

"Don't say any more. I've been there." Schwartzel scooted from the booth with an effort and came to his feet. "Put your wallet back, I've got this. And keep in mind what I said about your future. Good lawyers are tough to find, and we've got our eye on you." He offered his hand.

"Thanks…Harry. I'll definitely keep it in mind, and thanks for the beer."

"I'm going to stay here and work on my martini. Sorry I couldn't help you with the other thing."

"I'll tell Nick to forget it, then," Murphy said.

"Good advice."

16

Marietta reclined in a softly cushioned love seat below her first-floor bedroom window. This was her place, her room, and had been for many years. The area originally had been designed as a study with its generously-sized bath close to the kitchen. She had transformed it into a bedroom.

She greeted the morning in a cotton bathrobe, thick and pink and covering a flannel nightgown. Wool muffs warmed her feet, and an oversized cup of *café con leche* warmed her hands.

She took a sip while she examined the thick reams of documents she found the previous night in Clifford's safe. She was not a lawyer. That did not present a problem. Her father was a lawyer, or rather had been a lawyer until the day he was thrown into Castro's prison. His term of incarceration was initially three years, a price he had expected and gladly paid in return for her opportunity to seek freedom during a visit to Canada. But her father's jail term was increased to four years, then five, and that was as far as the authorities were able to extend his punishment, because he died in prison in that fifth year.

Before her successful bid for asylum her father had held an important position in the Ministry of the Sugar Industry. Afterward, her mother could only find work as a maid. *Gracias Dios,* Marietta had been able to help with monetary assistance via the Canadian postal system.

Clifford's will was not in the safe. If he had one she assumed it was kept in the lawyer's office. Therefore, she decided to concentrate on what she had. The five-page instrument in front of her recorded a transaction of convertible securities. Apparently, these were the proceeds when the assets of a corporation called The Wolverine Company were sold. Three small leather portfolios contained investment accounts that she could examine later. The remaining two documents appeared to be identical trust agreements, except for the different dates on the signatory lines.

She had been her father's legal secretary for several years, and though transcribed in another language, legal documents all had the same arcane verbiage, the same flow, and the same formatting. Navigating through the pages was as easy as reading a recipe. The challenge was in understanding the puzzle in the relationships.

By the noon hour, light snow flurries shimmered in cold sunlight streaming through a broken overcast. Marietta changed into warm corduroy pants and a turtle neck sweater. She moved to the kitchen table and pushed the money and pouch of gold coins to the side to make room for everything else.

One thing was clear. The Driscoll children were the legal beneficiaries of the Wolverine Mining Company's assets. The heirs had to reach the age of thirty, of course. She thought back. On several occasions during the past eight years Clifford had mentioned something about kids in regard to an undeserved inheritance, kids living with his sister Doris. Was he referring to *these kids?* They would have to be…well, she wasn't sure how old, but they certainly were not children anymore. And he mentioned a fortune. Was he referring to *this* fortune? What other one could there be? And why did he seem to think he would be the one who inherited the assets? There were other questions.

She compared the two trust agreements. Clifford was the trustee of the children's fortune on both documents, but listed as the contingent beneficiary only on the earliest agreement. The later document, and legally the one that mattered, listed his lawyer, a Donald Rhinehart, as the contingent beneficiary. Why would he do that?

She began to wonder what all this had to do with her, and whether she was perhaps being a bit too nosey. However, the legal rhythm drew her back to a comfortable remembrance. As long as she had the documents in front of her, she could almost imagine she was sitting in her father's office.

Marietta took a break and moved around the kitchen on autopilot for a while as she prepared a lunch of mild *palacios chorizo* sausage slices, hard cheese, and Ryvita rye crackers. Absorbed as she was in the minutia of a simple task, her thoughts were free to bounce around. They always returned to the documents.

She filled an electric teakettle with cold water and measured a portion of loose leaves into the infuser. A thought struck her, and she stepped to the table and leafed to the last page of the most recent trust agreement, the one that listed Clifford's lawyer as a contingent beneficiary. Sure enough, Clifford's signature was dated less than two years before, well into his mental befuddlement caused by a lack of oxygen to the brain. Chances were good that he never knew what he signed, and that brought up a raft of new questions.

A few minutes later Marietta poured boiling water into a teapot, immersed the diffuser, and sat down to a small lunch that reminded her so much of Cuba.

17

Lenny had to move his pickup truck. His usual parking spot between the barn and the well was taken over by the arrival of the drilling crew and all their scaffolding and cranes.

The foreman stood bundled next to the wellhead in a hat with the earflaps pulled up and tied. He wore a green, quilted, army surplus jacket and heavy-looking Red Wing boots. "I know you from somewhere," he said in a raised voice as Lenny walked over.

Lenny flapped his arms. "I worked at the R & J for a while. I seen your trucks out there."

The man nodded and yelled at the driver of a vehicle backing an air compressor, "The other way, Gene! You'll scissor the fucking thing." Then to Lenny over the popping bark of the engine, "Yeah, somewhere. I guess it was the R & J."

"So what's all this? What's going on?"

"Mrs. Blackwell. Is she your mother?"

"Nah, my aunt."

"Well, she wants a new well. We're putting in a deeper submersible pump. Going down another fifty feet, and that's a lot out here."

Lenny stood for a moment. "Didn't know we needed one," he said.

"I guess she thinks you do."

Lenny removed his ball cap, swiped his hair, and set the bill down closer over his eyes. "You guys are getting a late start today."

The man gave a thumbs up to the driver and directed his comment sideways, "We're not scheduled till Monday, but since weather's coming in I thought I'd at least get the scaffolding in place, maybe pull the well cap. Mrs. Blackwell said to bring our equipment on out and get started."

"Well, my aunt's not here. I think she's in Grand Forks. Said she was buying a new car."

The man nodded and looked at his watch. "We'll just do our thing then. Be gone by three-thirty, maybe four."

Lenny stood over the sink a few minutes later and pushed a soft, spongy marshmallow into his mouth. He compared his own pickup to the bright green models visible through the window. Clarke Drilling had new trucks. The two in the yard were heavy duty, four-by-four diesels. He had already asked Doris to help him out with a new one, but she wouldn't say. All she talked about was going out and buying a new car for herself.

A wisp of scalding milk rose from a pan on the range top. He scooped two rounded tablespoons of cocoa powder into the hot liquid, dumped in a half-dozen marshmallows, and gave the mixture a stir.

The phone rang. It'd be Doris. Maybe he could ask her about the pickup again. He poured the hot chocolate into a large mug and grabbed the wall-mounted phone. "Doris?"

"Hello. Is this the Blackwell residence?"

"Doris?" He squeezed his brows into uncertainty. A woman's voice came through clearly, but the tone was off, and she had an accent.

"This is not Doris," she said. "And may I ask who is speaking?"

"You want to know who I am?"

"If you don't mind. I'm a friend of the family, although you would not recognize my name." The voice added, "I know your Uncle Clifford."

Lenny viewed his hot chocolate on the counter. The marshmallows needed another stir to really melt into the chocolate. "My name is Lenny."

"Are you Lenny Driscoll?"

"Yeah, but everyone here knows me as Lenny Blackwell. That's my aunt's name. This is actually her residence." *Residence* sounded official, and he was pleased he thought of it.

"Ah… There was a pause. "Lenny, is your aunt around?"

"She went to buy a car. To Grand Forks, I think."

A sigh of relief came over the line. "Good." Then, "Could I ask you how old you are?"

"Why do you need to know that?"

"It's just…it's just that it may mean a lot for you and your sister."

He removed his cap, tossed it into a chair and scratched his head. This was the strangest phone call he had ever received, but the woman sounded nice. She reminded him of his grade-school nurse years ago, the time that he fell from the top of the monkey bars. The nurse was gentle as could be when she bandaged his head, and she didn't yell at him for falling. "Well, I'm…my sister and I both are going to be thirty this coming May. We're twins."

"Actually, I thought that, although I didn't know for sure. Is your sister there also? Perhaps I could talk to her."

"Juliet doesn't live here. She lives in Minot, but she works at the Crossroads."

"And what is the Crossroads?"

Lenny smiled. Everyone knew the Crossroads. "That's a saloon and kind of a restaurant over on Route 83. It's a huge place."

"Okay. Would you mind if I called you later this evening at your place? Do you have a work phone?"

"I live here and help out," he said with a twinge of embarrassment. "And who are you?"

"My name is Marietta Santa-Donato. I have—"

"You're foreign."

"I'm from Cuba, but I have known Doris' brother, Clifford, for many years. I have something I think is important for you to know. Do you know what a trust is, Lenny? Can I call you Lenny?"

"A trust is when you like someone, and they depend on you, like that."

She didn't speak for three or four long breaths. "Lenny, I'm going try and reach your sister. Do you have her number?"

He shrugged. "It's in my cell phone, but I lost it. I tried calling the number, but I don't hear anything ring."

"Do you think she's in the phone book?"

"I guess. Her name is. Juliet Driscoll. Or you can get her at the Crossroads."

"Fine. I'll call her, but I'd like you to know that you might be…I'm not sure what to say. I want to warn you about something. There is a chance that you and your sister are in danger."

"Danger? What kind of danger?" He had a vision of wild animals, wolves in the area. According to the Discovery Channel, a single pack could roam over ten thousand acres.

"It's complicated. Perhaps I explain to Juliet. Would that be all right with you?"

"Yeah. Okay." His hot chocolate was getting cold.

"It is important that you do not tell Doris about this phone call. Can you keep a secret?"

He tipped his head. "Yeah."

"Okay. Good. But if you see your sister, you can tell her what I said, that you both are in danger. That okay?"

He nodded again. "Yeah."

"Remember. You can tell your sister."

"Okay." He replaced the receiver and reached for the hot chocolate. Fortunately, the milk was still hot, and it looked like the marshmallows had melted in after all.

The Crossroads Saloon was closed on Sundays and Mondays, so that always gave Juliet a two-day break. She had slept late and arose rested and relaxed on this Sunday, chiefly due to the slow Saturday night. A thin snow flurry had whirled around earlier outside the windows, but nothing more seemed to be imminent, although the skies were gray. Even so, she'd have to watch the weather closely. Tonight she was preparing dinner for Nick at his place. On the way she intended to stop by and see her brother.

At five o'clock in the evening a thick cloud cover blanketed what was left of the setting sun. Still, the roads were clear as she drove to Doris' place. She turned on the headlights and wondered again what the hell Lenny was trying to explain to her over the phone. Doris was in Grand Forks for the weekend. She got that much. The rest of it was gibberish.

The yard was a mess of pipes and scaffolding when she arrived. Juliet parked the Toyota in the driveway and walked inside to find Lenny in the kitchen hovering over the stove.

He looked up. "Hi, Sis. Want something to eat?"

"Whatcha got?" He was flipping something on a skillet. The object looked like burned toast held together by God knows what.

"Grilled cheese. I can make another one."

She shucked her parka. Underneath she wore a black cardigan sweater over a white collared blouse. She still had her jeans, but she'd slipped on a necklace beaded with small gold and imitation pearl clusters. The jewelry was expensive, at least for her. She had never worn it before tonight.

"Whataya think? Do you want one?"

"No, and Lenny, there's a non-stick, electric skillet around here somewhere in a drawer. It'd be easier to cook on."

"This one's already done." He gave her a second glance. "You look nice, Sis. What? You going somewhere?"

"I invited myself over to Nick Olsen's place. I'm—"

"Why him?"

"He's a nice guy, Lenny. I owe him for the use of the Toyota *and* dinner. He brought steaks last week to my place, so I'm returning the favor. I should have brought an extra one by here for you. Sorry, just wasn't thinking."

"That's okay. This is one of my favorite meals anyway." He took a bite of his sandwich and quickly sculled the hot, melted cheese side to side with his tongue. "Need milk," he got out in a rush.

Juliet poured her brother a glass and moved him to the table. "What's going on around here, Lenny? What's all the stuff in the yard?"

He took a huge gulp of milk and plunged his hand into an open bag of Cheetos. "Doris wants a new well," he said as he cleared the swallow. He crunched into the Cheetos and licked the orange residue from his fingers.

She waved a hand toward the window. "Why the hell did she run off to Grand Forks with all of this stuff going on?"

He shook his head. "Don't know. All she said was that she was going to buy a new car."

She sat back for a moment and watched her brother plow through a dinner that a four-year-old would like. She and Lenny were fraternal twins. They came from separate egg and sperm combinations. That much she knew. They were essentially two siblings gestated inside the same womb, but in separate placentas. What she could not fathom was the difference in mental acuity between herself and her brother. Both parents were smart. She knew that now, so the probability of a genetic misfire did not seem plausible. That left the thirty-minute time lag in the delivery.

However, if Lenny's narrowed mental ability was the result of oxygen starvation during the birthing process, or perhaps some other delivery problem, what difference would it make now? He was who he was, even if she had once regarded her brother as shiftless and lazy. That would stop. If he did nothing more than live out his life on this shitty piece of real estate piddling with his pickup truck, well, that was all right with her. She'd find some way to look after him.

"You're thinking something, Sis. What?"

She shook her head slowly. "Nothing. Lenny, I need you to help me get the attic stairs down when you're through. I need the rest of those papers I came for the other day."

"Whataya need all that for?" He frowned and concentrated on picking off the blackened crust from his grilled cheese.

"It's stuff about us, and Doris has been hiding it. That's all. And what were you trying to tell me over the phone? A woman called?"

He looked up. "Yeah, from Cuba. We talked about trusting people and danger. She said she wanted to call you, and that I had to keep the secret, but not from you."

She studied her brother. He did not make things easy. Making sense out of a conversation with him was sometimes like trying to read code. "Okay, she'll call me, I suppose, and we'll straighten everything out. But Lenny, she couldn't have called from Cuba. They don't allow that."

"She *said*."

Juliet sighed. "All right. Why don't we go get the rest of those papers before Doris gets back from wherever?"

Thirty minutes later Juliet held the leather binder close to her chest. She had found exactly what she expected, but as she hovered above the topmost attic step the distinctive quality of the house seemed to change. She called her brother's name in a quiet voice. There was no answer. The air took on a heavier weight. A dull silence came over the place. The skin prickled at the back of her neck. She said again, "Lenny, I could use your help."

Nothing.

She took one step down and listened carefully. Several heavy thumps reverberated on the ground floor level of the house. A hiss of breath pushing through clenched teeth reached her a moment later, as though someone was being shushed. Her stomach tightened. Shoes came into view on the landing below her. They were not her brother's scuffed boots. These were black, lace-up, service Oxfords, something female cops might wear. But these shoes did not belong to a female cop.

Her heart raced. Blood thrummed in her ears. Doris had to be the individual wearing the shoes. She must have shocked Lenny into silence with her stealthy, quiet approach. And now she was waiting like a mother reptile from hell, drawn by a disturbance in her nest of dark secrets.

They'd gotten by Doris once already, but now with Nick's Toyota in the driveway a second time the old lady was evidently not going to be caught out again. Juliet steeled herself. There was nothing for it except to continue down the stairs. She looped her hand securely through the handle of the leather satchel and pulled it close to her pumping heart. That's where it would stay.

A voice crackled with the hiss of wet logs in a fireplace. "What you doing up there, child? Come on down here."

Juliet stepped from the last shaky rung onto the firm support of the hallway floor. Doris took a stance three feet in front of her, placed one hand on her hip and smirked. "Looks like you're stealing from me, little girl. Still trying to cause trouble, like you always did? Don't you ever learn, honey?" In her other hand she grasped a kitchen knife. The eight-inch steel blade had a rime of cheese on the cutting edge.

Juliet's breathing went deep. She trembled inside, but at the same time she felt her muscles tighten, her body stiffen. "Get out of my way, Doris, unless you want to get this in the side of your head."

Doris brandished the knife, but held it blade downward with a chopping motion, as if using an ice pick. She put a foot forward. "You're an intruder, and I believe I'm going to defend myself. I don't think you remember whose house this is."

"And I don't think you remember lying on the rape deposition years ago," Juliet said." She patted the satchel under her arm. "See. It's all right here. At least some of it. I've already read about your lies."

Doris laughed low and mean. "I think your brother and I can stop you. He lives here and you don't. Right, son?" She turned her head.

"He's not going to help you, Doris."

"Oh, I think he will, especially if he wants a brand new pickup truck. Won'tcha, Lenny?"

"Juliet's not doing anything wrong, Doris," he blurted. "You had our birth certificates up there."

Her brother remembered! Juliet watched as the dawning took place on the old woman's face. She had no eyebrows anymore, and her flat eyes were set in the gray, melted plastic of approaching cataracts. Doris took a step toward her. Juliet took a step back, her eyes on the knife.

"You're trespassing, don'tcha know, and after I finish with you, well, I'll just call for the sheriff."

Juliet's mouth was so dry she could barely form the words. "I'm having dinner with Nick Olsen's tonight, as a matter of fact. I'll let him know all of your concerns."

A surprised sound came from Doris and she lunged for the satchel. The knife flashed wildly in the air and Juliet swiveled away.

"Give me that, you little whore!" She kicked out and caught Juliet below her kneecap.

A flash of pain erupted on the inside of her leg. Juliet swung the satchel in response, a roundhouse pivot full of hardened, aged leather that smacked Doris in the elbow and drove into her shoulder. The knife flew from her hand and she screamed and went down on her knees. A loudmouthed rant full of filth exploded from her cracked and parched lips.

Lenny yelled something and reached for Doris's shoulders. He grabbed a handful of her dress and tried to drag her away from Juliet. "Don't hurt my sister!"

Doris came awkwardly to her feet and struck out blindly behind her. She caught Lenny with a backhand to the face. "I'll do any fucking thing I want. This is my house!"

With the attic steps lowered the path to the hallway stairs was blocked. Juliet said in a loud voice, "Help me get around her, Lenny."

"You might want to think about this, Juliet," Doris said breathing heavily. "There's nothing in that carryall that concerns you."

"Oh yeah? Except the answers to my entire life." Juliet was surprised by her readiness to strike out again. She was younger and stronger. "I already know about my parents, about the mining company and the other things you've been keeping from us, so move away. I'm taking this."

Doris snorted, "Your idiot brother still lives here. You might want to remember that."

Juliet's eyes flamed red, and in a short circuit of muscle tension and fury she charged toward the nightmare individual in front of her. She hit Doris with her arms, threw her against the wall, and pinned her face with an elbow. "Don't you ever, *ever* threaten my brother. You understand that? *Do you?*"

Doris took a noisy breath and expelled a stench of tobacco into Juliet's face. One gray eye opened wider than the other, as though the woman's brain was wired in separate halves. "Let me go you little bitch. Just get out of my house."

Juliet increased the pressure on her neck, and Doris' nicotine-stained tongue extended. She made a garbled sound.

"Sis, let her go. You'll kill her!"

"I'm thinking seriously about it," Juliet said breathing hard.

"Sis, please!"

Juliet withdrew her arm. Doris gulped air in a series of ragged inhalations as she stared at Juliet. The single eye returned to a normal squinty profile. After a moment Juliet turned away and moved toward the stairs.

"You'll pay for this, you little slut," Doris croaked through a spittle of saliva. "I promise you you'll pay!"

18

Juliet was frazzled. Her hands trembled on the steering wheel. Her cardigan had been ripped at the shoulder, and her nice necklace—the most expensive one she had ever bought—was destroyed, the pearl and gold beads scattered over the upstairs floor. She could feel the tension draining as the after-effects of the confrontation set in. She fought tears as she reached for a tissue. Would her life ever straighten out? Why was everything such a complication?

Lenny had settled down when she left, but he wouldn't leave the house and come with her even though she pleaded. She worried about his safety. Doris had refused to come down the stairs, and that gave her the opportunity to have a talk with her brother in a shaky voice. She made him take her cell phone, along with a promise not to lose it like he'd lost the last three or four she had bought for him. Her apartment number was programmed in the contact list. She could pick up a disposable on Monday or Tuesday at the Radio Shack in Minot and swap it out later.

The decision to continue to Nick's place after the fight was not one she made easily, but she needed the comfort of his presence, and his voice, and his quiet explanation of what the hell was happening. The truth was she wanted his arms around her, and that was a big admission to herself. She had never had a relationship in her entire life. The slightly ridiculous wrist massage had been in her mind for almost two weeks. That and the goodbye kiss behind her ear. She especially liked it when he played shrink and doctor, and she realized she wanted more.

Juliet came to an intersection and tried to concentrate as her tears dried to a sniffle. Nick had given her explicit instructions, which were not difficult to follow in North Dakota: Take the dirt road at the point Route 5 joined Route 83. Well, here she was at the juncture and it was beginning to snow. Should she return to Minot while she had the chance? The drive would not be difficult if she turned around at this moment. She realized that she had left her parka with Lenny in the confusion.

The car seemed to make the decision for her as it turned apparently by itself onto his isolated drive. Was this her inner self on some type of autopilot? She steered the 4-Runner to Nick's house feeling more like a passenger than a driver.

The satchel lay on the seat beside her. She hoped the contents would provide more information about her life, take her one more step toward figuring out who she was. She needed a sense of stability and saneness, and a way to move forward. That was asking a lot, as though she expecting the contents of the briefcase to be magic documents full of mystical powers. Well, that's what she needed, but if she couldn't find what she wanted then screw it, she would manage anyway.

The bright lights of Nick's house illuminated the landscape like a beacon in the icy wilderness. The complex had to contain half of the light bulbs in North Dakota, she was certain.

She stopped squarely in front of the house, set the parking brake, and killed the ignition. A minute or two of quiet would be nice. She could rest her head on the steering wheel and maybe gather her emotions. What little makeup she wore was ruined. Her necklace was destroyed. Her hands were still shaking. So what else was new?

Nick stepped out from the front door wearing a cloudy expression and a soft-looking herringbone jacket as gray as a Dakota overcast. A blue, Oxford cloth shirt was open at the collar. Did he own any color except various shades of blue?

"I tried to get you on your cell," he said as he opened the car door. "I got your brother."

"At least he answered it," she said in a voice bruised with fatigue.

"Come here, Juliet." He reached in, unsnapped her seat belt, and took her in his arms like a baby from a car seat.

"Nick." Her feet touched the ground, but her body was wrapped in his powerful frame. He was not going to release her and she didn't want him to. A hint of peppermint lingered on his breath.

He said nothing for a few seconds and she felt the press of his chest, his waist, and his thighs lower down. She could hardly think in his arms; the sensation of his complete embrace was overwhelming. "Your brother told me what happened," he said into her shoulder. "I wish to hell I could haul her ugly butt to jail."

She raised her eyes to his. "I had to fight for my life." Her voice sounded choked, even to her, but he held her now, and she was going to stay in his arms at this spot until she got it all out. "But I found the rest of the papers," she said. "I don't think I'm..." was all she could manage. Her eyes started to tear against his chest, and he tightened his arms around her, as if he had waited for the moment all of his life.

"Let's go inside," he said at some point. You can tell me about it where it's a little warmer. I've opened wine. It's good for this type of thing."

She shivered at the cold seeping into her thin sweater. "I brought steaks," she said, "and a check for the use of your car."

"I was afraid you'd try and do that. Totally not necessary."

She nodded. "Aren't you cold?" She broke away, her eyes wide, taking her bearings. A lazy scattering of snowflakes drifted down around them.

He took off his herringbone jacket and draped it over her shoulders. "I'm Norwegian," he said. "But this'll warm you up. Leave the steaks and come on in. I'll show you the house." He helped himself to a kiss in the small indentation below her right ear, as though he couldn't prevent himself from touching her. She shivered again, but not from the cold.

"North Dakota has a statute called The Castle Doctrine," he explained a few minutes later. "Most states have the same thing. Basically, it gives a homeowner the right to use force, even deadly force, against an intruder."

"And I was the intruder," Juliet summed it up.

"I'm afraid so," he said. "Even if you made the argument that Lenny let you inside the house, which would not be precisely correct if you let yourself in while he was in the kitchen. Point is, you no longer live there, and your theft of the briefcase during the struggle practically guarantees that no prosecutor will touch your case under the circumstances. Sorry."

"But they belong to me. They're my papers."

"I know. Here, make yourself comfortable on the couch. It's all yours." He brushed snow off his shoulders.

Juliet moved to a deeply cushioned sofa covered in a heavy beige fabric. She eased into soft comfort that held her more like a bed than a piece of furniture. She closed her eyes and went quiet. For the moment, maybe for a fleeting millisecond of time, she had what she wanted. Lenny seemed to be safe. And Doris was afraid of her. The last realization brought her lips upward in a smile.

"What?" Nick remained standing.

She glanced up at him. "Me fighting Doris. I didn't think I had it in me."

"I could have told you that you do. Would you like some wine?"

"Yes, please." He was giving her time, she knew. A re-entry window before the chapter and verse mystery of her life began again. She glanced around. When she entered the house she had expected to see oversized leather recliners with side levers sticking out like shift knobs on a sports car, and big, flat-screen TVs, and maybe animal heads on darkly paneled walls. What she encountered was a large comfortable living area that did not appear at all that different from her own small place, except for the size. Sturdy, wicker-oriented furniture was scattered throughout. A thick pile carpet washed in crimson, and bordered in a lustrous cream coloration lay under her feet. Mahogany bookcases lined walls painted in light hues. Large colorful oil paintings hung as a counterweight to small needlepoint pillows tucked against sofa cushions.

Nick killed the outside lights, ignited the gas logs, and returned to a room with less illumination. What remained had the effect of candlelight, and he poured wine into large goblets reflecting an orange glow.

Juliet was running down, falling off a cliff, out of gas, as drained of energy as a glider floating to a landing, and she did not want to think any more about what had occurred earlier. Nick's presence, his home, and all the things she could touch and visualize were what she wanted in her world for the time being.

"Where did you get these pillows?" She could hear the exhaustion in her voice as she slipped off her shoes and tucked her feet under her legs.

"My mom made them."

Juliet ran her hand over the cotton threads stitched into one of the pillows. Microscopic loops in multiples of unbelievable numbers were woven into a rendering of purple irises. She said, "You never told me about your mom."

"She passed away not long after my dad." He shrugged. "I wanted to keep some things…you know."

"I would have wanted the same," she said and tipped the wine glass to her lips. "Um… Good."

"Thanks. Wish I could take credit for it. Alice and Buzzy keep me supplied."

"And what kind of rug is this?" She extended a foot and allowed her bare toes to sink into the deep pile.

"Persian, although sometimes people call it an Oriental carpet. Stylistically it's a Bokhara. They're all from the Middle East."

She leaned her head back, ran a hand through her hair, and closed her eyes. "I knew you were like this."

"What? Like what?"

"Like this."

"You're the mysterious one, Juliet."

She raised her head. "I figured out what 'BSO' stands for, your ticket stubs in the car? The Bismarck Symphony Orchestra. Right?"

He gave a small nod. "I don't go very often."

"And your date? She must've meant something. You saved the ticket stubs."

"She ended up being a little pretentious, to tell the truth. I forgot the stubs were there."

"See? This is who you are. I'm a saloon girl, Nick. And I'm—"

"Smarter than me."

"Yeah?"

"Yeah. I still can't figure out that goofy refrigerator magnet at your place, and I did look at it more closely."

"Which one?"

"The chicken's head, followed by what looks like a flower vase, followed by the Greek character for the circumference of a circle—for *pi*—the little symbol that looks like a stool."

She raised an eyebrow and experienced a pleasant feeling inside. "My favorite dish, Nick: chicken...pot...pie. Get it? And the symbol '*pi*' actually references the *ratio* of the circumference of a circle to its diameter, not just the circumference."

"See. That's what I mean. You're smarter than me. That's one of the things I find so appealing about you."

He had a habit of making her smile. "Some guys would feel threatened by that," she said. "In fact, almost all the guys I've ever known."

He had no response, evidently feeling that none was required. She watched as he drank off some of his wine.

"Nick, I'm still not sure where I fit in all of this...with us. You seem so much more sure of everything."

"If it doesn't feel right don't force it. Life is complicated enough. We have time to talk about this, Juliet. We're adults. Talk."

"You mean now?"

"If you want."

Another slow sip of wine wouldn't do it. She would need half a bottle to fortify herself. She made a serious attempt on what remained in her glass and coughed with the alcoholic finish. "Okay. Well, with other guys—and please don't think there have been that many, because there haven't been—I've always felt like things were pretty superficial, that I could enjoy what I wanted on my terms. Nothing too binding, nothing too deep. You know what I'm trying to say?"

He nodded. "I've felt the same way. In fact, most of the time I feel that way."

"With you there's...there's a growing weight to this relationship. And since, as you said, we're adults here, I'll say what I think. I don't believe our—let's face it—our lovemaking, when and if it comes to that, would be light and carefree. It would mean something, and I'm not sure I want it to mean something. The idea is a little scary."

"That's what guys usually say. But Juliet, the more you put into a relationship, the more you get back. Don't you want that?"

"Yes. No. I don't know. I couldn't wait to get here tonight, to feel your arms around me." She sat back and looked away. A slight, annoying wetness began to creep into her eyes. God in Heaven, was she going to weep all the time? "I'm just afraid of the deep water, Nick. And I'm a little shaky tonight."

"Look. I *know* what you went through tonight. You could have been killed. Who in the hell can think straight after that? If you'd rather wait, we can get into all this you-and-me stuff once you've settled down." He fingered what looked like a razor scratch on his clean-shaven jaw.

"No. I want to get through this now. You said 'talk', Nick. I'm talking. I think for the first time in my life I'm sitting next to a man I want to be with. How's that for a start?"

"But you just said the idea of a deeper romance—lovemaking—was scary."

"See? That's how confused I am."

"Okay. Here's what I think," he said. "Sometimes you just have to jump in. However, if the sex thing bothers you, the lovemaking, the closeness, whatever, then we'll just operate on a platonic level for a while. You make the overtures, if and when you feel comfortable. I won't try to push you into any intimacy whatsoever. I'll be, I don't know, maybe a little standoffish physically. Give you some space. How's that?"

"What about your other, you know, entanglements? The woman in Bismarck?"

He made a motion with his shoulders. "It's not very serious. Never was. I'd rather take you to the symphony anyway."

"I've never been to a symphony concert in my life. Are you trying to change me into a classy woman? They made a movie about that, as I remember." She shot him a peculiar look. "Richard Gere played you."

"Juliet." He laughed. "Yeah, I saw that movie, but I flunked my Richard Gere impersonation a long time ago. Anyway, the story line wouldn't apply to you because you already *are* a classy woman. You just don't know it."

She went quiet for a moment. "Okay then, so we're going to have a deal?"

"Yeah. I'd like that."

"Don't be too standoffish, Nick. I'm flesh and blood, not made of iron."

"Don't worry about it. We're hardly off the ground anyway in that department. A couple of pecks on the cheek? My God, Juliet, third-graders on a playground are more physically expressive." He shook his head. "No, if you don't feel anything, then I'm not going to return anything, at least until I know where I stand."

"You make it sound like I'm totally passionless and cold."

"You're not used to someone who wants to be just as intimate emotionally as physically, who wants to know you. That's throwing you off kilter. I can sense it."

"So you're the shrink again?"

"No, but I can see the walls you've put up over the years."

"So what happens when you know where you stand with me? You said, 'until I know where I stand'."

"I'm going to try and not think about that. If we end up apart it won't do me any good."

"And if we end up as lovers?"

"I can't go there either, especially not now. No way I could sleep tonight with the thought of you in bed next to me."

A quivery butterfly seemed to take flight inside her. She placed a hand on her face, glad that he couldn't see the slight flush of heat.

For a few minutes no one spoke. "I'd better get the steaks," he said finally.

Nick turned the range top off and placed the cooked steaks on a plate. He doubted they'd get to them. Juliet was wiped out, and as he peered around the corner of the kitchen into the darkened living area, he saw that she was already asleep.

He turned the radio volume up. The NOAA Weather broadcast had been what passed for mood music during the past several hours. The arctic blast was almost on top of them. Manitoba and Saskatchewan were already in the chiller. The front was nothing Dakotans hadn't experienced before, but the roads would be dangerous. That was almost a guarantee. He'd tried to get through to Juliet early on—that's what he'd called about—but her brother had the phone. He wasn't going to wake her up now. As it was, he would have responsibilities throughout the county as the weather worsened.

His phone buzzed in his pocket. Two calls later he realized his evening with Juliet was headed toward a rain check on several levels. She would be staying for the night. However, he would be leaving.

19

An hour later, Clifford Blackwell groaned over a ball of seemingly indigestible lasagna in his gut as he watched the snowfall from the library windows. He had overeaten, but only because Ida was doing her bitch routine during dinner. All he wanted was a second small portion of lasagna, just a half-serving. Not allowed, she snapped. Oh yeah, he yelled back? No one was going to tell him what he could and could not have. He told her to piss off, go fix her face if that was possible. A few minutes later, as if on a dare, she slapped a second full order almost in his lap. Fuck it. He ate the whole thing for spite.

He tried to focus on the night outside, take his mind off of the block of cement inside his stomach. The landscapers had actually done a good job with their strategic illumination under trees and bushes. Spotlights broadcast yellow cones of light upward into lazy swirls of snow gathering on tree branches, many of which were already heavy with accumulation. The grounds were covered with six, maybe seven inches of white powder, and the scene took him back to a Grimm's Fairy Tale, something his mother used to read to him about little kids in snow-covered woods.

He dropped his hand to the oxygen canister, opened the valve another half turn, and tried to concentrate on the gauzy memory of that childhood tale. There was a cabin in those woods, and in his mind's eye he entered into that dark and gloomy shelter.

His chest began to hurt, as though someone inside the place was pressing a hard object against his sternum, so hard he had the feeling it was coming out the other side. But who else was in the cabin? He tried to focus, to make out the presence, but the blackness of the place seemed to envelope him. He *could* say that the blackness was *becoming* him, although that didn't seem to make much sense. And where was his mother? She used to wear white dresses, although he was unsure why. Had she been a nurse? Why couldn't she fix this terrible pain in his chest?

He had another thought just then, one that seemed important. Then the piercing torment seemed to explode inside his body and darkness covered him completely.

20

Nick was gone, and Juliet had the sense that the previous night was a dream. She padded to the gray half-light of the kitchen window wearing an oversized, tan flannel robe obviously belonging to Nick. The cotton fabric smelled fresh from a washer-dryer and she liked it. Especially since the robe might have been a small, pink bit of lacy afterthought left behind from a woman's visit. A small towel wrapped her wet hair. She wore a pair of large, woolen socks.

Snow in deep blankets and drifts covered Nick's 4-Runner and the fields as far as she could see. The precipitation was still falling, a soft, gentle storm of intricate icy crystals designed to screw up everything but the ski slopes, and she didn't know of any of those close by.

She read a note on the counter top. Some of the information repeated his instructions from the night before when he'd gently shaken her awake. He had shown her the layout of the guest room, where to find extra blankets, towels, soaps, shampoos, and he'd even provided a toothbrush in hard-to-open plastic. The message presently on the counter encouraged her to look around, search closets if there was something she felt she needed, and in general make herself at home.

First and foremost, she was hungry, *really hungry*. She tried to remember the last time she'd eaten. It wasn't the night before. She pulled one of the cooked steaks from Nick's fridge, found the eggs, the bread, the orange juice, the coffee, and proceeded to warm, fry, toast and percolate the entire smorgasbord.

The kitchen had the look of a well-thought-out remodeling job. Pots and pans hung from hooks above an island range top. A planter sprouted plastic leaves from the overhead basket. The cabinets were constructed from blond hardwoods, the counters layered with granite. This was the Nick she was beginning to know, not a knotty pine and Formica type of guy. Still, she could not define his occupation or lifestyle by using the sparse clues in this most important of rooms. A small shadow box of nautical-style knots hung beside the entry from the living area. Was he a sailor? There were wildlife prints on the walls. One depicted a stag in a copse of woods, as if the photographer had at that moment surprised the animal.

A rack of cookbooks adjacent to the refrigerator contained a well-thumbed copy of *Joy of Cooking*, and beside it something titled *Crazy for Casseroles.* Several stained Italian cookbooks were stuffed into the shelf, along with *The King Arthur Flour Baker's Companion.* Did he make his own bread? Nothing in the collection suggested an occupation in law enforcement or an almost-career in medicine.

A few minutes later she sat down to a warmed-over steak topped with two eggs fried with soft, runny centers. She cut a bite-sized portion from the steak, balanced a bit of egg on the top, and followed that delicious morsel with buttered toast dredged through the yolk. She repeated the process three times as she re-read Nick's lengthy note.

She wasn't going anywhere. A glance outside told her that much. The 4-Runner was suffocated in a drift produced by over a foot of snowfall. Could she even get the car door open and retrieve the satchel? She'd have to try.

She poured coffee and watched the steam swirl clockwise before it evaporated. The inside of her thigh hurt where Doris had kicked her. Just one more deep bruise added to all the others. She was beginning to feel like a punching bag. Had the witch actually pulled a knife? The incident seemed like a nightmare.

Twenty minutes later, and wonderfully charged with protein and glucose, she reached for the wall phone. She needed to check on her brother, a call that would be made to her own cell phone number. Hopefully, he hadn't already lost the thing. She sipped coffee and waited through six rings before she heard the dull voice of her sibling.

"You woke me up, Sis."

"How'd you know it was me?"

"Because it's your phone," he said.

She made a sad smile. The logic was completely backward. "Doris didn't bother you last night, did she?"

"She was outside most of the time, worried about her new car. Kept trying to brush the snow off."

"You have to be careful around her, Lenny. She's a crazy person."

"I got that, Sis," he said with a yawn. "That woman called again last night. The one I told you about. I wrote her number down. She said for you to call."

"The one you said was calling from Cuba?"

"Yeah."

"Hang on." A junk drawer was always near the phone. All kitchens had them. She tried two and hit the mother lode with the third she opened. Pencils and pens of every color in the rainbow were stuffed into plastic dividers. She scribbled the seven digits her brother gave her on a full size legal pad held to the refrigerator door by a magnetized strip. She repeated the number back into the phone. Then she asked, "The Cuban lady say anything else?"

"No. Don't think so. Just said it was important."

She envisioned him scratching his head. "Okay. Stay out of trouble, Lenny. Call me if…you know, Doris starts getting weird or something. And keep the phone in your pocket. Promise me."

"Okay, Sis. You with that cop? Olsen?"

"Not *with* him. He's gone. But I'm snowed in at his house. He's a nice guy, Lenny."

She rang off and determined the first order of business had to be cleaning up the mess in the kitchen. Nick was clean and orderly. So was she. After that, she would call the mystery woman, then examine the satchel in the car, and *then* proceed at full speed solving the puzzle of her life.

She placed the remains of her steak in the fridge and noticed several brands of foreign beers on the lower shelf of the door. There were German and Italian brews along with a solitary bottle of Tsingtao. She'd have to talk to him about that. If the male voters in the county knew he turned up his nose at domestic beer they wouldn't vote for him again as sheriff. Some men were as simple as that.

Lenny had been partially correct, she realized a few minutes later on the phone. The woman did have a Spanish accent, but since Juliet wasn't that familiar with the language, Marietta could have been from almost any Latin country as far as she could determine.

Juliet replied to the woman's introduction with the obvious, "My brother said you wanted to warn us?"

"Yes, I—first of all, I would like to explain who I am. Did you have acquaintance with a man named Clifford Blackwell?"

Her stomach tightened. Did everyone in North Dakota know about her now? "We were told to call him uncle," she said, determined not to let the conversation darken her mood. "But he wasn't our uncle."

"I know that, Miss Driscoll. Please, before I say anything further, may I ask about your birthday?"

"What? How is that important?"

"If I can give you the date, will you tell me your age?"

"My brother Lenny and I will both be thirty—"

"On the fifteenth of May, hardly more than two months away"

"And how would you know that?"

"Because I have legal papers—trust agreements—here in front of me that were drawn up by your parents who must have passed away years ago when you were a small child. Everything was spelled out. Perhaps…I am sorry to be impolite, but do you understand what a trust is? My language is not perfect, so I ask questions."

The room was not cold, but the hair began to prick on the back of her neck. She could feel her mother looking over her shoulders, a benign, soft presence she had never been aware of before. Her voice wavered. "I'm pretty sure I know what a trust is, but I'm not certain I know what you're talking about. You said you would explain who you are."

"Yes, I go too fast, I think. Again, my name is Marietta Santo-Donato. For eight years I have lived at Clifford Blackwell's house. I was his housekeeper during that time and came to know him quite well. He was not a nice man."

"You said 'was'."

"He died last night."

She briefly closed her eyes and waited for a mental image of the man to come forward, but her thoughts were as formless as a ball of dough. There was nothing inside anymore. A reaction might bubble to the surface sometime later, but that time was not now. She said nothing for a moment.

"Miss Driscoll, if I can—"

"My name is Juliet. You can call me Juliet."

"Yes, Juliet. You are unaware of these trust documents?"

She shook her head into the receiver. "I suspected, but I never knew for sure."

"Well then, I can say that, according to what I am reading, you and your brother evidently will inherit the assets of a trust on your upcoming birthdays this May. I cannot say how much money it will be at this time. However, clearly you had parents who made sure their children would be provided for."

Juliet swallowed. She had spent an entire childhood as an orphan, most of the time living in a sadistic hellhole surrounded by repulsive, vicious people. And now all of the arrows were pointing toward a mother and father who had loved her and her brother with a depth of devotion she could not imagine. Was she finally beginning to know them? Even though they were long gone a circle seemed to be closing, and for the first time in her life she felt linked to a family, her family, and she was in the center of the circle. Tears welled up at the discovery and the knowledge of her simultaneous loss.

"Are you there?" The voice was remote yet comforting. It belonged to an unknown and unrelated woman whose intervention was frankly puzzling. Why was all of this happening now? Someone suddenly appears connecting the threads in her life at the precise time that her parents would have wanted? It didn't seem logical to her engineering mindset. Was her mother—and this was a concept she could hardly manage—still caring for her, some spiritual guardian who had never left her side all this time? There were those who believed in angels, and perhaps this was…she couldn't complete the thought. A stirring, something deep and emotional inside her welled upward and she began crying. Her parents had loved her and her brother. Even in death they had always been there. She and Lenny had never been cast adrift.

Juliet tried to blink back tears in front of this individual she had never met, but she couldn't help herself. And, as if everything in her life had been building for this moment, her sobs broke forth going full tilt over the dam, releasing all the backed-up emotions she had stuffed and buried and pushed into some hole outside of herself. She convulsed like a child in a slobbering catching of breath, and she couldn't stop. Maybe she had never been as strong as she thought, just a weak individual whose failure to cope with the real world was plain to everyone but her. She cried for her broken family, she cried for her parents, she cried for her children yet unborn who her mother would never know, but most of all she cried for the failure in herself, and the inescapable fact that she had let her parents down, squandered their gifts of drive and intellect through all these years.

Minutes passed before she realized that she had nothing more to give, nothing left to reconcile herself and her past. Her tears diminished. She blew her nose and wicked the moisture away from her eyes and cheeks. She grabbed more tissues. At length, she noticed the telephone handset lying unaccountably on the table. She did not remember placing it there, and she picked up the small device and spoke. "Hello?"

"I'm still here," the woman replied, as though she had experienced the most normal interruption in the world.

"God, I'm so sorry," Juliet said wetly, and blew her nose again.

"At least I was able to know my parents before I lost them, and I know that is what you are feeling," she said.

"That and more."

"My father gave up his life in a Cuban prison for my freedom," she said in a soft voice. "It's not something I will ever forget, so I understand."

After a pause, "Why are you doing this? Helping us?"

"I allowed myself to be used by an evil man, knowing he was evil. I am trying to make amends for myself, and that also means for you and your brother."

"You said earlier that we are in danger. Did my brother get that right?"

The woman released a long breath into the phone. "I believe there is a conspiracy, if that is the right word, surrounding this trust, and there are those who will take it from you if they can arrange your deaths. It's very simple, really, especially now that Clifford has died. Perhaps it would be better if you could write this down, take notes on what I tell you. Have you got a pad and pencil?"

21

Her brother Clifford had finally come to the end of the road. He was stone cold dead. A massive coronary the attending doc had informed her. Well, so what? Was she supposed to feel something?

Doris lit a cigarette and examined the matchbook cover. Truth was she didn't feel anything. He had been a bully when they were children and she was going to go with that memory, hold it nice and clear, make sure he stayed in that box. Hell, even Rhinehart had trouble commiserating when he had called earlier. He hemmed and hawed, but it was obvious he was having a hard time keeping the sympathy level *in* his voice and the excitement *out*. And his excitement was contagious as they discussed the financial brochures she had received in the mail, the glossy pamphlets showing gold bullion stacked in a pile. Shit. She took a deep drag and snorted smoke out of her nostrils like a bull in a cartoon drawing. Two small steps and she would inherit everything. Actually, there was only one step that took any planning. Lenny was the easy part of the undertaking, and time was a-wasting on that dimwit. She could do the job today. Stick the kid in the well. He would freeze to death.

She moved to the kitchen sink and looked out through the window. The drilling crew wasn't coming anytime soon, not in this March blizzard. The cap of the reservoir would be off for days. She pulled on the cigarette again, this time allowing a lazy exhale to drift from her tarred nasal passages. So how exactly would she get the kid in there? She had a plan, and the lawyer's telephone call was the best part.

Nick stomped into the Office of Public Safety brushing snow from his jacket. The wind had moderated, but now large wet flakes were raining down like parachutes at the Normandy invasion.

Even at ten o'clock in the morning the sun couldn't break through the thick layer of overcast. It had been a long night and the day was going to be a bad one. He aimed his remarks at his deputy sitting with his feet propped beside the telephone. "George, get your feet off the goddamn desk. You've got to get here on time. Otherwise you're no good to me."

The deputy rolled back and forth in his chair and ran a finger down the spine of a law book on the corner of his desk. "Couldn't get the garage door open, Nick. And Marge needed help with the kids... Anyway, I thought Larry was supposed to come in."

"Larry's got the Crown Vic. You know damn well he can't make it until the plows clear Route 5 West. The county only provides two four-wheel drives. If you can't use yours effectively then I'm going to swap you out with Larry."

Murphy opened and closed the cover of his book in a flip-flop motion. "Great timing for those two new guys to be on vacation. I'm thinking about leaving anyway, Nick. I've got some interest from a law firm in Bismarck."

"How about thinking about your legal future after the day shift is over. Snow's gonna get bad and the state wants us to keep track of these roads. Get your ass out of here and call in the ones that are clear. You need to check the road plows once in a while anyway. The guy on 83 nearly got run down by an eighteen wheeler last night."

He shrugged and slouched to his feet. "Yeah, yeah. I know the drill."

The computerized chirp of the telephone came from both desk units. Murphy reached for his in an unhurried manner and checked the caller screen. He frowned. "It says 'Nick Olsen'. This is from your house, Nick." He punched the talk button.

"Murphy here." After a short pause he glanced over. "It's for you." And then with a tone and a smile Nick didn't like, he said, "Guess it's private."

Nick grabbed his phone and watched as Murphy slowly cradled the extension. "Olsen."

"Nick it's me." Juliet's warm breath came through the receiver. "I've got a huge amount to tell you."

"Juliet—"

"I've got *the* original criminal complaint. The one I filed when I was eighteen. It was in the satchel that Doris had in the attic."

Nick ran a hand through his hair and pressed his thumb and forefinger over squinty eyes that felt dry and sandy. He needed a couple hours of sleep. "Are you sure it's the original? Supposedly that can't happen."

"It's got my signature in blue ink. Everything's in blue. They did this so they could tell the originals from the copies way back when. I remember signing this, Nick, right below the signature of the guy I talked to. Someone named Schwartzel. I think he was an assistant district attorney. But that's not all. There is a trust document in existence, just like you said there would be."

"Wait, wait, wait," Nick cut in.

Murphy came to his feet, grabbed his parka, and made as if to leave. Nick waved him back to his seat and spoke in a voice loud enough for the man to hear. "I've got an almost lawyer here who swears a criminal complaint could not possibly be lost," he said. And then directly to his deputy, "Hey, didn't you tell me a guy named Schwartzel was one of your law professors?"

"And a damn good one," Murphy said. He lowered himself into his chair.

"A good friend of mine is on the phone," Nick said to Murphy. "She's in possession of an original criminal complaint filed in front of your Schwartzel guy—"

"Who was the assistant DA at the time," Juliet reminded him.

"Who was the assistant DA at the time," he repeated to

Murphy. "She says she has the documents right in front of her and they aren't copies. They're the originals."

Murphy replied. "I doubt it. She doesn't know what she's looking at."

"I heard that," Juliet said to Nick. "Tell him I'm bringing them with me in the car and taking them down to the federal building in Bismarck. Maybe the sitting DA would like to see them."

Nick smiled. God if the woman didn't have a little spunk. He repeated her threat to the deputy.

"Nick, there's more. I need to get to Doris'," Juliet said. "I think Lenny may be in trouble. I called him earlier, but now I can't get him on the cell phone. It keeps going to voicemail."

"Why would he be in trouble?"

He could hear her draw a long breath. "The trust document. I've been talking to a woman who lived with Clifford Blackwell—by the way, he died last night in a nursing home—and he was the trustee of the proceeds from the Wolverine Mining Company supposedly held for Lenny and me. Remember, we talked about that possibility."

"Yeah, but Juliet hold on. What could be so critical that a ten, twelve-hour delay would make a difference? I've got my hands full today, plus I've been up since I left you at the house last night. I've got to grab a few hours' sleep."

"I'm going to drive to Doris' to check on Lenny. She tried to kill me! I think she's going to try the same with my brother."

He rubbed his eyes again. "Juliet, I don't think you can make it there even if you tried. Route 28 hasn't been plowed all the way, and my driveway out to the state road isn't even marked. You'd be lucky to stay off the shoulder in these drifts."

"Nick, listen. Please! I found out Lenny and I are due to inherit the trust the day we turn thirty. That's only a few months from now. Doris believes she will inherit if Lenny and I are dead. She thinks she is listed as the contingent beneficiary."

"What do you mean 'thinks'? Hold on, Juliet." He covered the receiver and said to Murphy, "See if you can get through to the Blackwell place. Check on Lenny Driscoll."

"You mean the good-for-nothing—"

"Move your ass, George! *Now.* Hit your light bar, make it a Code 3."

"Okay, okay. You know my take on those twins."

"Frankly, I don't give a shit about your opinion. Either give me your badge—right now—or get your ass up there. Make sure the kid is safe. There's something strange going on here and I don't like it."

A departing, sideways glance told Nick all he needed to know. His deputy had the look of someone who was no longer a part of the solution. He was part of the problem.

Back again to the phone, "Okay, Juliet. I'm listening, but take it slowly."

"I heard you Nick, shouting."

"Yeah, well…go ahead."

"All right. Let me get my thoughts and facts straight. The woman I talked to this morning found two different trust agreements in Clifford's safe last night. The older one had Clifford listed as the contingent beneficiary—the man who would inherit the assets of my parent's mining operation if Lenny and I never made it to age thirty. It was probably written in that way because he was the trustee of our estate after his brother Jonas died."

"Makes sense. And?"

"But that's not who is listed in the most recent trust document. A while back everything changed, and a man named Rhinehart listed himself—and not Clifford—as the contingent beneficiary. So now *he* inherits everything if Lenny and I are dead."

"Clifford agreed to this?"

"He was probably half conscious and signed whatever was put in front of him. Besides, nobody reads the fine print on anything."

"So how does Doris think she's going to inherit?"

"She would've been the natural beneficiary if Rhinehart hadn't changed the contingent beneficiary to himself. Keep in mind, she was Clifford's sister, his sole blood relation, and with no one left, she would've hit the mother lode. I think she had that in mind when she pulled that knife on me last night."

"And because legally you were an intruder that might have worked. Rhinehart's got to be egging her on, encouraging her to do the dirty work."

"It's not that hard to do if you think you're going to inherit a fortune."

"So with Clifford already out of the way, Doris figures she'll be the beneficiary if she can remove you and Lenny. But guess what? She doesn't inherit a penny. Rhinehart gets it all. Slick."

"Yes! That's what I'm talking about! That's why I think Lenny's in trouble."

Anger boiled up. "Like I said before, we've got a nasty little parasite that's trying to hide, and we're uncovering the ugly thing." He grabbed the keys to the vehicle. "Okay. Listen, Juliet. I'm going to follow my deputy on up to Doris' house, see if I can get through on 28. Then I'm going to backtrack to my place in case you're stuck somewhere. You don't even have a cell phone, do you?"

"I gave Lenny mine before I left Doris'."

"Shit. Look, if I can't talk you out of going, go back into my closet and grab a couple of heavy down parkas. They'll keep you warm even if you get into trouble off the road somewhere."

"Thanks, Nick."

"I've always had a gut instinct about you and Lenny, and Doris Blackwell. I think I've had it ever since I was in high school. Maybe it's time that I did something about it."

George Murphy was heading north on a road that might be covered with a foot of new snow in the next twelve hours. The plows had been through once already, and for now the going was satisfactory. His wipers cleared large flakes that melted as soon as they hit the glass. The temperature was just at the freezing point, which meant that the road surface would pick up heat, then harden into glass-like black ice with nightfall. He could accelerate, but really, why bother?

The sheriff had things completely backward. Olsen had been away for too long during his stint in the military, and after that college and med school. And that's when the Blackwell twins had gotten into all that trouble. Reading a rap sheet about Lenny's priors was different than being around town, hearing about things first hand. And the girl had run away several times. Did Olsen know about that? Probably didn't make any difference. When you're screwing a thin little fox with a tight ass every night, well, who in the hell would question anything?

He had seen Juliet at the Crossroads from time to time. She had an attitude that seemed a little too *uppity* for a bar waitress. Who the hell did she think she was? However, there were plenty of guys, himself included, who wouldn't mind spreading her legs on a mattress for a weekend.

What he really needed to do was concentrate on working into Schwartzel's law firm in Bismarck, become the perfect young lawyer. He would keep his head down, stay late, and maybe hit Webster's Tavern now and again. That might give him a chance to check out that Lila babe who was giving the come-on to Schwartzel. Life could be everything he dreamed of, once he got out of this shit hole.

He flipped his cell phone open, pulled Schwartzel's card from his wallet, and punched in the number manually. He'd enter it into his contacts list once he got to know the man better.

A woman picked up with a smooth voice. "Schwartzel and Rhinehart."

He cleared cleared his throat. "Harry Schwartzel, please. This is George Murphy. He knows who I am."

"Mr. Murphy, may I tell him what this call is in reference to?"

"Ah…it's personal. He'll under—"

"Hold on."

The bitch cut him off! Was he still connected? He waited. The Mamas and Papas drifted through the phone. They were better than elevator music, but the receptionist had definitely earned a notch on his payback list. Maybe someday.

A plug of static disconnected *California Dreaming* from the hold function. A second later the big, round voice of Schwartzel burst over him. "George Murphy! What can I do for my favorite law student today? You here in Bismarck? Let's meet for lunch."

"Can't do it today, Harry. I'm up here in the north part of the state trying to keep my boss happy."

Schwartzel laughed. "Do what the boss says. That's what I like to hear. We're gonna have to get you down here for an official interview. So, what can I do for you? Billie—she's my secretary—says you've got something personal to discuss."

"Hang on a sec," he said into the phone. The front wheels tracked into rut, and he let the vehicle work itself to the other side of the ice. He bounced back onto a layer of snow and firmed his grip on the wheel. He said, "I've got some information that you might find interesting. It goes back to our discussion at Webster's the other night."

"Lemme think back." Schwartzel's tone held an air of contemplation.

"We were discussing a criminal complaint from a number of years ago."

"Oh yeah. That. Something about one being misplaced?"

"Harry, I'm not sure you want to hear this, but apparently one has surfaced with your name on it. It's the original document, according to the woman who's got it. I can't tell whether she knows shit about it though."

"I don't know how that could be, George. You'd better explain." His voice took on the dry, flat tone of an interrogator. Murphy recognized the quality; he used it himself.

"This was, well, it had to be ten, maybe twelve years ago. You remember a girl named Juliet Driscoll?"

There was a silence. Murphy waited.

"Maybe. I'm not sure," Schwartzel replied. "Tell me what you know, then tell me what you suspect."

22

Juliet had never been inside a man's closet. Lenny did not have one. His clean clothes were piled unpressed into an old easy chair. Dirty items were dropped in a corner, and anyway, it wasn't the same. She calculated the square footage of this one. Four feet by ten feet yielded forty square feet. Was this normal for a guy? She didn't know, but she gawked with curiosity as she stepped in to look for Nick's heavy parkas.

A whiff of leather and oil struck her right up front, along with a vague scent of something she assumed belonged to metal things like rifles and pistols. He was the sheriff, after all.

A laundry hamper sat next to the entrance. One T-shirt lay over the rim and one lay on the floor, as if he had tossed the articles from the bathroom hallway and missed with the first, and rimmed the hamper with the second. Men. On her right were jeans and flannel shirts on hangers along with uniform tops and trousers. Oxford cloth shirts separated by dividers were arranged in three Crayola shades: white, blue, and sea green. Just as she suspected, Nick was totally color challenged. She pressed her nose to a blue sleeve and took in the clean, linen smell that came from a dryer sheet. How would a guy know about those?

The heavy coats were toward the back, and Juliet grabbed a dark blue parka with a hood attached. She moved sideways back to the front and stopped at the hamper. The white cotton T-shirt draped over the tall basket did not appear especially soiled, and she tentatively held the fabric between thumb and forefinger and brought it to her nose. She came away with a sense of outdoor work and fields of hay. He wasn't a farmer. Was this just the North Dakota imprint on a man?

Ten minutes later she slowly and carefully steered the 4-Runner westbound along the state road. With the raised, grassy strip running through the center of Nick's driveway the problem of staying on the path hadn't presented much of a challenge, especially with four big snow tires gripping the surface. If the snowfall didn't increase she could get to Doris' with no problem.

Harry Schwartzel leaned back in his chair and scratched his testicles pinched beneath the center seam of his underwear. He rearranged them protectively, as if to thwart this stunning, unforeseen threat to his job, his lifestyle, and his very existence as a free man.

"Billie, bring us some fresh coffee and then take a long walk," Rhinehart ordered. "There's got to be a shoe sale somewhere. Don't come back until after lunch."

"Yes sir. Give me a minute." She executed a rapid about face and engaged her large hips into a cyclical forward motion.

"What the fuck, Harry," Rhinehart said at once.

The door came to a soft close. Rhinehart's countenance was a squall line of black energy. "I said what the fuck, Harry! How in the hell did a document like that walk out of a federal office building and into the arms of a bar girl."

Schwartzel glimpsed his partner's nostrils flared wide, a truly ugly slice of ill temper. He looked up and away, as if he attempted to peer back through the fog of many years. In fact, he remembered exactly what he had done. "You asked me to make it go away," he said weakly and somewhat defensively. "I thought I had."

Rhinehart drummed his fingers on the mahogany desk and glared at him. "You gave all the papers to Clifford, didn't you? Let that dickhead tell you he was going to burn them or something?"

Schwartzel said, "He sure as hell wasn't going to let a charge of rape against him ever see daylight. My God, Donald, I had to figure he was going to destroy everything as soon as he got home. Wouldn't you?"

Rhinehart leaned back, but he kept Schwartzel pinned in a narrow gaze. "Maybe. Except—how much did he pay you?"

"What?"

"I said how much did he pay you? Ten, fifteen, twenty? You think I can't figure out something was offered in return for that favor?"

For an instant Schwartzel said nothing. He drew inward showing a weak turn of body language, but he couldn't help it. "He gave me twenty—"

"Twenty thousand?" Rhinehart swung upright.

"He *wanted* to, Donald. I didn't force him. Besides, that was before you took me into the practice. I didn't cut you out of anything. It's not like you were directly involved."

"Except for the fact that I was Clifford's counsel, and a deposition with my name on it was attached to the criminal complaint. Did that walk away at the same time?"

Schwartzel nodded slowly. "He took everything. I couldn't very well have the deposition lying around referencing a missing criminal complaint."

"Shit." Rhinehart ran a hand over his scalp. "So how did all of this end up in the hands of the Driscoll girl?"

"Clifford left that day with his sister Doris, is all I can remember. The guy had a give-a-shit attitude, throwing papers around. Maybe the sister just somehow ended up with everything. And the Driscoll girl lived at the Blackwell woman's house, at least some of the time. There could have been all kinds of connections. We'll never know. Point is, she's got the originals now, according to my contact in the sheriff's office. I've got a deputy working for me, and he says she's got them with her in her car."

"No copies of anything?"

"I think I made one of the deposition. The Blackwell woman wanted one of her own, seeing how it was her testimony."

Rhinehart swore again and let out an angry breath. "I'm not sure who the biggest dumb shit is, me or you."

Schwartzel let the comment ride, whatever was meant by the statement.

His boss went on, "We don't need any more complications coming up regarding those twins, especially now that Clifford is dead."

"Dead?"

"They called yesterday from the nursing home."

"So that's…now you've got the trust agreement to settle?"

He flared again. "You don't know the half of it!"

Schwartzel went quiet. Rhinehart owned fifty-one percent of the partnership and could dissolve the lucrative arrangement if he wanted. Better to let the guy cool down.

"And if you think your own ass is in the clear, you're dead wrong," Rhinehart said. "You'll be hauled before a court and disbarred at the very least if this news gets out. Interference in a federal, judicial process? Shit, Harry, you'll be living in the homeless center on Pike Street for the rest of your life. No more expensive dinners at Webster's, and say goodbye to screwing that Lila hostess. Think she's going to come looking for you at the shelter? Think again."

A knock sounded, so discreet that it barely registered. Schwartzel jumped at the diversion and raised his voice. "Come in Billie."

She opened the door and peeked around the jamb. "I just didn't want to intrude. I've made your coffee."

"Set it down on the sideboard," Rhinehart instructed.

"Very good," she murmured. A moment later she vanished.

"You know what you need to do? Tell me you understand this, Harry."

Schwartzel nodded sharply. "I've got to get the documents back, ASAP."

"Fucking-A. And you're going to call that deputy sheriff of yours to get 'em. You got that?"

Schwartzel stood. "I know what to do. Deputy Murphy won't be a problem."

Nick Olsen punched on his flashing beacons and headed north on Route 83. The car had GPS built in to a navigation system, but he never turned it on. The handful of roads from Minot all the way to the Canadian border had been fixed in his mind almost from the time he could drive.

He hit the transmit button on the Motorola and the radio burped with a squelch of static. "Where are you George? How are the roads?"

His deputy came back after a long pause. "I'm north of Route 5, but the snow's getting heavier, Nick. Not sure I can get up there."

"Has the snowplow cleared 5 yet? He should be working west toward Mohall."

"He's still on 83. I think he's broken down. I would've stopped, but you gave me the Code 3 to the Blackwell place. I was about to call the plow in for rescue anyway."

At that moment Nick caught the orange rotating beacon partially obscured in a flurry of white downdrafts. As he approached closer, he realized the road equipment lay angled off to the side.

The radio squelch broke through. "Nick, you there?"

"Yeah, I've got the plow in sight. I'll handle things."

Murphy radioed back, "If you've got it, do you want me to run east on 5, check on your friend, Juliet?" A scratchy sound came through, like the guy was changing hands on the wheel while shuffling his thoughts. "I can make sure she's not off in a ditch somewhere. Look, Nick, I heard enough of your telephone conversation. She's trying to make it out from your place, and if the plow can get stuck then anybody can."

Nick slowed as he approached the stationary plow. The operator's single, rotating light reflected orange strobes in a 360-

degree arc around his own vehicle. Combined with the Durango's red, blue and white rooftop pulses, the small hemisphere of swirling snow seemed a mad carnival of colors. He doused the light bar and rubbed at his grit of overnight stubble. There was a quality to his deputy's voice, something that seemed a little pushed. It could be that his fatigue was spinning shadows out of nothing. He thought about it and came to the conclusion he was being paranoid. He pressed the transmit button. "All right. She doesn't have a cell phone, so if you don't see her headed west then she's off the road somewhere. Backtrack all the way to my driveway turnoff and keep me advised."

"Got it, Nick." The transmitting side tone ended abruptly.

Murphy drove slowly. The median strips and shoulder markings were completely covered and invisible, and there was no way one could avoid the drainage ditches without taking extreme care. Thirty minutes elapsed before he spied the dark green mass of Nick's Toyota 4-Runner. The girl had found a ditch with the right front wheel, no surprise there. As he closed on her position the driver's side door opened and a figure in an oversized blue parka jumped out and began waving energetically.

Murphy doused his rotating lights and pulled to a stop beside the other car. He ran the window down and witnessed a rapid deflation in the girl's expression. She peered at him with curiosity.

"I was...I thought you were Nick," she said in a voice that blew out a puff of condensation. She stepped toward his patrol vehicle and pulled back her hood.

"Not this time, Juliet. Nick couldn't make it. A snowplow driver got stranded. But I see you got his car in a jam." She was not quite the woman who he recalled serving beer in the dim light of the Crossroads Saloon, but a few years had passed since he had glimpsed her in daylight. She was prettier than he remembered, with irises that reflected green in spite of the overcast. Her expression was inquisitive, and her eyes darted back and forth in continual motion, as if she might be making calculations.

She frowned and drew back a strand of hair peppered with snowflakes. "Nick warned me about the roads, so I'm not going to blame the weather."

"No need to stand out in the cold," he said. "Get in the car with me and we'll get Nick on the radio."

She made a slow gesture that seemed almost condescending. "I'm fine for now. Do you think you could pull me out? I see you've got a winch on your front bumper."

There was that attitude again. He could read it as plain as day. Did he have to remind her she was a bar girl? "Don't know yet, sweetheart," he shot back through the open window. "I'm going to have to get out and take a look. But I'm not going to do that until you get in this car and out of the cold. Understand?"

She leveled a thoughtful gaze and said, "Okay then." She moved to the passenger side, opened the door, and slid into the seat along with a brace of cold air. "Sorry to be a bother," she said with a smile that appeared forced. "It's just that I'm really concerned about my brother."

"I tried to get up to the Blackwell place. Couldn't make it. The plow hasn't been able to clear the road yet." He grabbed the radio mike and punched the transmit button. "Olsen, you there?"

The crackle of a carrier tone broke through after a moment. "Whatcha got for me, George?"

He checked the girl with a nod. "A one Juliet Driscoll here in the car. She put a wheel in a ditch, but your car's not in too bad. I think I can winch it out."

"And how is my friend?"

Murphy said, "Your girlfriend's okay."

"Yeah, well. Have her follow you back here to the office if you get the 4-Runner going. We'll talk then. Thanks, out."

Murphy replaced the handset and turned to the girl. "Stay in the car. I'm going to hook you up. I'll put the 4-Runner in neutral and we'll see what happens."

"Don't you want me to…you know, gas it when you're pulling me out?"

"I want you to stay here. Understand?" Murphy slid out of the seat, slammed the door, and trudged toward the disabled vehicle.

Olsen's 4-Runner smelled like a woman's car. That's the first thing he noticed. The combined scent from the girl's perfume and maybe her body lotion raised a distinct urge and a single dark fantasy. "If only…" he murmured.

The second thing he noticed was an old, brown leather briefcase lying on the passenger seat, except the briefcase looked more like a large lady's handbag, open at the top with dividers and side pockets.

He pulled the driver side door partially closed to shield the woman's prying eyes from what he intended to accomplish. He illuminated the headlights, started the engine, and in general made it appear he was busy preparing the car for the tow.

Schwartzel's instructions had been precise: Look for a single sheet of paper with the lettering 'United States District Court' along the top. A case number and the words 'Criminal Complaint' would also be prominently visible, along with lots of signatures inked in blue. Additional documents would look the same, however the deposition would consist of two or three pages and would likely be attached to a cover sheet entitled 'Subpoena To Testify at a Deposition in a Criminal Case'. According to Schwartzel, there would be four or five pages in all.

Murphy thumbed through the side pockets of the briefcase. Nothing there. He glanced out the front windshield. The girl was staring back with that irritating, inquisitive watchfulness. Murphy switched on the wipers and placed the shift lever in neutral. He turned the wheel in the direction for a tow line. More noise, more commotion as he thumbed open the center partition and reamed a finger through the mess. Old newspaper clippings and bits of paper and cardboard scrap were visible, but nothing stood out that seemed official. He glanced again at the girl. The bitch was opening the passenger side door.

The remaining pocket was half-sized and closed with another flap. He reached in and grabbed a handful of papers.

They were folded accordion style with the top portion of the first page in view. He read, United States District Court, and in smaller script, *United States of America vs Clifford Blackwell.* Signatures were in blue ink. Bingo! He slipped them into an inner pocket on his coat. The girl was halfway to the car when he closed the leather flaps. Tough shit, bitch. He gunned the accelerator and spun the wheels for good measure. Nothing moved. It was time to get back out and hook up the winch.

Juliet decided that the deputy's behavior was erratic. Yeah, he did pull her out of the ditch, but did he have to be such an asshole? He scarcely slowed on the drive back to the Office of Public Safety in Sherwood. She was able to follow, but only just. By the time she hit Route 5 she was comfortable enough to let him speed up out of sight. Murphy had been inherited from the previous sheriff's staff when Nick was elected. She knew that much. Otherwise, she doubted Nick would have hired him. She didn't like the guy. He always wore his uniform top when he came into the Crossroads Saloon, as if he wanted everyone to know what he was. Nick usually wore jeans and a tucked-in Oxford cloth shirt—in one of his three colors—when he was off duty. She smiled. Now *that* was something she had to address.

When she arrived at the sheriff's office the deputy's SUV was already parked in front of the building. So much for helpful public servants.

She entered the office complex, followed the signs along a short, linoleum-floored hallway, and glimpsed Nick through a glass-paneled door. He was relaxing with his backside against a chunk of gray plastic and steel that had the definite appearance of a government issued block of office furniture. He held a cup of coffee in his left hand as he addressed an older man who appeared to be straight out of a homeless shelter.

She banged through the door. "Nick?"

"Juliet." Nick's expression brightened.

The happy rapture on her face probably told him everything about her. She didn't care anymore. An overwhelming urge to touch him took hold, as though her desire was finally surfacing. Perhaps the time had come to stop analyzing herself and instead acknowledge what she felt.

The strange man at Nick's side tempered her approach. Instead of an embrace to end all hugs, she forced herself to offer a hand in a formal, jailhouse greeting.

Nick held her fingers in a warm grasp, and that told her what she needed to know. "You were right about the snow," she said in a rush. "I got stuck." Her remark was a little stupid, a little idiotic, and a little *obvious*, but that's what rolled out.

"Murph arrived a few minutes ago. He told me he pulled you out," he said.

She couldn't help herself. "You scratched yourself a little, Nick. And here…" She took her thumb and wicked away a tiny spot of toothpaste from the corner of his mouth, her excuse to touch him again.

He tipped backward for a second before giving up. "Okay. It's been a long night. I needed to wash up, brush my teeth, shave, the usual things." He turned to the man standing close by. "And Juliet, this is Andy, the snowplow driver. I rescued his butt. Andy, meet Juliet."

"Not much heat in them plows," the man offered. "You get one stuck an' it gets awful cold and lonely out there on the road." The old man showed no inclination of moving away. Instead, he seemed to welcome her as a part of a happy, conversational threesome.

Nick inclined his head and pointed. "You can hang up that big parka in the annex if you want. You're going to get hot in here pretty quickly with that on."

"I'm already hot," she said. "Plus, I'm wearing one of your big sweatshirts underneath. I just had that thin sweater otherwise."

Andy looked at her with renewed interest and appeared slightly troubled, as if the focus of the discussion might be drifting away from him. "Now I coulda used that last night on the plow," he said. "Nick, that yours?"

"Yeah. The lady borrowed it," he said. Juliet picked up a glint of humor in his eyes.

"Well now." The old man seemed to run out of conversational gambits.

"Look, Andy. I'm going to get my friend a cup of coffee. I'll get the deputy to run you down to the state garage in a minute."

"No hurry, Nick. I'll just wait." Somewhat deflated, he moved to the hard chairs and took a seat underneath the back windows.

"Where *is* the deputy?" Juliet asked. She unbuttoned and unzipped the oversized garment.

Nick nodded toward the annex. "I think he's in the restroom now. There's also a ladies room that way, past the copier and the wall with the coat hooks."

She shucked the coat. "Just what I need. Back in a sec."

The annex fed off the back corner of the office. She assumed the lock-ups were in the other direction as she entered a narrow, poorly lighted hallway. She racked Nick's parka alongside a damp, heavy coat that promptly slipped from the adjacent hook. The garment fell to the floor. She frowned. The place needed more hooks for these bulky winter clothes, and they should be spaced farther—a grunt of surprise came from her as she glanced to the floor. Surprise turned into a shocked disbelief at what lay before her eyes. The deputy's coat had fallen open exposing the inner pocket, and stuffed inside was a sheet of paper with her signature upside down in blue. She remained frozen for a moment. She could recognize that document anywhere on earth. Her hands began to tremble, and she fought her body's reaction as she reached down and retrieved the sheaf of papers that had been in her possession not thirty minutes before. That asshole deputy Murphy... Now she understood why he seemed to be screwing around for too long in her car.

The toilet from the men's room flushed, a distinct sound of a hydro-mechanical valve being tripped by a strong vacuum force.

Juliet held off a surge of panic and hauled the deputy's coat back up to the hook. Was the guy going to wash his hands? There couldn't be more than seconds remaining before he opened the door. Something fired inside her, and she grabbed the documents and stepped rapidly to the copy machine. Paper was stacked on the in-tray. She pulled out the top four sheets, creased them into a quick fold and scrambled back to the coat. She slid the blank pages into the inner pocket and stepped away. Her original documents went into the pouch in her oversized sweatshirt just as the door swung open.

The deputy stepped out checking his fly. He gaped at her.

She stammered, "Uh, is the ladies' room this way?"

"To the left," he said slowly.

After a few shaky steps further on Juliet swung through the entrance to the women's room. She leaned back against the door and heaved through a couple deep lungfuls of air. Safe. There were questions to be answered, to say the least. But meanwhile, she had pulled off a really clever, really sneaky, double move that was going to shock the shit out of the deputy, and maybe others. A smile formed on her lips. She couldn't wait to tell Nick what she had done.

Nick stood alone in the office when she returned. He slouched against his desk with a look of inward concentration, tapping his front teeth into a yellow pencil.

That's not good for your gums," she said. "Or so I've been told. Where is everybody?"

He examined the pencil and pinched a fleck of yellow paint from his tongue. "The deputy's on his way to the DOT garage in Minot. He's got the snowplow driver with him."

She moved closer to him. Prior to today she had never been in his office, but he kept things as neat and tidy as his house. "You look really tired," she said.

"Goes with the territory. If I was doing a hospital rotation I'd be getting a lot less sleep than this."

"Nick, I've got tons of stuff to tell you, but I really am concerned about Lenny."

He shook his head and tossed the pencil on the desktop. "We can't get up there yet, and I can't get anyone to pick up when I call the house. According to the NOAA broadcast, the weather system is supposed to play out by tomorrow, warm up a bit. Meantime, I've got the other snowplow working on Route 28. That's the best I can do."

The phone rang. He picked up the handset and listened, occasionally offering monosyllabic replies. Juliet focused on a slice of the parking lot visible through the door and front hallway windows. The distraction allowed a space for her thoughts.

Lenny was her major concern. Suppose he was okay after all? Then none of this sordid, family history was Nick's problem. He could arrest people for misdemeanors, felonies, break up bar fights, issue traffic tickets, but…according to Marietta, the lawyers behind all of this weren't even in Nick's jurisdiction. They had offices in Bismarck. And what of the criminal complaint she had just recovered from the deputy's coat pocket? Did it really matter anymore? After all, the man who assaulted her had just died in a nursing home. So why did Nick's deputy want to steal the documents when Clifford was already dead? There was only one reason. Murphy was under orders from someone.

She glanced at Nick. He was examining his pencil with an ear to the phone.

There was something else, something personal: She felt changed. The fight with Doris had unleashed something. And the call to Marietta had…well, she was not sure what that had done, but the knowledge of her family made her feel stronger and more capable. She could ride a bull right now, charge right through Doris and her sleazy lawyers. She wondered why on earth she had taken such a back seat in life. If her mother and father were up there somewhere looking out for her, then she was not going to let them or herself down any longer.

And Nick? She had withheld so much of herself from him. Here was a man who desired her on a level of intimacy that she had never expected or thought she wanted. Yet now she wanted him the same way, and she was not going to hide herself from him any longer.

Nick replaced the handset to the side and faced her. "What?"

She took a breath. "Nick I want to explain things...about me. All the stuff you don't know. Everything. All of it."

"What brought this on?"

"Are we alone in this room? If we're alone I want you to kiss me."

His expression was that of a man shaken awake. He glanced at his pencil and focused on her. "Juliet, this is a change. I thought you couldn't do that, couldn't kiss a man, your issues with intimacy and all. Remember our deal? It was just last night."

She nodded. "As I recall I'm supposed to make the overtures. You're just supposed to, what?"

"Be standoffish," he said.

"Don't tease me, Nick. Are we alone? No cameras or anything around here?" She scanned the room.

"There's one in the corridor by the lock-ups. It loops all the time, even if no one's in there. That's the only one. We are alone." His voice held a different tenor. A breath seemed to catch inside him, or was it hers? A pulse beneath his open collared shirt became visible: a vein, an artery, something that he could name but she could not. She reached for him and slid her arms around his waist.

"Nick, I wanted you last night. That's the first thing I need to tell you."

"You were emotionally exhausted. I knew that. You needed some sleep."

"I dreamed about you...touching me, in bed with me, everything. I almost thought you'd be there when I woke up."

"Juliet, in a few minutes..." His voice was uneven, his breath a warm caress on her face. "That was another deputy just then on the phone. He'll be coming in."

"And I want you now. That's the second thing you need to know." She could feel his body hardening lower down, and in turn she responded with pressure. "We have time for a kiss," she said in a voice that trembled. "I want you to start with a kiss like the one you gave me behind my ear. You know, when you were standing at my door that night saying goodbye. I've thought about that."

He raised her left hand, turned her wrist palm side up and placed his lips over her white scars.

"Nick?"

"I'm going to get there." He opened her fingers and kissed her palm.

She cupped his cheek. "You think you still want me?" she said in a strained voice. "Along with all of these scars?" Tears welled up. Dammit, was she losing control again?

"All my life," he said, as he bent his head and kissed her eyes and her straight nose, and ran his lips lightly over her cheeks. He worked a path behind an ear and nuzzled her for a moment with his mouth and lips.

"Nick." She shuddered and pressed her hands along his back pulling him inward, closer against her body. "That's...that's what I need."

His voice became thick. "You're supposed to make the..."

She brushed the corner of her lips against his mouth, a sliding movement that barely touched him. She felt slippery, smooth, soft in his arms.

He held her back for an instant. "I'm sure of this, but are you?"

Juliet nodded and allowed his lips to make the softest contact with hers, a slow movement along the line of his mouth, as if gauging her response. She inhaled a fresh scent of aftershave on his skin and a touch of mint on his breath. She parted her lips a millimeter, then more, then fully as he took her in a slow consummated union. Her whispers were no longer hers, but moans from someone she barely knew. The instant he touched her tongue her breath evaporated.

The sound seemed to come from a great distance, a
faraway galaxy as it slowly intruded into her consciousness. Nick
pulled away with a breathlessness that matched her own. He
looked toward the sound of someone stamping off snow in the
outer hallway.

"He's here," he said, grabbing a lungful of air that came
out all erratic.

Was she as flushed as he? She put her cheek against his
for one final caress. If she couldn't hold onto him she was going
to float away this very minute, especially since she could feel his
hardness against her.

"God...I'm...can you walk, my Nick?" The knowledge of
his arousal heightened her longing. "Maybe, if you take a seat for
a minute or two..."

"You think that'll do it? I'm not sure this is ever going
away."

She sighed and pulled back her hair with a shaky
movement. In that moment they had become lovers in a sense,
even if their longed-for consummation would have to be delayed.
She could wait, but only barely.

The inner door opened, and Larry Hudson staggered into
the office.

Larry was downright portly. Juliet could not figure out
how he could ever chase down a thief. He had never been thin,
even in high school, but he was a whiz at creating or repairing
anything mechanical. She recalled their after-school science club.
Larry had been the vice president of the club second to her, the
president.

She stabilized her breathing and joked, "Deputy Hudson.
You put together any metal detectors lately?"

He headed for the coffee pot. "With three kids? You think
I've got time?" His holstered weapon flapped on his hips as he
walked. Over his shoulder he asked, "When are you going to
settle down, Julie? I thought you'd have kids and a huge
mortgage by now."

The remark was unintentional but it hurt a bit. "I'll get to it, Larry. Actually, I'm working on someone right now. Just don't want to be rushed, is all." She avoided Nick's gaze.

Nick came to his feet. The exit of blood from his cheeks left a rouge-like shadow. He jiggled his pocket change, evidently making a final, inward adjustment to his arousal problem. She smiled. If he thought he was in trouble now, she had big news for him later on.

Nick cleared his throat. "Larry, you and George have the shift. Close up at midnight unless something develops. The plow is up on 28 working toward the Blackwell residence."

Larry turned with a question mark on his face. "That's your place, Julie."

"It used to be, but that was a while back. Aunt Doris and my brother live there now."

"Let me know if it gets through," Nick said. "We're worried about him."

"Who, Lenny?"

"Yeah," Juliet added. "It's complicated, but I can't get him on his cell…and some things have been developing that I believe could be trouble for him."

"Nick? What's this about?"

"I'm not sure. I can't brief you until I know more of the facts. Just keep a watch. I'm going to leave you the Durango."

"Right, boss. Where's George?"

"Running Andy back to the garage in Minot."

"You want the keys to the cruiser?"

"Yeah, but not this minute. We're going to walk over to the diner. I haven't eaten since last night and I'm hungry."

The table by the café window toward the rear was a perfect place for a private conversation. One other table was occupied, which was actually a surprise, considering the weather.

Nick glanced at the menu and stuffed it back in the metal holder. "What's the biggest and best dish you've got going today, Becky? Fix me something good."

The waitress was young. Juliet didn't recognize her. "Burger and fries," the girl said. "You know those are good. Or I can do breakfast. We do that all day long."

"Breakfast special, I guess. Eggs over easy. Sausage. Pancakes on the side."

Becky worried her brow. "You want the sausage links or the patties? We've got both."

"Patties, I guess."

"And hash browns? I can add 'em if you want."

He grinned. "Yeah that'd be good."

Juliet giggled. "Jeez, Nick. I didn't know a little sex made you so hungry, and we hardly started. "

"Juliet, for crying out loud."

"I'm just getting back once in a while."

The girl glanced away with a thin line of amusement on her face, as if she was unsure where to focus. "Coffee everyone?"

"Yes, please," Juliet answered with a sweet smile.

"Aren't you hungry?" he asked.

"I'm fine. I had the steak that we didn't get to last night," she said with another glance at Nick's waitress friend.

Nick shook his head and reached for her hands on the table as the server walked away. "Now who's the comic," he said.

"I think I'm starting to have a little fun," she said.

"You didn't tell her that you actually fell asleep last night."

"I won't make the same mistake twice."

"That could be taken two ways."

"I'll let you figure it out," she said.

With the coffee's arrival Nick's expression went serious and she withdrew her hands. "Take me through everything slowly," he said. "You said you've got a lot to tell me."

Juliet nodded. "You won't believe it, Nick. But let's start with these." She reached into the sweatshirt pouch and pulled out the legal documents, all signed in blue.

A short time later Nick pushed away the plate. "It's like everything else," he said. "Once you understand the larger picture, all the little pieces fit together. We need to look at the trust agreements that this Marietta woman has found."

"She's in Bismarck. Can we get there?"

He tipped his head. "Not a problem. The roads are clear to the south. You ever meet her?"

Juliet shook her head. "No. But she seemed helpful, even nice over the phone, and she did try to warn Lenny that he might be in danger. She's got it all figured out." Juliet smoothed the tablecloth with her hands. "I'm not sure Lenny understood anything. He thought she was calling from Cuba."

"This is the woman who was living with the man who raped—sorry, assaulted you?" He reached for her hand again, felt the return squeeze.

"You can use the word. It is more accurate. Now that you know everything, it doesn't hurt so much inside."

He nodded slowly, then, "Two things: we've got to check on Lenny, and we've got to get the trust documents. Since we can't get through to Doris', we're going to Bismarck to see Marietta first."

"What about George?"

Nick stared at the nearly empty parking lot outside. "That's the one problem I didn't see coming, but I'm trying to think back. Weeks ago I asked George about criminal complaints, if one could simply disappear. He took the question directly to his law professor, Schwartzel, the very guy who signed on as the assistant DA in blue ink." He pointed to the signature on the form. "See? Exactly what you told me over the phone."

"He's in with Schwartzel. That's what I think."

"That would explain his actions. He's been blowing around the fact that he's going to be made an associate in the law firm. So when he overheard your phone call this morning—"

"My God, Nick, you repeated almost everything I said to him."

He nodded. "Most of it, including the fact that you said you had the criminal complaint and deposition in the car. George must have dialed Schwartzel from his cell the moment he left the office, and the lawyer would have been in a panic. You just can't bury that kind of legal complaint. Schwartzel knew if the complaint surfaced he would be disbarred or thrown in jail, or maybe both."

"So that's the reason?"

"Yep. Makes sense to me."

"Well, they *are* going to surface," Juliet said with a smile. "I can guarantee it."

"That's my woman," Nick replied. "And I hope Murphy enjoys his last day of work as a deputy sheriff." He stood and retrieved his cell phone from a pocket. "Speaking of my ex-deputy, I think I'll call him and tell him he's fired."

"Nick, no wait. That'll tip him off about the documents. He may not know he's carrying blank sheets of paper. Let him make his big presentation, fall into his own trap."

Nick laughed. "The lawyers will explode."

Juliet nodded. "Then he'll lose two jobs in one day."

23

George Murphy swung through the pebbled glass revolving door of the Lyman R. Casey Office Building in Bismarck, North Dakota. He was immediately confronted by a telephone stand in the marbled foyer. He patted his interior coat pocket for the reassuring crackle of paper and scanned the marquee next to the bank of elevators. This is where he wanted to work, for now and forever more.

He punched in the two-digit extension corresponding to the Rhinehart and Schwartzel law firm and found himself connected to the same irritating secretary that had cut him off much earlier in the day. He made his words short and purposely rude. "Mr. Murphy for Harry Schwartzel. Buzz the elevator."

"Should be opening now, sir."

He stepped into the car and rode up three floors while considering his new life. Once he was made an associate he'd get a small, in-town apartment. If Marge and the kids wanted to make the move later on he would have to consider selling the house. But that would take at least a year, maybe two. A timely divorce might be something to consider, but only if he could get out without too much financial damage. Meanwhile he would be here in the city on his own. A hot, young lawyer! Christ, if an old geezer like Schwartzel could tie into that nice tail at Webster's, just imagine what he could do.

The secretary was a plain-featured sixty-something woman with a big ass and pasty, overstuffed legs. However, she stood and shook his hand in greeting. That was something, at least.

"Detective Murphy, nice to meet you at last. Mr. Schwartzel has a very high opinion of you."

"I'm a deputy, ma'am, but thanks for the promotion."

"Can I get you a coffee before I usher you in to the conference room? Mr. Rhinehart is also waiting to meet you."

A slight increase in his heart rate disconcerted him. This was obviously going to be a heavyweight interview, a first look by the partner on the heels of Schwartzel's recommendation. "Coffee sounds good," he said. "Could you bring it in?" Gripping handshakes around a cup of hot liquid did not seem the wisest approach.

"Certainly, sir." She stepped to the dark-paneled door, gave it a light knock and smiled. "If you'll go right on in…"

Murphy stepped into an office cushioned in a thick carpet with lots of creams and pastels woven into the pile. The room had the smell of a new car, but one trimmed in expensive wood and leather instead of cheap plastic and cloth.

Schwartzel rose from the end of a long, mahogany table inlaid with a blond hardwood veneer. A second person came slowly to his feet.

"Well, George," Schwartzel said and offered his hand. "You haven't even passed the Bar and we already need your services. Looks like I had my eye on the right man." He turned to the other individual. "This is the managing partner, Donald Rhinehart."

A hawk-faced man in a nicely tailored suit extended a hand. "Harry tells me you've brought us something that could save the firm from an embarrassing situation."

"Got it right here." He patted his coat pocket again.

The secretary materialized at his side wielding a silver tray crowded with steaming coffee poured into three porcelain cups. Sugar was piled into a sterling container, cream in a small, crystal decanter. "Here you are, sir."

"On the table will be fine, Billie," Rhinehart directed.

Murphy raised a hand for the offering, only to see the platter quickly removed.

Rhinehart cocked his head in the direction of the table. "Why don't we have a seat ourselves?"

If Schwartzel was neutral to positive in his behavior towards him, then Rhinehart was neutral to negative. However, they both shared a marked condescension when dealing with a deputy wannabe lawyer from a hick county in the north of the state. He had to remind himself what he was carrying in his pocket. If they wanted the papers they damn well would start showing a little deference to him, and not the other way around. He was not going to be treated like a fucking lap dog.

He was ushered to the end of the table. The two men settled on his left and right.

Rhinehart drummed his fingers on the table. "What have you got for us, Murphy?"

George steeled himself and glared at the lawyer. "Rhinehart, you're either going to call me George or Mr. Murphy. Take your pick. Otherwise I'm leaving here without showing you or Schwartzel anything. Clear? And I believe I'll have that cup of coffee before we go any further."

The man's eyes narrowed. A faint smile appeared and faded to a flat line. He held his hands in a bullshit gesture of supplication, a disciple at the foot of Jesus. "By all means, please help yourself."

Murphy stirred cream and sugar into his coffee with deliberate slowness. The long period of silence was broken only by the clink of his spoon. He took a sip of the beverage.

Schwartzel broke in. "I told you, Donald. He's what we need at the firm. Aggressive new blood."

"Before we get started," Murphy said, "I'd like to know how this criminal complaint along with a deposition came to be separated from the normal schedule arranged by the clerk of courts. After all, I'm trying to learn the law here."

"And break it at the same time?" Rhinehart put in. "Or am I misinformed that you stole those documents from the Driscoll woman's car?"

There it was again. The guy was addressing him as if he was trailer trash. "I actually consider this bending the law more than breaking it," he said. "Aren't these documents supposed to be a matter of public record? And if they're for public use, how can they be stolen property?"

"Gentlemen," Schwartzel interjected. And to Murphy, "I appreciate the favor. You know that. I'm afraid this situation has been primarily my fault. Donald has a right to be irritated over the mess." He played with the coffee cup in front of him and seemed to categorize his thoughts. "I'll level with you, George. I never bought into the Driscoll girl's allegation of rape when I was the assistant DA. We all knew—" he glanced at Rhinehart, "—that she had run away twice, and that her brother had done jail time. Yet here she was accusing Clifford Blackwell—an upstanding individual and a valued member of the community, along with his sister Doris, of course—of a despicable crime that could send him to prison. Yes, it was wrong of me to bury the complaint and deposition, but as you put it so well, sometimes bending the law is not quite the same thing as breaking it." He puckered his lips underneath an arched brow. "We need, and I'm being frank here, someone in this law firm who's not going to be squeamish when it comes to bending, hell, maybe even breaking a few of those rules. Let's face it, you can take the high road all the time, or you can make lots and lots of money by taking a more *reasoned* approach. Your choice."

"The reasoned approach sounds more my style," Murphy conceded. He took a final swallow of coffee and experienced a light-headed fizz of excitement. He reached for the papers inside his jacket. "And now you probably want to see these. I give you your original criminal complaint and deposition," he announced with a flourish as the papers hit the table between the two lawyers.

The sheen of paper appeared sharper and carried an odd whiteness that wasn't there before. It had to be the overhead florescent glare in the office, he reasoned.

Rhinehart reached for the papers and with two fingers parted the folds. One eyebrow went up. A puzzled expression registered on his face, and for a long moment he said nothing. A cold gleam settled in his glance when he looked up. "Do you mind explaining this?" he asked in a voice as needle sharp as an ice pick. He slid the papers across to Schwartzel.

"What?" Murphy responded with bewilderment.

Schwartzel paged through the sheets. "Is this your idea of a joke? These are blank sheets of paper."

Murphy drew forward and encountered a split-second of disbelief. Something was not right, but his brain could not accept what it was. His mouth hung open as he focused on the blank pages now held in Schwartzel's hand. "What...?"

"Good fucking question, Murphy," Rhinehart snapped.

"I..." He reached for the papers, and as his fingers slid over the empty sheets he felt a cloud of blood redden the base of his neck and continue upward in a prickly spiral. An image flickered through the sluggish nerve endings in his brain. The girl. The fucking Driscoll bitch in the bathroom hallway. She'd done the switch right there. But how could she have known? He shook his head.

Rhinehart stood. "Out. Get your worthless ass out of this office and back where you came from."

"The girl," Murphy enunciated through a dry mouth. "The Driscoll girl tricked me. I should have caught it."

Rhinehart laughed. "Tricked by a slut. I'll remember that tagline next time I need a good joke."

Murphy glanced toward Schwartzel in the hope of a reprieve. The overweight man was on his feet and looking down with a bleak expression at the crumpled pages in his hand. He turned a pale face toward the deputy. "You have no idea what you've done. Don't bother driving down here for my nightly lecture series," he said glumly. "It is my pleasure to inform you that you've already flunked Contracts. If I could make you pay further I would."

"I can get them back," Murphy said in a thin voice. "She stole the documents from my coat pocket, and there's no reason I can't get them back."

Rhinehart grinned. "You know, with your curious, legal take on thievery, it is almost a shame we can't somehow find a place for you. Tell you what. You get the criminal complaint back *and* the deposition, and I might—*might*—give your employment prospects a slight reconsideration. Now get your ass out of here."

24

Doris had to get something in her mind, to work up her pulse, her irritation, and her fortitude, and she'd had all damn day to do it. She focused on an image of Cliffy from years back. The little prick was always shoving her around, acting like the normal bully he was. But this time he was making her undress behind the bushes in back of the swing set. She was crying, and he kept pushing and pulling and making her show her private parts. God, if that still didn't make her blue in the face, just the thought.

Yeah, she could do it. All it took was substituting Juliet's idiot brother for Cliffy in her mind. He probably would have done the same thing if he'd gotten the chance. She knew what he was about when he went over to Park River every so often. "Lenny!" She shouted upwards from the stair landing.

A muffled reply accompanied by a couple of thumps on the floorboards told her he was responding in his typically sluggish manner. A minute later his head appeared over the top of the banister. "What?"

"Turn off that TV and come down here to help me." What the hell had the kid been doing all day? Damn if she wasn't going to take a two-by-four to the satellite dish...afterwards, of course. With all the money coming in she would be moving someplace nicer anyway.

"Whataya want, Doris?" He was still leaning over the bannister.

"You hear the phone ring earlier?" she asked in a raised voice. The damn thing had been ringing off the hook ever since Rhinehart's morning blabfest informing her about Clifford. As if she didn't know her brother was dead? And three of the incoming calls showed Sheriff Olsen on the caller ID. Not like she was going to answer those.

Lenny rubbed his eyes and raked a hand through his hair that stuck out every which way. "Yeah, I heard the phone a couple of times," he replied in answer to her question. "Sis called earlier. Was there something else for me?"

She cocked her head and gave him an owl eye. "The foreman on the crew fixing our well called. Said he can't get out here with the roads the way they are, but he told me that unless we can get the cover back on, all the pipes at the bottom are gonna freeze. You hear that?"

"Yeah? So what'll we do?"

"We got to get the cap back on. It's too heavy for me to manage by myself. We've got no water if the pipes freeze, Lenny."

"I was just trying to take a nap. You know, relax today, with the snow and all."

"Help me out, and maybe we'll talk later about that new pickup you want. How's that?"

Thirty minutes later he trundled beside her in a bovine sort of way. The well was halfway down the incline towards the barn and Doris watched him as he looked here and there. What the hell was he thinking about? Nothing much was tied down behind that thick forehead, she knew that much. His upcoming loss, disappearance, unavailability, *whatever*, would be small in the scheme of things. He was wearing boots and jeans and a sweatshirt, and at the last minute had slipped on a thick-waffled parka he had picked up somewhere. She couldn't talk him out of the extra jacket, though it wouldn't matter in the long run. She raised her voice and put some urgency into her tone. "The guy said to get as much of the snow and ice off the rim as we could, even on the inside. Everything helps, he said."

He shuffled through the white powder. "We need to talk about my new pickup, Doris. After all, if I'm helping out around here all the time…"

"After we get through with this chore, Lenny, we'll discuss things. I think I kinda know what you've got in mind."

The water well had been designed as a picture-perfect structure with a small A-frame roof. The original supports for a bucket with its turn of rope around a wooden spindle were long gone. Doris stepped onto the slightly raised stone platform around the well. The protection afforded by the roof was negligible, and snow packed the rim like drift on a picnic table. "See this, Lenny?" She brushed at the accumulation with a gloved hand and leaned into the opening. "We need to clear this stuff off, break loose those icicles on the inside and get them out of there so the cap will fit back on."

"How we gonna do that?"

"Well, let's start by just getting the snow off the rim. Then we'll get to the inside stuff." Damn she was good. She should have been bossing a construction crew of her own.

Ten minutes. That's all it took to clear the rim. Now came the part that took a more subtle approach. She leaned over and poked her head far down. 'Lead by example' was the turn of phrase that hit her out of the blue.

"Careful, Doris. You don't want to lose your balance."

His consideration was touching, especially since what he was probably thinking was: no Doris means no pickup truck. She leaned even farther in. Damn if the hole wasn't just a black void. There were, however, a few icicles clinging to the inside rim. She snapped one off and backed out. "See," she said with a breath. "These are what the guy said to remove before we slid the cover back on. And your arms are a lot longer than mine."

"I'm not sure I want to lean in like that." He scratched his head and rearranged his cap. "Makes me kinda dizzy."

What? Was this kid she had raised a total *pussy?* Jesus! She'd known *women* with more balls. Hell, she had 'em herself. "Okay. Look, Lenny," she said with another deep catch-up breath—and she could use a cigarette right now. "If you can just sit on the rim and dangle your legs inside, that way you can kick at the ice, loosen it up, and I can lean in and grab it where it breaks away." She gave him her most sincere look and attempted a smile, even though she was not exactly sure what a smile looked like on her face. Probably scared the shit out of him. "The rim's plenty wide enough, and you can't fall in that way," she said.

"Well, I guess that'll be safe," he mumbled.

Until I push your ass off the rim, she thought.

He scanned the yard and the long drive out to the state road with a hopeful look, as if the drilling crew might be coming right around the corner. "Alright, let me climb over..."

"Careful now." She gave him room, went to the opposite side so as not to spook him early on.

Lenny kicked at the ice. "I can hear some of it cracking, Doris. You got to reach in."

"Yeah, okay." She leaned in again and grabbed a sheet of ice about to break loose. She held it up, actually a bit surprised. "Now, see? This is what we're talking about! Good job, Lenny."

Lenny extended his legs and put more energy into his kicks.

"Swing around just a little," she said. "You've got to work all the area."

He scooted his butt in her direction while she moved toward him. Just a step, really, until she was directly behind him. She took a deep breath, recoiled back a half-step and shoved a straight-armed blow at his belt line with both of her gloved hands. He yelped in a full-throated cry as he slid from the rim and dropped. That was it. The entire deed was simple in the end.

She listened for a few minutes, took in the emptiness of the woods and the isolation of the state road to the south. The wind had died. Earlier it had been blowing like a freight train from the north. Now stillness settled over the place. A couple of crows squawked from the roof of the barn. She peered down into the well and yelled for good measure, "Lenny, you okay? Lenny!"

She heard something. Did he answer? She couldn't tell. Anyway, time would take care of the lingering issues. She stepped from the open shaft and swung her arms to get the circulation back. Actually, her wrists hurt just a little, but nothing that a few Tylenols wouldn't fix. She trudged back to the house. The farther she walked from the point of *the accident*, the better she felt about the whole thing. Really, she just fell against Lenny, slipped on the ice. It wasn't as if she had pointed a gun at someone's head and pulled the trigger.

She spied her silver, BMW 7 Series sedan in the front drive under a thin covering of snow. She experienced a jolt of both pleasure and concern. The new car was a joy to drive, but the navigation system was damn near impossible to get the hang of. Could they make anything more complicated?

25

The woman at the door was not originally from Bismarck, North Dakota. She had on a pink, soft wool dress that was tailored to accentuate her figure and look both casual and formal at the same time. A lustrous fall of dark hair was pulled back and held with a clip. She wore nylon stockings with one-inch black pumps.

Juliet noted Nick's appreciative glance, and she had to agree that Marietta was an attractive woman. She felt shabby in Nick's sweatshirt. However, if the woman could read her thoughts she gave no indication.

"Marietta Santo-Donato," she stated with a heavy accent and a smile that seemed genuine. "And you are Juliet."

"How do you know?"

"Because I expected your visit, especially after our phone call this morning. You are doing exactly as I would have done."

Juliet sighed with fatigue that was suddenly overwhelming. "Was it just this morning that we spoke? It seems like last month."

"I see you brought an officer of the law. I hope I am not going to be arrested." She extended her hand, first to Nick.

"He's a close friend," Juliet said to her. "This is Nick Olsen. And Nick, this is my new friend, Marietta."

"We should apologize for the last minute call," he said.

"No reason to apologize. I feel that Juliet and I are no longer strangers, and I have discovered some things since this morning that you both might find interesting," She said. "Come in, come in. We can talk in the kitchen. America is like Cuba I have found, in that all important business is conducted in the kitchen."

They moved as a group through the foyer hallway. "Does your police officer understand what we are here to discuss?" she asked over her shoulder.

"He knows everything, at least everything that I know," Juliet answered as they entered a large eating area, possibly the largest kitchen she had ever seen.

Marietta seated them at an equally large table and allowed her focus to stabilize for an instant on Nick. "I believe a uniform makes a handsome man more attractive, and by the same measure takes away from one who is not so...beautiful. May I use that word?"

Nick laughed. "I have never been called beautiful before."

"No? It is a word that must mean the same in Spanish as English."

"Not the same, but close," Juliet answered for him. "He's handsome and also beautiful, in my opinion. But I'd never say that to him." She laughed and observed a slight, almost undetectable blush creep onto the face of her strong protector.

Forty-five minutes later Juliet sipped the remaining milk and sugared residue from her strong cup of Cuban coffee. She stacked the unbound pages from the second trust document back into the correct order and exchanged a glance with Nick that acknowledged and confirmed all of their suspicions.

"As you can see," Marietta remarked. "The lawyer made a very sly and ingenious change to the latter document. I was a legal aide to my father back in Cuba. This was obvious to me."

"It makes clear what you were explaining earlier," Nick said to Juliet. "The part about Rhinehart inheriting everything if you and Lenny don't survive to age thirty."

"And he's got Doris thinking she'll inherit," Juliet pointed out. "Rhinehart gets her to try and murder us, yet he keeps his hands clean and ends up with...who knows how much money?"

"That is something else that I have to tell you," Marietta put in. "I have found more of Clifford's records. As the guardian and trustee of the estate, he was responsible for managing the assets from the sale of the mining company. His records indicate accounts at three institutions. "This would be your money, of course, Juliet. Yours and your brother's."

The sugar seemed to catch in her throat. She coughed lightly. "And what did you discover?"

Marietta smiled. "Perhaps I offer you both a large glass of wine first. I have some chilled white wine from the Albariño area of Spain. It is—" She turned and glimpsed the wall clock— "almost six o'clock in any case, and I feel you might need something to accompany my answer."

The wine produced a frost of condensation on the glass, and Juliet took a sip as her hostess dropped three black leather folios heavily on the table. "Everything here comes from Clifford's accountants. He was much too sloppy to keep records as organized as these," Marietta said. She took a seat and gave Juliet and Nick an expression of satisfaction.

Nick touched the spine on one of the leather binders. "These represent the assets from the sale of the Wolverine Mining Company?"

The woman nodded. "Checkbooks are in each holder. Clifford made huge withdrawals over the years."

"So what remains?" Juliet asked. "If anything."

Marietta helped herself to a long sip of wine. "From what I could determine today, twenty remains in one account, thirteen in another, and only four in the Wells Fargo account. Clifford used that one for most of his withdrawals."

"Thirty-seven thousand." Juliet summed the numbers and made a small grin. "Maybe I can take some college courses in residence now."

Marietta cocked her head, a light in her eyes. "Oh, I don't believe your college will be a problem, my dear Juliet. The correct dollar amount is thirty-seven million."

26

Donald Rhinehart rolled back his sleeves and made an attempt to stop grinding his teeth. Another massive headache would steamroll him later in the night if he couldn't dissipate the building tension. The pain was so everlasting that he often staggered around until mid-morning of the following day before he felt like a normal human being again.

He needed to…what? What did hippies do? Some type of Zen meditation accompanied by a marijuana joint and the open legs of a Berkeley coed? Well, hell. Good luck finding a willing coed in Bismarck, North Dakota. As for the marijuana joint, he had something better. He angled a look at his Rolex. Six-thirty in the evening and Billie had disappeared. Schwartzel was nowhere to be seen, probably at Webster's trying to nail the hostess one last time before he was arraigned on charges. Tough shit for the fat lawyer; he made a bet and lost, that is unless the deputy could somehow return with those documents.

Rhinehart splashed three fingers of J&B over cracked ice and returned to his office recliner. He levered the backrest into a recumbent position and gazed at the ceiling. Thinking back, both of them should have seen something like this coming. The Driscoll girl was eighteen the day she marched into the assistant state's attorney's office. That took a lot of balls. And she was smart, obviously, since she had outwitted a deputy who thought he was God's gift to the legal profession. Could the pieces of his plan still fit together? He craned his neck forward and sucked in a full swallow of scotch accompanied by small bits of ice.

A blinking light on the phone bank caught his eye. He craned his neck further and read Doris Blackwell's name on the incoming line. What the hell was she calling about? Guarding his drink, he inclined forward and grabbed the receiver.

"Donald Rhinehart here."

"Mr. Rhinehart?"

"Call me Donald, Mrs. Blackwell. I was just thinking about you."

"Well, Mr. Rhinehart—Donald. After your call this morning, I maybe have some news you might appreciate."

Her voice held excitement, electricity virtually humming over the wires. His pulse ticked upward in response. It was about fucking time for some good news. "I'm listening, Mrs. Blackwell."

"Doris, I guess would be fine," she said with a chuckle. "You can call me Doris."

"Doris," he said, and helped himself to another swallow.

"Well…Donald. I think that Lenny is probably unavailable now. Like we, uh, talked about. And that's official. One down and one to go." Another small laugh spilled out.

He could do the math, the silly twit, but he did feel a stirring. "Maybe you'd better let me know how exactly he became unavailable. There may be some legal angles we need to cover." He crunched on a piece of ice and listened carefully as she explained her trickery at the well.

"So what do you think?" she inquired after the interchange.

"I think you're well on your way to becoming a wealthy client of mine. And remember," he added with motivational bullshit, "I'll be the one managing your funds. That kind of goes without saying."

"Of course," she said in a voice that inched upward a full octave.

"However—and let me be very clear about this, Doris—there are some steps you need to take right now. It sounds like you haven't exactly thought this through."

"Well, I'm not a lawyer, for Christ's sake."

"Yeah. Okay." He rubbed a hand over his mostly bald scalp. "First, you need to reinforce the fact that this was an accident. That means you need to call 911 as soon as you hang up the phone. It's what a normal person would do if something like this *accidently* occurred."

"Hold on," she interrupted. He picked up the flinty scratch of a cigarette lighter in the background, followed by the labored pull of overworked lungs. A *whuff* of air blasted past the receiver as she exhaled. "Okay." She coughed. "Now why should I do that? I mean, no one is ever going to find him."

"I thought you said guys were digging a new well." He had the sense she was transfixed by the glowing end of her cigarette.

"Shit. You're right."

"Then they'll find him, or maybe his sister will come looking for him. And look, Doris, there's a chance he could still be alive. But even if he is, it'll be your word against his. There's no way they can touch you *as long as you call in the authorities.* Got it?"

"Got it, Donald. And the girl comes next. I'm really on top of this thing now."

"Right. Well, that's where you need to be, but you've got to be smart about it."

"I've been thinking about my portfolio, maybe putting some of my fortune in gold coins. The kind you can stack on a table. You know, stuff you can actually look at."

He pitched irritation into his rising voice. "We can talk about that later. Just make the damn call, Doris. And don't call me until *after* everything is settled with the remaining Driscoll kid."

Nick Olsen's cell phone burped at the same moment his radio issued a loud squeal that meant either a be-on-the-lookout—BOLO—alert, or something equally serious. He came to his feet and stepped back into the foyer.

Radio first: He toggled the transmit button and connected with the dispatcher. "Jenny?"

"Nick, a 911 just came in from the Blackwell place up north."

The conversation went downhill fast. Juliet's brother, Lenny, had apparently fallen into a well, or been pushed. The EMTs were already on the way.

"Get a hook and ladder unit up there," Nick ordered. "I've seen that well, and we'll need some cranes and support units. Call the State. See if the troopers can get a chopper on the property." Then, "Larry, George, you guys on the dispatcher frequency?"

A pop of metallic static came from a keyed transmitter. Larry's voice came over. "I'm on, Nick, and I'm already close. Be there in ten, but roads are not actually clear yet. You'd better ditch the cruiser and pick up George's Durango if you want to be sure and make it."

"Got it Larry. Make it a Code 3. George, you on?"

"Yeah, I'm back at base. Want me to follow?"

"I want you to stay there. I'm on my way back and I need your 4-wheel. Give me thirty minutes." He pulled out his cell and scanned the backup text from the dispatcher.

"Nick?" Juliet stepped into the foyer, a cloud of concern on her face. "Nick, what's happened?"

"Grab the documents, Juliet. They belong to you in any case. We've got to go now."

"But, at least—"

"It's Lenny! I'll explain in the car."

Nick used the sequenced flashers northbound on Route 83 in order to clear the occasional vehicle that poked along through the flurries. Juliet sat stone-faced beside him as he explained what he knew.

"Why can't we go directly to Doris'?" she said.

He shook his head. "Not sure the roads are completely cleared. We're going to swap this vehicle out with Murphy's Durango. It's got four-wheel drive." He looked over. "It'll be a good time for you to pick up the Toyota anyway."

"I'm not riding up there with you?"

"You need your own car. You can follow me. And Juliet, we don't know what exactly has occurred up there, except that Lenny's in the well."

"What are you saying?"

"I'm saying our primary goal is to get your brother out of the well. You've got to let the law take care of Doris. It *could* be an accident. We don't know yet, and the last thing I want to see is you taken into custody on assault charges. Understand what I'm saying?"

"I understand the law is good at picking up pieces. Not so good at preventing anything," she said in a biting tone.

"Let's focus on one thing at a time, is all I'm saying, and right now Lenny is the priority."

Forty minutes later Nick crunched against the snow bank covering the concrete stop bar outside the Public Safety Office. His Toyota 4-Runner was ten steps away. "Take the Toyota," he said to Juliet. "I've got to get the keys to the Durango."

She opened the passenger door. "Murphy's in there, right?"

He nodded. "I might have a word or two with the deputy."

Juliet trudged a few steps toward her car. Just as quickly she turned and fell in step behind him. "I'm coming in with you."

"That's really not a good idea," he said. "Go on up to Doris'."

"First I want to say something to this slimeball."

He came to a halt. "You're staying right here."

"What?"

"I said you're staying right here. Now stay."

She firmed her lips into a line. Strands of black hair fell over her forehead. "I'm not your pet poodle, Nick. You can't give me orders."

"Take it any way you want. I'm the sheriff here." He swung open the door to the building and pulled it closed behind him. He was well along the corridor when the scuff of the weather seal opening at the entrance reached him. "Shit." He didn't have to glance behind.

Nick threw open the door to his office. Murphy had his butt planted in a government-issued, high back executive chair, feet on the desk. He appeared comfortable.

"You're fired, Murphy. I'll take your badge and the Glock 40."

"What?" He brought his feet to the floor.

"Funny how people keep saying that to me. I said you're fired. You get two weeks' severance starting today, Monday."

"You can't do that."

Nick laughed. Murphy had carried a sense of entitlement from his years under the previous administration. He had expected, in the natural order of things, to follow on as the next sheriff. Only thing was, he lost the election to Nick, and by a margin that wasn't even close. "I can and will," Nick said. "You removed a legal deposition and criminal complaint from my car early this morning. That's called stealing, a basic convention we try to avoid as officers of the law." The door opened behind him and Murphy's eyes shifted.

"A couple of pieces of paper? They didn't even belong to you, Nick. You could say they were part of a public record."

Behind him Juliet blurted, "You lying asshole! You stole the documents when you were helping me out of the ditch this morning."

Murphy came to his feet. "Why you little—"

"Creep, slime ball, jerk!" Juliet shot back. "How'd your friends like all the blank pages?"

Nick angled his head. "Stay out of this, Juliet."

Murphy put his hands in his belt, cleared the corner of the desk, and leaned slightly forward in his stance. He had an average build, but Murphy had never been toughened by the military. He buckled his belt over a pudgy-looking middle that had gone soft from the lack of physical training. The deputy might have been handsome in his youth, but these days his face was cut by a slack, bitter-looking mouth.

"So this is the little piece of fluff you've been keeping out at the place?" he said in a sour voice. "I've heard about her. Maybe we all have."

A wire snapped somewhere inside Nick. He closed the two steps and drove his fist hard into the man's solar plexus, an in-and-out before the deputy could wheeze a reaction. He swung around the desk, planted a leg in back of Murphy's heels, and threw his forearm around his throat.

"I...who the fuck you think you are, Olsen?" he gagged. "You..." He sputtered saliva on Nick's forearm. "I'm going to sue the fucking shit outta you! I'll—"

"I'll keep the arm bar loose," Nick said. "Just so you won't choke to death. Now I need your shield, the Glock and the C-2. Got that Murph?" He unholstered the firearm from behind, tossed it on the table, and pulled the Taser from the man's equipment belt. "I'll have Patricia cut you a severance check," he said as he released him.

Murphy straightened and took a deep breath. "You're in more trouble than you know, Olsen."

"Bullshit. Nothing happened here. Now give me the keys to the Durango and your badge." He waited as the deputy slowly fished the keys from his pocket, tossed them on the desk. He flipped the shield in the trash.

"Dig it out yourself," he said. "And you'll be hearing from me."

The frosted glass set into the office door shivered hard against the frame with the force of Murphy's departure. Nick shrugged without concern. A shattered pane would simply have been deducted from Murphy's severance check.

The office became quiet. He took a couple of restorative breaths and regarded Juliet positioned behind and to the right. Her hands were balled into fists. She obviously did not follow orders very well. "I thought I told you to stay outside," he said.

"I was going to help if you needed me." Her cheeks were flushed.

He noted her fists again. "And what exactly would you have done?"

"Kick him in the balls, then poke him in the eyes. That's how women fight, Nick."

"Jeez. Maybe it's better I don't know these things." He picked the keys off the desktop. Something hung in the air. She had more to say. "What?" he asked. "Juliet, we need to go."

"Nick, I probably won't be thinking straight when we get up to the well, so I want to say this now. If Lenny is…gone, and I…and I'm not myself for a while, I just want you to know that I meant what I said and what I felt earlier…you know, when you held me here in the office."

"We're going to think positive, Juliet. And I'm not sure I remember much about that moment, except I couldn't think of anything but you. I still can't."

"Exactly." Her eyes were wide and open. "That's what I meant."

"You've got your mother's look again. You know that?"

She blinked. "Maybe it's because I know what she felt for the first time in my life. That's all I really wanted to say."

27

The flurries were dissipating in the gathering twilight when Nick arrived at the Blackwell property. The bright, intense white of Klieg lights already in position around the well had the effect of creating darkness outside the circle of their coronas, and he looked out onto a gloom of cranes and activity.

Nick parked beside the EMT van and stepped onto a layer of slick ice packed and rutted by dozens of vehicles. The medical technicians were comfortably hunched in the warm cab with the diesel engine clacking a tail of black exhaust from the rear. Before he interfered with the team around the well he needed a briefing. He approached the left side of the van and recognized the driver. Emma ran the window to the bottom and an upwelling of heat surged from the interior of the cab. Nick peered in. "Emma, glad you're on duty. What do we have so far?"

"Nick! You're not going to believe this, but he's alive. He's evidently got a phone and they've been getting some type of weak cellular reception after the crew up there pulled the roof off of that stupid pile of bricks."

"Has anyone given you a time frame?"

"For what?"

"For getting him out."

"Yeah. That's why we're still here in the cab. A commercial outfit has already got some equipment in place. They were going to drill a deeper well, according to the Blackwell woman. The guys from the fire department have got the crew coming on out ASAP. They're the ones that have all the know-how to get the rigging in place."

"Any details on his condition?"

"He's got a broken leg, he thinks. Maybe some other injuries, hypothermia for sure, but he's talking. That's something."

Nick looked toward the site of the rescue attempt and glimpsed Juliet running to the scene. He said to Emma, "Why don't you and Jimmy back on up while you've got a clear space. You'll never get the van up there once these other vehicles arrive."

"Got it, Nick."

He pushed away from the van and walked quickly up the slight incline toward the well. Juliet was hanging over the rim shouting into the narrow vertical tube with two guys holding her arms. The rotors of a helicopter created a *whump-whump* somewhere above. He looked upward into a blanket of opaque gray. They'd never land the thing in this overcast.

A squawk on his radio at that moment confirmed the bad news from the state troopers. According to the dispatcher, the pilots could make out a diffused glow at the GPS coordinates of the Blackwell property, but could not make visual contact. The powers that be were cancelling the chopper. Nick took the sign-off as Larry waved him forward through a small crowd of responders and observers, several of whom he suspected had no official function.

"Skipper, it looks like he's alive," Larry yelled over the racket of a massive generator thumping power to the Kliegs.

"Thank God, Nick," Juliet unbent from her position as he ducked over the rim. She held a mobile phone to her ear. "He says he can't move his arms much, legs hurt…"

"Could be broken ribs," he said. Reflected light way down in the shaft glimmered against a circular tube of damp, algae-covered bricks. He couldn't make out anything further.

The fire chief edged in and Nick straightened from the rim. Troy had graduated from the local high school some time before Nick, had been away for a good number of years, and returned to take administrative command of the emergency unit in Sherwood. "I just heard about the chopper," he said to Nick. "Damn shame."

"Maybe we won't need it after all. Your guys drop a rope yet?"

The older man nodded. "We've lowered a light and a rope. Nothing much down there except pipes and mud. Maybe just enough water to break his fall. The bottom is seventy-five feet down, but the kid says he can't hold on to the loop."

"You guys can't get a ladder down there?"

"Yeah, but he couldn't climb it. And there's not enough room for another man to carry him to the top. The construction foreman's bringing up a bosun's chair to the site. Says they use it for getting down and working in wells and shafts. Lenny can just sit on the canvas strap and ride it up."

"Oughta work, even if some ribs are crushed."

"We just gotta wait. Probably be another fifteen, maybe twenty minutes till they get here."

Nick peered into the crowd. "Where's the Blackwell woman? She supposedly witnessed the whole thing, called 911 right off."

"She's got to be up at the house," Juliet said, close against his shoulder. "Probably hiding out. She's a bitch, a mean, evil bitch."

"Juliet, we don't know—"

"We know goddamn well, Nick!" she yelled.

He made his voice heavy with emphasis. "Listen to me. Legally we don't know exactly what took place here, unless Lenny has already said something. Has he?"

She shook her head. "He says he can't remember what happened. I'm sure he's not...you know, altogether now anyway."

"Maybe it'll come. Troy, you guys squared away for now?"

The fire chief nodded. "For now."

"I'm going up to the house to ask a few questions. I'm taking Larry to corroborate any statements. We'll keep a watch out for the drilling crew."

"I'm coming with you," Juliet said.

"No, you're not."

"Yes, I am," she insisted. "I know her. I used to live here, Nick. It would be helpful to have me along."

"You're not coming, Juliet."

"First I've got to stop by the car," she said. "I'll meet you at the front door."

"Ah, shit."

Doris Blackwell sipped Bowman's Vodka through a soda straw striped red and white like a peppermint stick. She watched the curious proceedings through the kitchen window. All the lights and the crowd? Hell, that boy was done. What were they making such a big fuss about? Her cheeks went concave with suction as she drew a blast of Bowman's into her gullet. The slushy ice in the glass added just the right amount of water to the beverage, although by now she should have been way beyond drinking this cheap vodka. Here she was driving a Beemer and buying Bowman's by the case. It didn't make sense. At least the cops couldn't tell she'd been drinking, not that it mattered, but they were sure to come around, by and by.

Thank God she had called Rhinehart in time. Now the authorities couldn't touch her. She chuckled and reached for a cigarette. Hell, accidents happen, and what she needed was just one more. She toasted herself with another pull of Bowman's and felt the alcoholic buzz percolating. The ship was plowing through the waves now, sails set, forward ho. Maybe the vodka wasn't all that bad.

Seriously though, she would have to think about using the car on Juliet. Mash her underneath real good. What with the brake pedal so close to the accelerator, and with the different new-car feel and everything. Why, she was just an older woman who thought she was hitting the brake. What could be easier?

The rap at the front door sounded like bare knuckles on wood. That meant a man and probably a cop. Couldn't they leave her alone for a while, let her celebrate with a drink or two in private?

"Doris Blackwell," the tall official stated as she swung open the door. "We'd like to come in and talk to you for a few minutes."

"Nicholas Olsen." Doris projected her voice out into the cold. "Why you being so formal? I knew your mom years ago and I remember you coming around."

The three individuals standing under the weak porch light regarded her with determined expressions, and her eyes flicked to Juliet. The inclusion of that troublemaker in the group shouldn't have taken her by surprise—her brother was in the well, after all—but somehow the girl's presence knocked her off center. Maybe it was a delayed reaction to the fight the previous night. Was it only the previous night? "And why'd you have to bring *her* along, Nicholas?"

Juliet butted front and center, a sheaf of papers under her arm. "I thought maybe you'd like to try using the knife on me again, let the cops witness the attempted murder this time."

"What are you talking about, child?"

"Juliet," Nick cautioned.

"You know damn well what I'm talking about. The same thing you tried to do to Lenny out in the well."

"Now I had nothing to do with his death, the poor boy, but accidents do happen." Her tongue seemed a tad thick. Was she slurring words?

Larry chimed in, "Mrs. Blackwell, I'm Deputy Hudson. You'll be delighted to learn that Lenny is alive, and actually in pretty good shape, considering."

She watched in stunned amazement as he mouthed the words. Did she hear that correctly?

"Thanks to your quick call we got here in time," he said.

Her stomach twisted. A garbled acknowledgement came from her lips as she cracked her facial lines into an upward, pleased expression.

Juliet snorted loudly. "I know that development makes you *sooo* happy, Doris. I've got some better news, if we might come in for a moment."

"We'll need a formal statement from you regarding the accident," Nick said.

She turned on her heels, mainly to get control of herself. They followed. What was she to do? Five steps inside, she remembered her manners. "Now I know the place isn't exactly clean and tidy like I usually keep it. 'Course, I wasn't expecting company."

"Larry, have you got a flashlight?" Juliet asked.

"Yeah. Why?"

"Because this witch doesn't have a single table with enough light to read by, and she's gotta see something I've got."

Doris staggered a half turn. "You watch your tongue, young lady. I'll be treated with respect in my house."

Nick groaned. "I'll give you ten minutes, Juliet, then out. I know where you're going with this."

Doris rounded the kitchen doorway and glimpsed the straw poking out of her glass. Damned if she was going to offer a round to the cops. They seemed more inclined to gather around the corner table anyway. She cupped a hand around the tumbler and leaned toward the group. Juliet was placing documents into piles. "I think I know what this is," she mumbled over her glass.

Juliet glanced upward. Larry's flashlight beam skimmed her face before settling on the documents. "There are two trust agreements here, Doris. They're dated. See?" The light illuminated the sequential months and years. "As you probably know, only the most recently dated trust agreement counts in a court of law. Do you know that?"

She jiggled her ice. "Of course I know that, girl." What in the hell was she getting at?

Juliet paged over as Larry panned the light. "On the *older* agreement—the one that doesn't count—your brother, Clifford, was named as the *contingent beneficiary*."

"Yeah, I know. That's the way the thing was set up, I heard." Nicholas was breathing over her right shoulder. Damn if he hadn't grown into a big, solid cop.

"That meant that if Clifford had passed away during the life of this document, and Lenny and I had also died—or been murdered, which is probably closer to your heart—"

"Juliet, watch it now," Nick warned.

"Then you, as the surviving blood relation would have inherited the entire worth of the trust my parents set aside for Lenny and me. Got that?"

Doris cleared her throat. "Well, a course I never paid all *that* much attention to the legal ins and outs of the arrangement. All I wanted to do was raise you kids in a decent and loving environment." She vacuumed up a slug of Bowman's.

"What you don't realize Doris, is that this later document—pushed through by a lawyer named Rhinehart and signed by Clifford—changes all of that. In this most recent agreement, Donald Rhinehart, the lawyer, is the contingent beneficiary. He dropped Clifford from the agreement."

"He…what do you mean?"

"I mean that instead of *you* inheriting all of the estate after Clifford's death, and assuming Lenny and I were to die also, the lawyer Rhinehart gets all the money."

"Okay," she responded slowly. "But Clifford is dead, God rest his soul, so you and Lenny will get all of his trust. Isn't that the same as before?"

"Aside from the fact that the trust never belonged to your brother in the first place—our parents, my mother and father, set that aside for Lenny and me—you are correct. But let's say we had been murdered yesterday. Clifford's already dead, so the way it currently stands, you don't get a penny. Rhinehart gets it all."

Something slowly fused in her mind, a thickening in the maze of capillaries that nourished whatever brain cells were currently alive. A dawning that came up red with heat flushed her face. *Rhinehart.* That slime of a lying, asshole lawyer. The slick brochures he put in the mail, the fact that he sat back and let her do the dirty work, all the while, *all the while*…she couldn't even bear the thought, and she realized they were watching her. She shrugged and said tight-mouthed, "So?"

Juliet smiled up at her sweetly. "Just thought you'd like to know. Maybe it'd be something you'd like to discuss with your lawyer."

"Come on, you've got to wrap it up, Juliet," Nick said.

She rolled the papers together. "Just wanted her to see this. Thanks for the light, Larry." She stood and kissed Nick on the mouth. "And thank *you*, Sheriff Olsen. I'm outta here."

28

Yellow morning light exploded through the windows in a cascade of brilliance, a counteroffensive of the sun after so many days of snow and overcast skies. Doris recoiled with shock and gradually became aware of the pool of saliva on her pillowcase.

Not a big deal, considering what she had lain in before, and after a few minutes she sat upright and allowed the systems in her body to slowly stabilize for another day. What time was it, and what the hell was all that commotion about last night?

They pulled Lenny from the well at about one o'clock a.m., and the boy was alive and kicking. She remembered that much. Channel 12 News out of Bismarck was on the scene, a real fucking celebration. Meanwhile, Rhinehart had tried to pull such an evil, despicable double-cross that she was going to make sure it was his last. Her pulse rate burned higher with just the thought. If it took her final breath he was going to pay. Now that the dream of a mega-fortune was over, she was going to crush the lawyer under the wheels of the BMW instead of Juliet. It was all about tidying up loose ends at this point in her life, achieving a healthy emotional closure. Hell, according to what she'd learned on *Oprah*, it was almost required.

Donald Rhinehart pulled the draperies together in his office. There was too much morning light and his head was still blocked with pain from the preceding evening. He poured a glass of water from the carafe on the sideboard. Two more Tylenols would help, and to hell with the cumulative effects of the dosage.

He donned his Bvlgari sunglasses and tried to relax in his lambskin recliner. The telephone rang in the outer office. Billie picked it up and a second later buzzed his desk.

"A call from Mrs. Blackwell. Do you want to take it, sir?"

"Tell her I'm…oh hell, just put her through." He heeled a palm against his throbbing forehead and closed his eyes for an instant before he picked up the receiver. "Donald Rhinehart speaking."

"Donald Rhinehart. And how are you this morning?" The voice was as hard and flat as the woman's face. Occasionally, God gave the sultriest telephone voices to the homeliest of women, voices that had the power to produce an almost instant erection. Not the case here.

"Got a migraine that won't let up. What can I do for you this morning, Doris?"

"Been watching the news?"

"Haven't had the set on. What happened?"

"They got Lenny out of the well last night. He is alive. Channel 12 even covered it."

"Shit." He massaged his forehead. "Well, you're in the clear, Doris. We talked about that. You called 911 so there is not a damn thing they can do. It's just a temporary setback, is all."

"I thought, considering everything, that we might actually meet somewhere and talk. We've only got a couple months left to complete the items on the agenda, if you know what I mean. Also, I'd kind of like to discuss your commission rate. We're dealing with a lot of money here."

"We could do that, I guess."

"How about you take me to lunch around noon? It'll give you time to get over that headache."

Was she nuts? He could lose clients just by being seen in public with her. "I…I'm not sure I'll be up to it, Doris."

"Okay, maybe these agenda items are not all that important anyway."

"Hold on a second. I'm not feeling so well. I told you that already, but maybe I can swing a light lunch somewhere close by. There is a diner around the corner."

"I was thinking of that place across the street, the restaurant called Webster's. I've driven past it, but never been in there."

Christ on a crutch. What was this about? "Doris, like I said. I'm just not—"

"*Fine*. I've been thinking about reviewing all these legal documents by myself anyway. With everything happening now I realize I'm not in the loop like I should be."

He closed his eyes and rubbed a hand over his face. "You'd...maybe you could put on a little makeup, you know. And you can't smoke in the restaurant portion of the establishment."

"Don't try and tell me how to fix myself up, Donald. Even though I'm a senior I can look pretty damn good when I want to."

A wave of nausea hit him. He really needed that to go with this migraine.

"Can I meet you there at, say 12:30 sharp?" she asked.

"That would be fine, Doris, I guess."

"You sound a little tentative. I'm not sure I want that in my financial advisor."

"No, no. I'll definitely be there. 12:30 sharp, like you said."

Doris sat in the comfort of soft, heated leather and blew smoke inside the ventilation loop of the BMW. She shook her head, as if the motion could tamp back the fury bottled up inside her. The pressure was explosive, even more so as she allowed little bits and pieces of Rhinehart's scheme to bubble to the surface. Unlike her deviant brother, this guy was totally vile, and if she went on about every little thing she was going to boil over before reaching the city.

An ash broke away from her Marlboro 100 and disintegrated. She brushed the residue into her butternut paisley blouse. She wore a shirttail hem over a pair of black designer jeans that had seen better days. Black pumps and makeup completed her outfit, although she was careful not to overdo the blush and lipstick. Too much rouge and greasepaint had the effect of hardening her looks and blanking out the coy, younger complexion that she wanted. She might, after all, enjoy a nice lunch before she popped the cork on her anger.

The drive to Bismarck was easy. She cruised past the Gateway Mall, shot under I-94, and drifted straight in to Rosser Avenue, which split into east and west avenues. Webster's was on the north side of the street. Rhinehart's office was on the south side. She rounded the block several times to get the feel of the traffic. Timing was the thing here and it had to be exact. She would have two chances: once on his way to the restaurant, and again on the way back to his office. If the first attempt went bad, she could leave the restaurant while he was settling the bill, fire up the Beemer, then POW!

"Are you okay, sir?" Rhinehart's secretary asked him.

"No. I feel like shit, but hopefully this will be a quick lunch." He took the elevator to the first floor and straightaway encountered a torrent of light coursing through the double doors opening to the outside. The sidewalks and streets were overwhelmed with sunlight. The white, reflecting power of melting snow doubled the intensity. He slipped on his Bvlgaris again and squinted into the brightness. Maybe a dark, corner booth in Webster's wouldn't be so bad after all.

Sun glinted from the windshield of a silver, BMW sedan as the vehicle nosed around the corner of 7th Street. The car caught Rhinehart's eyes. The Beemer was obviously brand new, and he likened the vehicle to an expensive silver bullet. He would buy one, maybe two, once this stupid Blackwell woman finally got around to doing a proper job on the twins. God, if she didn't make a case for the natural selection of the species.

He held a visored hand over his eyes to block the glare from the car as he stepped into the crosswalk. An agreeable purr from a powerful engine cut through the fugue of traffic noise that thrummed in his head. A woman screamed somewhere. A yell from a man reminded him of a football game. An instant later the throaty growl of an accelerating engine streaked toward him. Rhinehart glanced toward the racing car and froze with horror for a split second as an impossible nightmare seized him. A shot of adrenaline surged into his muscles. He cried out in terror, then tensed and jumped, a high vault that carried him forward and upward. The driver anticipated the movement, swerved, and took him chest high with a crushing thump into his midsection. Rhinehart lay on the hood for an instant in shock and unbelievable pain. With a slow dawning he recognized the face at the wheel. But nothing made sense. There was some mistake. Weren't they having lunch together? His arms were useless, just two nothing appendages that didn't respond to the order to hold on, and in any case, there was nothing to grip on the sleek surface. But maybe she would slow down and stop. He felt himself sliding off the hood. His feet touched the pavement. The friction increased the pull. She was not going to stop, he realized. A flash of the afterlife took him. Was this the final vision he would ever see, the hard, smiling face of Doris Blackwell? He prayed for something else, anything, but as he slid from the hood in the final seconds of his life, he realized his prayers were in vain.

29

The Crossroads Saloon was rocking. A daylong fireball of sunshine had baked a clear blue sky, and the temperature had climbed to sixty degrees. The crowd was thirsty, boisterous, and hungry, and buckets and buckets of beer thumped onto the tables. The aroma of Angus burgers, fries, and onions grilled in beef fat wafted from the kitchen. A whiff of jalapeños and tortilla chips blistered with cheese followed closely behind. The entire smoky mess hit the guys in ball caps like the smell of blood to a pride of starving lions.

Pete had once again pulled Glenn Campbell out of his secret drawer, and Juliet noticed a few sun-scorched guys in T-shirts happily singing along to *Galveston*. At six o'clock in the evening the temperature would be dropping again like a stone, and she expected to see the new arrivals wearing quilted vests.

She was tired but pleased when she considered the past twenty-four hours. Lenny was asleep when she left Trinity Hospital for her evening shift at the saloon. His arms were badly abraded from the bricks on the way down the shaft. He had broken bones aplenty, but not any more than if he had been tackled by, say, a bunch of pro football linebackers. She preferred to think of it that way.

With Nick and Larry's help she had finally gotten to Doris with her explanation of Rhinehart's slimy double-dealing. The expression of frozen disbelief on the woman's face was something Juliet would never forget, even though she wanted to. God, if she could just bury that projection of hate and never bring it to mind again.

Nick was asleep at home. He had been up for nearly forty-eight hours and had left the scene soon after Lenny had been taken to the hospital. If she didn't see him again until Wednesday or Thursday she could wait, though barely.

And what about all this money supposedly left in a trust fund for her and Lenny? Was that for real? Somehow it didn't seem so as she dodged the hands reaching for her butt. She had topped her dark jeans with a white, peasant blouse scooped at the top, and the combination seemed to drive the men crazy.

"Juliet, got something for you," Darlene yelled from the bar.

She plopped a second icy bucket of six frosty bottles in front of three guys who had just polished off the first. She spun out of reach with the empties and twisted toward the bar. "What's up," she asked over the end of the counter.

"Doris Blackwell. She's your aunt. Right? I know she's some type of relative."

"I lived with her when I was younger. I thought I took you through all of that."

Darlene nodded toward the kitchen. "Pete just caught a news bulletin. Seems earlier today a woman by that name ran down a man in Bismarck. Killed him. The state police are talking vehicular manslaughter."

"They give a name of the victim?"

Darlene shook her head. "They just mentioned he was a lawyer."

Juliet made a small grin that held a note of sadness. "I'm guessing that would be a guy named Donald Rhinehart, a nasty man exactly like Doris."

The time was seven o'clock in the evening and the word was out. Billie had stayed late to help deal with the press, police, clients, assorted colleagues, and acquaintances. Flower arrangements toting sympathy cards dotted the reception area of the Rhinehart and Schwartzel law firm. One basket oddly contained assorted cheeses, a jar of Major Grey's chutney, and Carr's Table Water Crackers, all neatly packaged in a pyramid of yellow cellophane. Schwartzel carried the offering into his office—he was a mourner, after all—unpacked the contents, and helped himself to port wine cheese with crackers.

On a thought he rose, uncapped a fresh bottle of J&B from his late partner's corner office and settled himself back into the comfort of his somewhat smaller, but now it seemed, temporary working space.

He had been given a reprieve by the fates, or by a benevolent, supreme being. Whatever. But now he intended to use it. Only one thing stood between him and the luxury and affluence that would mark the peak of his career, and that was the pesky criminal complaint. The misdeed was such a small thing, really, but enough to destroy his life. He thumbed through the class roster of his Contracts lecture group and found George Murphy's listing. He punched in the telephone number on his cell.

"Murphy's residence." There were kids in the background.

"George Murphy, please. Harry Schwartzel calling." More kids, more family squabbling. He was glad he had never settled down—bratty ragamuffins pulling on his pant legs, a wife telling him when he could and could not drink, the married sex, or lack of it. Was there decent screwing after a couple of years and two or three kids? Hell, he didn't know and he didn't care.

"George Murphy here. Is that you, Harry?"

"The one and only. I guess you heard the news."

"Just came over Channel 12. I'm sorry, man."

"Nothing to be sorry about, especially since you were present during that last little snafu. You didn't exactly cover yourself with glory, Murphy."

"I agree, sir. I let a skirt pull a fast one on me. Rhinehart was right about that, although he could've been a little more diplomatic about the whole thing."

"Rhinehart was an asshole long before you fucked up."

"I meant what I said. And I swear that's a promise. I'll get the original documents back."

"That's what I'm calling about. I'll obviously be taking over the partnership, and it seems we're a man short." He threw back the shot glass, drained half the contents in a swallow, and coughed as the bite of scotch fumed his palate. "So that means I may have a deal for you."

"I'm listening, sir."

"Stop with the sir. The deal is this. If you place the original criminal complaint and deposition in my hands by the end of the week I'll have a job for you, once you pass the Bar, that is. But if you blow through the Bar exam forget it."

"I'll get 'em, Harry."

"No mess, Murphy. I don't want any mess however you go about it. If you fuck this up we're done. No more second chances."

"I understand, sir."

The cleanup from the packed evening at the Crossroads pushed the hour to almost two o'clock in the morning when Juliet at last stepped outside. The spring thaw was underway and the air had a washed, freshly-scrubbed scent. Shallow ruts of standing water reflected light that could only come from stars because the moon was not visible. Another couple of days would take care of the snow banks if the warm weather continued. The roads were clearing. She could return the 4-Runner and start driving her Brownie.

Lenny was asleep, resting comfortably, according to the phone conversation with the charge nurse. Juliet flipped her recovered cell phone back into her coat pocket and one-handed a turn from the parking lot onto the state highway. Her parka was trashed after the muddy soaking at the bottom of the well, and she had uncovered her blue woolen Navy pea jacket in the back of her closet. She had always liked the anchors embossed in big, blue buttons of thick plastic, and the collar that flipped all the way up to completely cover the back of her head. She couldn't recall why she'd stopped wearing the garment, but she felt nice and warm with the rediscovery. The super-deep pockets were perfect for holding makeup and assorted items she normally carried in a small handbag.

Juliet accelerated the 4-Runner through the draining snow melt. For the first time in weeks, maybe months, she could travel at a normal speed and it felt liberating.

A vehicle or two splashed past going the opposite direction. The night was still cold and the road, but spring was on the way, and it seemed as if the seasons and her life had both changed drastically in just the past couple of days.

Was she going to be rich, wealthy? The concept was so alien that it seemed foolish to consider. Yet Marietta had the evidence, and apart from that she liked the woman. They were about the same age, and Marietta had a past full of difficulty and unpleasantness, much like hers. Juliet looked forward to another get together, and not just for a talk about money.

Then there was Clifford, already dead in the nursing home, and his slimy lawyer, Rhinehart. And now Doris might spend the rest of her life in prison. Did it matter that she might have pushed Lenny into the well? Even if Lenny were eventually able to recall what happened, would it make any difference? No.

The wipers caught a sprinkle of sleet as she approached the outskirts of Minot. She slowed the vehicle as a snow flurry followed, intense and temporary, as if the cold weather was not quite ready to release its stranglehold.

Still unresolved was the business about the criminal complaint. Was it worth dragging the paperwork in front of the current district attorney in order to expose a crooked lawyer? Yes. The process did not require much effort, even though her desire was to move on with her life. Both documents were still in the glove compartment. Since she intended to switch cars, she leaned over, popped the latch, and transferred the papers to her coat pockets.

She parked beneath the orange cast of a sodium-halide streetlight. The snow flurry passed, replaced by the thunder of a bomber roaring unseen in the darkness around the air base. She exited the vehicle, clicked the key fob, and received a return beep locking Nick's 4-Runner. They could swap the cars whenever, but from now on she would use her own vehicle. She slipped the keys into her deep pocket and walked across the lot.

The apartment complex featured a center flight of stairs inset within a foyer-like breezeway. She climbed to the second-story level and turned onto a balcony walkway securely lined with steel handrails. Not a light was on behind the curtained windows of her neighbors. She checked her watch. At two o'clock in the morning she expected nothing else, although she often wished the building had been designed with an interior corridor. Evidently, the original military occupants required no additional protection from the weather or potential intruders late in the night.

A post lamp was out at the far end close by the last apartment which belonged to her. Shadows created black voids in her path, and as she stepped carefully she noticed boot prints in the disappearing film of snow. Hair rose at the nape of her neck. The prints ran the length of the balcony and vanished in the vicinity of her apartment door. She checked closely for indentations coming the other way and found none.

Juliet came to a halt, took a quiet breath and peered twenty feet ahead to her door. Her pulse quickened. Warning bells were definitely ringing. Nick had once remarked on an oddity of the human eyeball, in that one's peripheral vision was much more light- sensitive than a direct focus because of the arrangement of cones and rods in the retina.

Juliet shifted her concentration, allowed her gaze to relax and play around the margins of her apartment entrance. Then she had it. A dark line creased the edge of the doorjamb. The latch had been released, just enough to permit a quarter-inch opening. Someone was inside her apartment.

A jolt of fear tightened her stomach. Her mouth went dry. She took a step backward, then two, and turned softly toward the stairwell.

"Where you going little girl?" The voice was produced in a low register, barely above a whisper, but it reached out to her with the hiss of a coiled snake.

She scrambled toward the stairs at a run, took the treads two by two, and cleared the rail over the final steps with a vault to the grade-level concrete slab. The impact stung her feet, but she raced around the back corner toward the darker, south side of the complex. The stairway vibrated with the weight of the man behind her.

A glance backward outlined a nightmare figure wearing a full-face ski mask and gloves. He banged a heavy pipe against the stair rail and stretched his mouth in a wide, frightening caricature of a clown.

She gulped air. Her heart pounded blood through her system as she ran across the patio onto a grassy area. A whimper of terror escaped. Was that her? A low and menacing laugh sounded somewhere behind her. She cried out again as she fought to control her panic.

A deep hedgerow of natural woodland bordered the rear of the property, and served as a separation from the government fencing around the perimeter of the military base. The woods were twenty yards away, a softball's throw in a woman's league. She rushed toward the deep cover.

The nightmare shuffled after her, but at a slower pace. A glance backward showed him holding a small penlight beam, as if the light could illuminate her at the increasing distance. She reached the forested area and moved into the trees. Her dark jeans and deep-blue Navy coat blended with the night. She flipped up her hood.

The environment changed. A dark, totally different world lay inside the thick band of forest. She could see her hands, but only because she knew they were there. With every footfall a fallen branch or a root hindered her progress. If her movements were marked by the occasional crack of a twig, they paled in comparison to the clumsy, thrashing footsteps coming at her from behind. Cold drizzle from bare saplings and evergreen fronds splattered her hair and ran in thin rivulets down her forehead. A grunt came from somewhere. Forest sounds were muffled, directions hard to pin down. The man still lagged behind her, but where? Or had he bypassed her and moved out in front? She didn't think so.

What in the hell was he after? She had no money, no jewelry in her apartment. The image of his club flashed in her mind. He wielded a two-foot long lead pipe, and there could be only one reason for that. She was not supposed to survive the night. Goosebumps pricked her arms. An acid coil of bile rose up. She imagined several knockout blows to her head followed by whatever he had in mind, and there were obvious assumptions on that score. After which, he'd place a hand over her mouth and suffocate her. The authorities wouldn't find her body for months.

But why was someone after her? She still didn't get it.

As quietly as possible she slipped deeper into the woods and began to control her quivery breathing. Nick's tip about the human eyeball once again came to mind, and she avoided a center focus and allowed her vision to pan side to side. A huge, fallen tree was barely visible silhouetted against the lighter shade of the night. The horizontal trunk provided a natural place of concealment, a shelter inside the lacework of branches and accumulated forest debris. Perfect. She could get in there and take cover. But as she maneuvered toward the hideout a premonition welled up. If the shelter appealed to her, whoever trailed behind would be drawn to examine it for exactly the same reasons.

Maybe she could make good use of that assumption, if only she could calm down and think rationally. Like her father she had the mind of an engineer. A problem existed. Therefore, a solution could be found, except this was not a classroom exercise. Her life was at stake.

She made herself completely still and inhaled quietly through her mouth. The man after her had evidently figured a few things out concerning the racket he was making. She could not detect his noise or movement.

A plan of action came to her. But was this a silly trick or a real solution?

Juliet reached into her left-side coat pocket and found her miniscule, glass teardrop of Yves Saint Laurent's Opium perfume, a twenty-ninth birthday present from Pete and Darlene. She could not afford to purchase another, but given the circumstances, she could not afford to keep the present one.

The man had gone quiet. If he thought he was being sneaky, she was prepared to teach him a few things. She withdrew the vial and unscrewed the cap partway. Hopefully the perfume would leak away once the small container was tossed into the brush. One more quick check behind her, and Juliet flipped her birthday present toward the fallen tree. A barely audible *snick* could be heard as the perfume fell into the overspreading branches. One drop, maybe two spattered against almost anything would create an overpowering evidence of a woman's presence. She backed against a thick, standing trunk, willed herself to become small and invisible, and waited.

The sound initially came from the fence. A run of steel mesh topped by barbed wire served as a natural guide in the dark. He was flat-footed and breathing heavily. Unfortunately, she was on the wrong side of the tree, and he could probably pick her out if he used his penlight.

She edged around the trunk, a hide-and-seek move that she performed carefully, molding herself to the bark and keeping her lighter face from his line of sight. A branch, a dead leaf, something directly above funneled a steady drip of icy water onto her hair and down her neck. She tried not to shiver, tried not to move.

The shadowy figure stepped closer and took a motionless stance seven feet away. The muted roar from a jet engine far out in the night rolled over her. A beating wing from a night bird fluttered the air. Juliet imagined herself a rock, an immobile hunk of inorganic granite that gave off nothing, was nothing.

A garbled sound, a low grunt that seemed to carry surprise and satisfaction came from the man, as if he had fastened on to the location of his prey. He switched on the light and moved in the direction of the fallen tree.

The scent hit her at the same time, a heavy, feminine fragrance of exotic oriental spices, peach blossoms, and mandarin oranges. Juliet cast a wary eye around her protective cover and followed his movements. He was concentrating on the fallen tree, swinging his light in one hand, the pipe in the other.

A stark thought abruptly crystalized: her cell phone was still on. A ringtone now would be the end. She stilled herself against the new fear and waited a final few seconds. The figure jumped over the fallen timber and down into the sheltered underbelly of the tree fall with a triumphant yell. She reached into her pocket, depressed the power-off button on her cell phone, and began quickly and quietly backtracking toward the parking area.

A sapling lashed her face slicing her with pain. Juliet bit her tongue and held back a cry as tears watered her eyes. A curse cut the still air behind her, and she heard the thrashing sounds of a man's rapid movement.

Thirty seconds more and her advance became faster. Unexpectedly she sensed her mother's presence. The feeling was strong and close and comforting, and she wondered why, in all the previous years she had never experienced the awareness. The pattern of her movements changed. She began to slip through the tangle of brush as freely as a wraith, with a warp and weave that hardly made a sound.

She glanced behind one last time before reaching the corner of the apartment complex. The man was clearing the line of trees and running toward her. Juliet inhaled a deep breath of cold, night air and felt a renewed burst of adrenaline kick into her bloodstream. She had another thought, a crystal-clear plan of perfect deception.

Her newly acquired Brownie car from Nick's aunt was going to save her life. Without breaking stride Juliet raced toward her second-hand vehicle, a forlorn hunk of metal that appeared all but invisible as it squatted on the far side of the lot. The trick would be reaching the car before her pursuer rounded the corner.

The keys to both the Brownie and Nick's 4-Runner were in her pockets. She withdrew the square key fob at a run and unlatched the Mercury's door with a beep. Forty feet remained, almost there. She grabbed a last deep breath, reached the door handle, and pulled. Nothing gave. She hit the latch with her fist. Still nothing released. Once more she punched at the cold metal and worked the latch. This time the door opened and she slid inside and flipped the manual lock.

Her hands were shaking as she inserted the key into the car's ignition. She turned the key to the 'on' position and ran the window two inches from the top. A quick glimpse through the crack revealed the man sprinting around the far end of the complex. He slowed and seemed to take stock of the situation. That meant he hadn't seen her. Now was the perfect time to unlock the 4-Runner's door and screw with the asshole's mind.

Did he know about the 4-Runner? Yeah. He probably watched her drive in and park. But she was certain he had no idea she was hidden in a second vehicle with temporary, cardboard plates.

Juliet hit the unlock button on the 4-Runner's key fob. The lights pulsed on the Toyota 4-Runner, and the man approached the driver's side with the club still in his right hand. She held her breath as he stood there.

An instant later he swung the pipe into the car's window. She yelped and put a hand to her mouth. Could he hear her small outcry?

He swung the pipe again and the 4-Runner's driver's-side window caved into a web of shattered particles.

Juliet shuddered. The attacker still thought she was inside, and had she been, he would have finished her in an act of cold-blooded murder. She switched on the Brownie's ignition. The engine caught and clanked for a moment before settling in to a smoother rhythm.

The Toyota's door was open and his head inside when she backed once and wheeled the car through a short radius turn from the lot. She looked left. Route 83 northbound would take her to Nick's or to Pete and Darlene's, both long, lonely drives. He might expect that, in which case he could overtake her before she could make the distance. A right turn put downtown Bismarck and Marietta's house in her sights. She swung right and hit the gas.

Two miles further on a check in the rear-view mirror showed no headlights. She let her breathing catch up and fished the cell phone from her pocket. The first call was a 911 blast to the authorities announcing a break-in at her apartment. In a shaky voice Juliet recounted her escape from an unidentified madman. Currently they were involved in a simulated emergency involving stolen nuclear weapons from the air base, the dispatcher told her, and hadn't she heard all the sirens? Stay calm, the woman said, and just wait for the local police to arrive.

"Bullshit!" she yelled. No, she had not heard the sirens, and thanks, but no thanks, she was not going to stay calm at the apartment and let the man beat her head in with a fucking lead pipe!

Her second call required some searching, but she finally found Marietta's number on an incoming log. The Cuban woman answered on the fourth ring with cotton of sleep in her voice. In less than a minute Juliet knew she had a place to stay.

She hesitated before calling Nick. To wake him at this ungodly time of night after forty-eight hours on duty would not be fair. And did she actually need his help after the fact? Nope. In spite of her rapidly diminishing ability to envision a day without him, she could handle this. And what could he do anyway, except maybe hold her hands, reassure her with his strong grip?

She thought about that, and other things Nick might do to her with his hands as she accelerated toward Marietta's.

30

Nick sipped scalding coffee from an insulated cup bearing the faded, purple logo of Sandford Medical Center as he scanned the text messages from Juliet for a second time. He held the hot liquid away from his face as he took a bump onto the asphalt pavement of Route 5 without slowing. The final paragraph read: *anyway—safe at marietta's—still shaky—up all nite—where r u? lenny's ok & getting better—can't wait to c u— getting to be an old lady at thirty—what wine do u like, i forgot— and omg, i might truly be rich. wdyt my love??? going to bed in a while—xoxoxo—j. ps—u don't kiss real well when ur on duty☺*

The text had come in at 6:30 a.m., but he'd slept late, and the sun had climbed well above the horizon before the smell of dark-roasted coffee on auto perc had rolled him out of bed. He'd reached over and checked his mobile with the lazy muscle energy that came from a good night's rest. Juliet's message lit a fire.

Nick had called the Ward County Sheriff's Department in Minot immediately. Tom Patterson was his opposite number in the neighboring county, and Nick knew the sheriff as a very capable individual. Tom had filled him in. "We got the 911 early in the morning," Patterson explained. "I'm not saying our response was anything to be proud of, but we had this exercise underway. You know how it is—back side of the clock, practicing alerts with the military, all the government rigmarole to deal with." And then he asked, "You know this Driscoll woman?"

"She's a friend. Close, like."

"Yeah? Well, you're welcome to look in on this one, Nick. Screw the jurisdiction thing. We've established the crime scene, but we can't get the dogs and we can't get the on-call detective yet. It'll probably be afternoon before he gets here. I'm standing in the apartment now. It's trashed."

"I'm on my way out the door," Nick said.

"What about the assailant? Any ideas?"

"Some."

"Well don't keep it all to yourself. And a verbal statement from the victim would help."

"Working on it, Tom." And he'd rung off.

The highway was in good shape. The snow had disappeared and he hit seventy. A solitary pickup passing the opposite direction provided a flashing image of firewood stacked way too high in the truck bed. The road ahead was clear.

Nick thought back to the text message and allowed himself a smile at her final sentence. Was she referring to the quick goodbye kiss at Doris'? He was definitely in the 'on duty' mode that night, and she was being a little bit of a pain. But now this?

31

Well into the afternoon Juliet finally padded downstairs. She noted the digital readout on the espresso machine showed two o'clock as Marietta handed her a cup of cappuccino. Juliet sat at the kitchen table and ruffled a thick, cotton towel through her damp hair with her free hand.

Marietta's guest room was stocked with all the amenities of a fine hotel. Was this the hospitality of the Latin culture? Juliet didn't know, but after a long hot shower and shampoo she felt loose and satiny in her borrowed pink flannel nightgown and white cotton robe.

"If you need it, there is a blow dryer in your bathroom, Juliet."

"Thanks. You've done so much already."

Marietta acknowledged the gratitude with a light laugh. "We are princesses, you and I, to sleep so late."

"Considering we stayed up all night, I think we can be forgiven." At three o'clock in the morning Marietta had opened her house with a sleep-scored face and a strained expression of worry for this woman who was not quite a stranger, but not yet a close friend. If the whirl of Juliet's adrenaline-charged nightmare had rocked Marietta's opinion of life in quiet North Dakota, the woman gave no further indication. Instead, she opened a bottle of chilled white wine. The one bottle became part of another as the horrific details of Juliet's escape came to light. Afterwards, the conversation shifted, ebbed and flowed, became part of Marietta's background, then Juliet's again. At some point they revisited the trust agreements, the financial documents, and the accountant's ledgers. One issue had not been dealt with as gray light washed through the windows and became brighter with the sun.

"I need to hide these papers I've got with me," Juliet had said to her.

"You're sure that man didn't follow you?"

She shook her head. They'd been over it five times already. "No, but I know what he's after now, and I'm pretty sure I know who he is."

The Cuban woman nodded. "There is a wall safe in the house."

The onset of fatigue overwhelmed Juliet as suddenly as the assault had hours before, yet she forced herself to pay close attention as Marietta took her through the combination sequence.

"There are many gold coins in here, along with stacks of bills. I will give you an accounting of the valuables when we are rested," Marietta had told her. "They belong to you."

Juliet yawned. "I'm not sure they belong to me."

Marietta explained, "I came to know Clifford Blackwell as one of the most selfish, devious, and abusive men I have ever met. I have examined closely the transactions from the accountant's ledgers going back to the beginning. The truth is this: Clifford built this house with money he withdrew from the trust your parents set aside for you and your brother. Your money, Juliet. Therefore, this is your house, legally as much as ethically I would think. Aside from which, I have no ownership claim here whatsoever."

Juliet shook her head. "I'm the one who owes you, not the other way around. You told me the truth about what my parents left my brother and me. This is your house and will always be your house if I have anything to say about it." The wine was still in her and she said, "You weren't the only one Clifford abused, Marietta."

Nick had never met the detective standing inside Juliet's apartment, a guy named Harold Bransom. "You're going to find my prints in here also," he said to him. The man raised his eyebrows, and Nick added, "Except in the bedroom. There won't be any in there."

Glass littered the floor, lamps and tables were overturned, and the refrigerator door lay open. The apartment had been turned upside down, as if there was a personal score to settle beyond whatever criminal objectives the man had in mind.

Nick retrieved a small item from the linoleum tiles, a refrigerator magnet painted with a chicken's head, a flower pot, and the Greek symbol for *pi:* chicken pot pie. He slipped it into a pocket.

"Careful, Nick. Let's keep everything sterile," Tom Patterson said.

"Yeah. Thanks for coming by." The Ward County sheriff had hung around. Nick owed him one.

Bransom shook his head with a puzzled expression. "What the hell was the guy after?"

"Whatever it was, he didn't find it," Patterson said. "It looks like the perp just went berserk."

"I've told you what I think it *might* be." Nick said. "My opinion. Maybe a stretch."

"Good thing he didn't catch the girl."

"He had a lead pipe, according to my information. He would have killed her. Look what he did to my 4-Runner."

"You need to debrief her, Nick. And if what you say about your deputy Murphy has any truth whatsoever, you need to call in the state DBI guys."

"Ah, that would be my *ex*-deputy we're talking about," Nick replied.

"Whatever. If you try and take this up on your own you'll screw the works. And we can handle things here. I know I asked you to help out, but that was before you told me about this thing with Murphy. This is a Ward County crime scene, and Bransom here is our best detective."

Nick tipped his head in acknowledgement. "I'll try and stay out of the way. Just make sure everything checks out here."

Patterson put a hand on his shoulder. "Okay. We'll do it. You just get the victim's statement."

Bransom broke in, "Actually, I was hoping I could come along, maybe take the statement myself." He looked from one to the other. "A pair of fresh eyes won't hurt."

Patterson looked over. "Nick?"

"Yeah. I've got no gripe with that." And to the detective, "What time is good for you? I'll call ahead, but we're getting kind of a late start."

The man shrugged. "Whatever. I don't want to inconvenience anyone."

Nick checked his watch. "Yeah, all right. Lemme call."

The Dakota sun had begun falling westward as Nick rang the bell at Marietta's front entrance. Shadows were long.

Juliet opened the door wearing a white, crocheted bolero over a red, floral top cut low. She had on a tight, dark skirt. Had he ever seen her in one of those? Had he ever seen her bare legs? He angled a glance at her legs and her cleavage, everywhere at once.

"It's about time you got here," she said. She folded herself into his arms and kissed him as though she had just discovered the pleasure, which she had.

"Juliet," he said with surprise in his voice. "And here in broad daylight?"

"I can do anything I want. It's the new me."

A pan hit the floor deep inside the house. He broke away. "We…" He took a breath and ran a hand through her hair. "Probably not the best place…"

"God, Nick. I want you so. I just can't hold you enough after last night."

"You know what people would say about this?"

"Yeah," she said in a playful voice. "Get a room."

He kissed her again, a light, formal kiss befitting the circumstances. "You know what'll happen to me if we keep going like this."

"Like in your office the other day?"

He nodded. "Like in my office the other day. And this has to be an official visit."

"You just wait, Mr. Sheriff. And how do you like my new Latin ensemble? My clothes from last night are still in the dryer."

"You're...sexy."

"Marietta and I are the same size, except she's a little bigger up here." She placed a hand over her cleavage. "Maybe a lot bigger."

"I like you just the way you are."

"You know just what to say to a girl."

She had that spontaneous, good-to-be-alive exuberance which sometimes lasted days following a near-death experience. He was familiar with the feeling. "The other detective will be here in a few minutes," he said.

"The Bransom guy you mentioned over the phone?"

"Yeah. He'll actually be taking your statement."

She offered her lips once again, another official welcome. "Marietta is in the kitchen. I guess you heard the racket with the pan. She did that on purpose, Latin decorum and all. Follow me. We'll walk slowly...to give you time," she said with a smile and a glance downward. "In case you need it."

Harold Bransom arrived a few minutes later. After introductions he placed a lined composition booklet on the kitchen table, took out a pen, and fiddled with a device that looked like a cell phone. Nick was content with his standard legal pad and number-two yellow pencil.

"Okay if I tape our conversation?" Bransom asked.

The detective was much older than Nick had first supposed. He reminded him of a country preacher, a man weary of his flock, with better things to do, yet not quite ready to make it without the weekly collection plate.

Juliet nodded her assent. Marietta sat somewhat apart but within hearing distance. "I'm afraid the lady must excuse us for now," Bransom said.

"Sorry, Harold, she gets to stay," Nick replied. "She's an excellent observer and a friend." And to Juliet, "This will be a little different from the statement I took when your car was smashed. The detective will cross examine on points where he wants clarification, or sometimes if he feels there is something important you are omitting, either intentionally or not. It's normal procedure."

She bristled. "Should I tell him that two people have tried to murder me in the past ten days? I mean, I wouldn't want to omit anything."

"Now, really," Bransom said.

"Really," she said. "Or that my brother was almost murdered by the same woman who tried to gut me with a kitchen knife?"

The detective removed his glasses and ran a hand over his face. "We're getting a little far afield here."

"Her name is Doris Blackwell. That ring a bell?"

Bransom caught himself in the process of replacing his glasses. He screwed his eyes toward Juliet. "The boy who was in the well? He was your brother?"

"*Is* my brother. He survived, as you probably know. And now the same woman has been arrested for running down and killing a lawyer with her BMW, not that the deed should be considered especially criminal. I assume she's in a jail somewhere around here."

Bransom looked at Nick with an unreadable expression. He turned to Juliet. "You mind if I start the recorder?"

She waved a hand. "Feel free."

Twenty minutes had elapsed when Nick checked his watch. Bransom was wrapping things up. "So you never saw his face, never clearly heard him speak, and can't really identify anything about him. Don't get me wrong, ma'am, I believe your chase through the woods actually happened, and I have no doubt we'll notice the perfume smell and maybe find the bottle around that fallen tree, but what makes you think he wanted to kill you?"

"He was swinging a lead pipe. That's a weapon in my book."

"Which hand did he hold the pipe in?" Nick asked.

She focused on the ceiling for a moment. "The right. He held the pipe in his right hand."

"And Murphy's right-handed."

"That doesn't really mean that much, as you probably know," Bransom said. "But it's interesting. I haven't seen a lead pipe for years. Everything is PVC nowadays."

"Still, we could get a warrant," Nick said. "Shouldn't be that hard to come up with. A right-handed man with a two-foot lead pipe in the garage or closet. Burglary or intent to burglarize is a felony."

Bransom sat back and released a long breath. "A warrant for whose house? You're thinking your ex-deputy Murphy is the culprit, but that's going to seem pretty thin to the DA. We've got no positive ID. Nothing but some circumstantial stuff and very little of that. I mean, plenty of guys might have lead pipes still lying around in their garage. Got to have more than that, Nick. And you know it."

"What about the criminal complaint and the deposition he was after?" Juliet asked.

"That's what I mean. You're telling me he was after a complaint dating back what, ten, twelve years ago referencing a man who has already passed away in a nursing home? What's the point? Nothing is there that would stand up as a motive. Sorry." The detective removed his glasses, clicked the temple ribs closed, and deposited the spectacles into a holder. He collected his items and rose from the table. "I do think…and Ms. Driscoll, this is off the record. However, there was evidence of a good deal of anger in the way he wrecked your apartment, as though he wanted to get at you, or get back at you for something. *If* the man we are talking about is George Murphy, then the way you tricked him while retrieving your documents from his coat pocket could've done it." He glanced at Nick. "Firing him from the force certainly upped the ante. Christ, Nick. Did you have to do that?"

"Not a question about it."

"Well, all that, and the way Ms. Driscoll outfoxed him in the forest last night may have driven him over the edge."

"You think?" Juliet pitched in with a tone.

"And..." Bransom eyed them both, "He evidently took it out on your truck when he finished with her place."

"Nick, your truck?"

He shrugged. "He made a mess of it. It's pretty much totaled, but that's what insurance is for. I'm more concerned about your apartment."

"I'm sorry."

"You weren't hurt. That's the main thing."

She sighed. "So when can I go back, get my things and straighten up the place?"

"It's a crime scene, Juliet," Nick said, and came to his feet. "You can't return there, maybe for a while."

Bransom moved toward the foyer. "I trust you've got renter's insurance, Ms. Driscoll. As I mentioned before, the man did quite a bit of damage."

Marietta followed a few steps behind. "I'll make my own way out," Bransom said. "Thank you." And to Nick, "You know what precautions to take. I would up it a level and make sure she's informed." He opened the door.

"Call me if anything develops, Harold."

"I want the same from you." He waved a backward hand moving away.

"What is 'upping it a level', Nick? Does that mean what I think?" She sat nestled against the opposing armrest of a sofa upholstered in a purple flowered fabric. Her hands wrapped a coffee mug.

"That means Bransom believes your statement. Plus, the evidence of rage is pretty clear regarding your apartment, even if he can't bring charges."

"So?"

Marietta spoke from a wingchair. "He wants us to be extra careful, Juliet. The person has been determined to be a threat."

"What do you mean 'us'?"

The woman placed her cup on a low table between them. "I thought of other things while you and the detective were talking, things that you might not have considered."

"Like what?"

"You must stay here. They say you cannot return to your apartment, and why would you? It is dangerous. Also..." She lowered her eyes and smoothed her skirt, "It is not possible for you and Nick to be together, for him to protect you all day and the night. He has a job. Therefore, you must stay here."

"She makes sense," Nick added. "Murphy knows about us, Juliet. He'll stake out my place looking for you sometime when he knows I'm not there. I don't believe he has any knowledge of this house. I'm thinking back and I don't see it."

"But, I can't just hide out here."

"You have to. He knows exactly where you work and what time you'll be getting off. Remember what those guys did to your car? No one even saw or heard them."

"Maybe we could run the criminal complaint and deposition over to the DA's office right now. Make it known that I don't even have them anymore. Then he wouldn't care about me."

Nick checked his watch but he already knew the answer. "Too late. We couldn't get there before the federal offices close. We're dealing with the government, Juliet, not a Walmart."

"Tomorrow then. First thing."

"First thing. But that leaves tonight and maybe a few extra nights to be on the safe side. I want you both to be prepared just in case."

"So we're talking a day or two?"

"I'm not sure. I'll work with these Ward County guys and maybe we can nail this down. Believe me, Pete will understand at the Crossroads."

"That sounds excessive, especially if I get the paperwork to the DA tomorrow."

"Juliet, two people have tried to murder you in the past ten days. *You* know that. *I* know that. Give us some time to do the job."

"Cops aren't real good at preventing crimes, just at picking up the pieces."

"Thank you for that vote of confidence."

She looked away with eyes that shadowed a deeper emotion. "Sorry. I...this hasn't been easy."

"No, it hasn't," he said. "But you are tough and you are smart, and you haven't let all of the shit life has thrown at you get you down. And those are three of the reasons why I...well, why don't we save the confessions for another time."

A sound like the surprised cooing of a turtledove arose from Marietta's wingchair. "*Dios mio*, such a strong man, Juliet."

Juliet smiled through eyes that glittered. "Nick. Jesus."

Marietta came to her feet. "Perhaps I go and make more coffee at this moment."

"I'd prefer that you stay here," he said in a more business-like tone. "I want to cover some basic self-defense tactics."

"Oh?" She settled back in the chair.

"I assume neither of you has a weapon? Maybe a handgun, a pistol?"

"You know I don't," Juliet said.

"For all these years, I had assumed I was an illegal. I would not get near a weapon like that," Marietta said.

"Unfortunately, it's too late to train either of you in the use of one."

"I carry pepper spray everywhere," Marietta added firmly.

He formed a thin smile. "I've got a better idea."

32

Murphy's wife was crying when the telephone rang on the kitchen wall. He fired a throw pillow against the back cushion of the living room sofa and escaped to the kitchen. He grabbed the receiver and spoke in a shout of irritation. "Hello."

"Is this a bad time, Mr. Murphy?"

"Who…Mr. Schwartzel? Harry?"

"The same. Can you talk?"

Murphy peeked around the corner, turned his back to the doorway, and lowered his voice to a whisper. "I can talk."

"It seems that someone broke into a woman's apartment in Minot last night. Was that you?"

"I'm not…why would you think that?"

"There is no tap on your phone, George. And as you probably know, only cell phones can be openly monitored. So I repeat my question. Was that you last night?"

"Yeah," he mumbled.

"And did you find what you were looking for?"

"The girl came home while I was there. I didn't get a chance to check things out like I wanted."

"I heard you chased her. Why did you do that?"

"I…I guess I let my temper get away from me. I got fired from my job because of that split-tail."

There was a pause and the sound of a slow exhale at the other end. "Under the circumstances, I've decided to give you one more chance, even though I said I wouldn't. I understand the anger when a man loses his job."

"Damn straight, Harry. Things are…they're just really bad around here now. My wife's trying to play the bitch martyr."

"Ah, married life. You need your own apartment in downtown Bismarck."

"Do I ever?"

"Okay. You know what you have to bring to me. Any questions on that score?"

"No, but where do I go? Her place is a crime scene now. I can't go back there."

A sound close to a laugh came through the line. Schwartzel said, "The woman actually had the documents in her coat pocket the whole time. You trashed her apartment and car for nothing."

"How could you know that?"

"Are you kidding? I was an assistant district attorney for six years. Believe me, I have my sources. And cops like to talk. You should know."

Murphy ran a hand over his forehead. "So what should I do?"

"Juliet Driscoll is staying in a big house on the outskirts of Bismarck. Belonged to a guy named Blackwell. He died, but his Cuban housekeeper still lives there. That means you'll be dealing with two women, so that should make it easy. You were a cop, George, and you'd better have a decent plan, something more than chasing a woman into the woods like a dumb shit. Got that?"

"When do I...?"

"That's up to you, but the sooner the better as far as I'm concerned. And one more thing: If you screw this one up you'll never hear from me again. Understood?"

"Yes sir."

"Here's the address. You got a pad to write on?"

"Of course." Murphy looked for a pad and pulled out a phone book. He scribbled the information in the white border, and that gave him an idea.

33

Juliet hit the mailbox on the first attempt, the second attempt, and the third attempt, in spite of the fact that daylight was fading. She shook the can of wasp and hornet poison vigorously and pointed the nozzle again. "I want to try it from twenty feet, Nick. The label says it shoots that far."

"You're fine. Keep in mind you'll be inside the house. I doubt if either of you would be more than ten feet away from an intruder."

"So this is really better than pepper spray?" Marietta asked.

"It's an open secret among cops. That poison incapacitates just as effectively as pepper spray and you don't have to be up close to use it."

"We just squirt him in the eyes?" She examined the tall, black and gold can.

"Aim for the face. Those things put out a lot of fluid. You'll get the mouth, the eyes, and the nose. He'll feel like he's being water boarded with gasoline."

"And then we can whack him hard with the cast iron skillets," Juliet added.

"Try to hit him from behind. You don't want him reaching out, even if he's temporarily blinded."

Juliet nodded.

"Have the skillets out and available. You cannot have them in a drawer. If everything works half as well as we've planned it will give the police time to respond to your 911 call. Also—"

"Nick, my love. We'll be fine." She moved to his side and offered her lips for a kiss. His return embrace was stiff and absentminded. She understood. Still, his touch uplifted her mood.

He continued. "I was going to say that you should remove all the knives from the kitchen. All of them. You won't use them but he might. Don't give him a weapon. Okay?"

"Okay," Juliet said. "I'm ready for the bastard."

"We are prepared, Nick." Marietta said. "I know how men break into houses. I saw enough of that in Cuba."

34

"Another six on the half-shell, Harry?" Lila stood close by, screening her body from the other patrons and offering the deep furrow of her cleavage at eye level. "I know what oysters do to you."

Schwartzel was too slow stifling a yawn. The hour was late and he and Lila had been thumping around on his king bed pretty energetically for the previous couple of nights. He was running on a mixture of positive delight at Rhinehart's timely but overdue exit, combined with a serious midlife apprehension about remaining a free man. Both emotions apparently fused together and created an electricity that, with a bit of modern chemical assistance and maybe the oysters, brought out a Neanderthal quality to his sexual endeavors. Lila certainly had no complaints, but then she was working from the angle of lover-becomes-wife. He smiled generously. Fat chance of that.

"Don't give me that smile and tell me you're not interested tonight, Harry Schwartzel."

"Interested in the oysters or something else?" A faint indentation of a nipple pressed through the layers of her bra and linen blouse. How could it do that? For a moment he was transfixed with the outline of an aureole circling the slight protrusion of a pencil eraser.

"Now you're teasing." She tweaked a sideburn with thumb and forefinger. "I may have to make you pay after I get off work."

He shook his head. "Seriously, Lila, I can't. I've got to read through some briefs. They're backing up, and that's if I can even stay awake tonight." He winked. "You've been driving me pretty hard."

"Ooh, you got it backwards, I think."

He frowned and shook his head sharply this time. "Let me recuperate for a night or two. I'll make it up on the weekend."

She shifted her tray to the crook of an arm and reset her expression. "As long as it *is* 'up' on the weekend, Harry, if you know what I mean."

"And bring me one more martini for the road."

As they began wiping down tables a short time later, Schwartzel found himself buried in the fuzzy, warm blanket of a third martini.

A thought abruptly made it through his woolly mental state and stoned him cold: For all intents and purposes, he had entrusted his entire future to an ex-cop with not an ounce of common sense. Granted, the guy was a good academic. So? That and another fuck-up or two would land him in the slammer as surely as though he had committed the insane acts of stupidity himself. Chasing a broad into the woods? God save the imbeciles. Was that from the Bible? Sounded like it. He took another sip of his martini.

"Harry, love. Time to go," Lila gently prompted. "I can walk you out if you like."

He slowly extricated himself from the booth. The whirling platforms of balance seemed to stabilize. "I'm okay, Lila. Need a little recuperation, like I said."

"Sleep it off, Harry. We'll catch up."

"One is only really safe with iron bars over the windows," Marietta explained. "Most dwellings in Havana have them, and that is how he will try to enter."

"Unfortunately, there are no window alarms in this house," Juliet said.

The other woman shrugged. "Perhaps we worry for no reason. He is not supposed to know about this place. How could he discover that you are here?"

Juliet shook her head. "I don't know, but you weren't the one he chased into the woods last night. The man is violent. He would have killed me if he'd caught me." A mental picture of a masked man dripping with cold water intruded. Had it only been last night, less than twenty-four hours earlier? It seemed like weeks before.

She placed her coffee on the end table and stretched her legs, back, and neck muscles. The time was past midnight, and there was only so much caffeine she could absorb. Her hair was pulled into a tight ponytail and her dark jeans had been washed and dried. One of Marietta's black cotton tops replaced the white blouse from the previous evening—a stealth outfit for tonight. Nick had promised to drive down during his overnight shift. She could use his company at this moment.

Marietta glanced at her watch, and Juliet picked out the motion of the small radium dial. Every lamp in the house had been extinguished. Light bulbs were missing. The outside eave lights burned brightly however, and enough illumination poured through the windows to see movements, shapes, and furniture. Nick called it 'dark adaptation', another advantage they were supposed to possess when and if something happened. She had his flashlight to boot, a black three-cell LED model that looked like a weapon and weighed a ton.

"This time of night the bars would be crowded in Havana," Marietta said. "We young people used to party into the early hours, but…" She yawned. "That was a few years ago."

Juliet was light years from yawning. She moved to the center of the carpet and performed deep knee bends. Normally, the Crossroads would just be closing at this hour. Two o'clock in the morning was her normal bedtime. "Nick says that most crimes occur from three to four a.m.," she said with a puff of breath. "But I'm thinking if this guy comes he'll be here well before that."

Murphy was beginning to think Schwartzel was a shit-for-brains. The guy was an office dork who happened to be a lawyer. Granted, he had screwed up the previous night with the Driscoll woman, but what in God's name gave Schwartzel the idea that he could tell Murphy anything about field operations?

He punched in the keypad code at the entrance to the gated subdivision and watched the metal grills swing wide. Impressive. With inside information like this, he could have taken care of business days ago.

A careful drive-through was in order, fast enough to appear that he was returning home, but slow enough to take in the general layout of the place. His surveillance revealed big lots with houses set behind winding drives. Lots of bushes and trees screened the residences. Most importantly, he spied three houses with real estate placards set in the yards. The dark, bunkered appearance of one such house had all the giveaway signs of a deserted property. Overgrown shrubbery brushed the bricks from the foundation to the first floor windows. Old newspapers scattered the driveway. Didn't homeowners have a clue about this kind of thing? The house was a crater in the earth compared to its next-door neighbor, which was alight like a gantry on a rocket launching pad. He couldn't miss the mailbox number. The brightly lit house was exactly the one he was looking for.

Murphy completed his circuit, swung back through the meandering subdivision, and dowsed his headlamps before returning to the vacant house. There was no moon, but the wattage pouring out from the neighbor provided enough second-hand illumination to read a newspaper. Once entering the driveway, he shifted to neutral, allowed the car to coast, and used the parking brake to bring the vehicle to a stop, a technique that prevented the taillights from illuminating. He turned off the ignition, reclined the seatback, and decided to take a much-needed nap. On the chance that he had misread the empty house, the occupants could challenge his presence during this time. If not, his wristwatch alarm allowed a solid hour of refreshing sleep. He closed his eyes.

"It's getting foggy outside. See?" Juliet focused on a middle distance through the window. The bright clarity of the yard and driveway no longer existed. A milky soup of dampness enfolded the house.

"What?" the other woman replied in a low murmur.

"Marietta? Were you asleep?"

She cleared her throat. "Yes, I might have been. It is after two o'clock. Do you still believe something will happen?"

Her pulse quickened. "We have to stay alert and stay smart. If it's Murphy he's carrying a lot of hate, and not only toward me. I remind you that he bashed in Nick's 4-Runner for the hell of it."

"You tricked him twice and made him look stupid and small. A man like that will never stop until he gets his revenge, especially against a woman."

"We need to trick him one more time."

Marietta said, "He will...what is the English word when someone looks around?"

"Reconnoiter. He'll reconnoiter the house, find the best place to break in."

"Exactly. I am guessing the small study at the back corner of the house. Clifford liked the room, but it was always dark because of the junipers blocking the light outside."

"We should have been back there already," Juliet said. She grabbed the spray can and swung the heavy, cast iron skillet through an arc in the air. "We've got to split up, Marietta. Let me take the back study. You can monitor the front side of the house."

"We need to listen for a window breaking, Juliet. It is not the sound you might think. There is no sound of a large, glass vase that crashes onto the floor. When I was a girl in Cuba I thought it more like the tinkling of glass wind chimes. A little tap as the pane is broken, then the tinkling."

Juliet hefted the skillet again. The weapon was formed flat, like a cast iron dinner plate with a handle. She could take off his head with an edgewise cutting motion. "He's got to reach in and unlatch something, and I've got five pounds of iron in my hand. I'll break his fucking fingers. Sorry for the language."

"You are angry and full of the charging bull. That is how we should be."

"The back corner study?"

"Down the hallway toward the kitchen. Take a right at the end. It's the small corner room. The drapes are closed to keep in the heat, but you should open them."

"Remember, Marietta. One of us yells, and the other one calls 911."

"I am as ready as you, Juliet."

The Casio watch on his wrist generated a series of bell chimes at precisely two-thirty a.m. Murphy awoke from a very light sleep feeling not so much rested as motivated. He sat upright, opened a small tin container of Altoids, and plucked a white tablet from the crinkly wax paper. The tiny hit of sugar along with a bracing charge of peppermint did the trick.

There were gates in life, forks in the road, opportunities that seldom came along twice. Tonight was one such moment. It was a small thing, really, just stealing a few papers. However, in this case the consequences were huge. He could either spend the remainder of his existence as a security guard with a two-bit law degree, or have access to the money and influence that came with a practice in a major law firm. Hell, he could go even further, become a district attorney, a judge, even a state legislator or beyond. Talk about motivation? Was there a shred of a reason not to take this to the limit tonight? Hell no. He sucked saliva through the crumbling peppermint and reached into the rear seat for the lead pipe. The mask and gloves that he used only twenty-four hours earlier should work again. Why change anything?

The ground was spongy soft from the last few days of melting snow and ice. Moisture radiated upward and condensed into a cloudlike mass of minute water droplets. He moved into the row of evergreen bushes screening the property line, peered at the Blackwell side, and squinted into the bright diffusion. His clothes were gray top to bottom, except for his head covering. The olive, three-hole mask had come straight off a shelf in an Army surplus store. Night snipers and Army Rangers used the same camouflage. Enough said.

First order of business: Check out the rear and both sides of the dwelling. There were shadowed areas between the cones of the eave lights, and several high wattage bulbs were missing entirely. He could work through the darker areas, and the fog would help. Had Schwartzel actually called him a dumb shit? The phrase rankled. The fat-ass lawyer had no clue about the world outside of his cushy office.

He stretched the mouth and eyeholes wider in the ski mask and hefted the pipe. Tonight's exercise required the kind of expertise that he had in abundance, if only his future partner could recognize the fact.

Juliet sized the room at twelve by fifteen feet, a neglected part of the house that stank of cigars and unwashed clothing. The draperies picked up and held the odors, which explained why Marietta must have kept the space closed off from the remainder of the downstairs area. She shot open the curtains, and on second thought, grabbed the fabric and tugged violently downward and outward, until the entire edifice came away from the overhead valances and pitched into a pile on the floor. A return upwelling of dust and mildew engulfed her, and she gagged at a cloud she could not see.

The window was a standard-sized, double hung opening. Marietta was correct about the foliage. Two Christmas-tree-like bushes were growing close to the house. The wash of illumination that leached between the overgrown branches shed dim light into the room. She kicked the curtains further aside and peered through the narrow aperture to the outside. A fraction of the side yard along with the neighbor's hedge line was visible. A fleeting movement, a shadow in the fog crossed her field of view. She caught her breath and blinked hard. Was this just her imagination? Like, she expected to see something and therefore she did?

The door to the hallway hung ajar, and she stepped to the opening and raised her voice. "Marietta, can you hear me?"

"Yes. I am looking out to the front yard."

"I thought I saw something, maybe moving towards the back of the house." A quiver in her voice betrayed a coil of fear just below the surface. Her mouth became dry.

"Should we call 911?"

Tension gathered in her stomach. What did she see outside? The answer was nothing. Yet she knew it was him. They were being stalked.

"Juliet?"

"No," she answered in a tight voice. "Not yet. What would we say? That we're just a couple of scared women? That'll give them a good laugh." She tried to swallow. "I'm going to check the other rooms." She moved through the back utility area to the kitchen. Her eyes had adapted to the darkness, and there were plenty of lighted green and blue dials, and winking, power-on lights around the counters to find the way. The bedrooms were next. A clear, brightly lit view from both sets of bedroom windows revealed a large area lacking both trees and bushes. Murphy was a roach, crawling in and out of shadows and dark corners. He would want cover, therefore the rear of the house could be ruled out as a point of entry. She completed the circuit and returned to the study. Still nothing moved outside. She stationed herself just outside the cone of light coming in through the window and waited. The skillet pulled at her wrist like a five-pound barbell.

Minutes passed, too much time to spend alone in a stuffy, smelly hideaway belonging to an old man she had long hated. But she felt nothing. He was gone to dust as if he had never lived.

And here she was in this darkened room, at this odd time and place wondering why she had carried the outrage and revulsion around with her for so long.

A burr of something scraping against the bricks reached her, and she turned an ear to a sound so slight she wondered whether she might be hallucinating. The foggy, cold night was expressly made for overwrought imaginations. They made movies about nights like this, and they usually featured a werewolf.

There it was again. She stiffened and leaned forward. This time a branch moved slowly away from the window. The movement was too slow and methodical to be caused by the wind. And there was no wind.

She felt the hair bristle on the back of her neck. She edged backward into the gloom and pulled in air quietly with a tremor in her diaphragm. A hand came into view. The hand was swept aside by a masked face with eyeholes peering into the room. She couldn't breathe. The devil was here.

Juliet watched his face moving left and right, gloved hands against the glass cupping his temples. Could he see her? Maybe not, as long as she remained motionless. He turned his head, lifted his covering, and pressed an ear to the surface probing for sound. That meant he was already aware that she was inside, and that being the case, she had to assume he knew about Marietta and the fact that they were alone. But he did not know their exact locations, and he needed to break in unseen and unheard. She tightened her grip on the skillet and readied herself.

The hands went away. He glanced downward and seemed to fumble with something below the level of the windowsill. She could yell to Marietta now, tell her to call 911, but he would hear the cry.

A bloom of blue light reflected on the outside glass, as if he had keyed a computer pad or cell phone. Then she knew. He was making a telephone call to the house. What could be easier? Someone inside had to move around and pick up the receiver, maybe talk back and forth. What better way to pinpoint the occupants of a dwelling?

He pressed his ear to the glass at precisely the moment she heard the computerized bell tone of an incoming call from the back bedroom and the kitchen. Marietta called out and stepped into the hallway. Footsteps tapped quickly toward the study and then slowed. The door stood open a hand's width from the post. If Marietta swung it further they both were in real trouble.

"Juliet?" Her voice was soft and barely audible.

The telephone kept ringing. Murphy's ear was once again pressed onto the glass. Juliet said nothing. Perhaps by some miracle of intuition her friend could sense the situation.

The man pulled off his ski mask. It was Murphy all right. He turned his head, presumably to give his right ear a chance to pick up sound. In this position the back of his skull was angled in her direction. The house phone went to a recorded message, and Murphy seemed to shrug as he slipped his mask back over his head. He bent to retrieve an object and straightened with the lead pipe in his hand. Like a hustle with a pool cue he tapped the end of the pipe lightly against the bottom pane of the window. The glass disintegrated, but Marietta was right. There was very little noise, and now the pipe was protruding four or five inches into the room.

She maneuvered to the window. In spite of the danger, the flood of adrenaline in her system fueled her muscles with savagery. With all of her strength she swung the skillet flat against the end of the lead pipe. The weight and inertia of the cast iron pulled her hand through the swing and the pipe shot backward with the gong of a church bell hit by a clapper. An agonizing bellow of pain and surprise told her that the opposite end had struck him somewhere, hopefully in the face. Maybe he would lose an eye.

A screaming torrent of foul language accompanied a series of wild swings of the lead pipe, and with each concussion exploding shards of glass and wood showered the room. Portions of the window began caving in as the panes shattered with a roar. She yelled for Marietta.

The woman ducked around the doorframe with a hand over her mouth. "*¡Ay Dios mio!*"

Juliet shouted over the racket, "Be a good time to call for help. Use the wall phone in the kitchen and leave it off the hook. Hurry!" She pointed the spray can toward an opening that was becoming larger by the second. "Then you can help me douse this asshole!"

In less than a minute Marietta reappeared at the door. The window was almost completely demolished. "They say they are coming, Juliet. I tell them please to hurry!"

Juliet caught herself breathing way too hard, as if she was readying for a fistfight. "He's going to try and get inside and we have to stop him."

"But, Juliet—"

"We can't run. He could catch us anywhere in the house. We have to stop him here. Have you still got your spray can?"

"And the skillet. Right here."

"Be ready with the spray when I say. Aim for the face."

His yells were indistinct guttural skips, as if he could not quite form the words. Did she hit him in the mouth? Whatever, the facts were plain: He would beat them to death if he could get through the window casement. His penlight swept over the destroyed window, flickered past their forms, and returned to settle on their faces. Juliet ducked, thumbed Nick's powerful flashlight on, and hit Murphy between the eyes with the blinding force of the halogen beam.

He grunted, dropped back, and threw both gloved hands onto the sill plate. A scramble upward put his head through the opening. A large tear in his ski mask revealed a bloody laceration in his jaw. He raised his head and eyed them with the look of a gargoyle.

Marietta screamed.

"Now!" Juliet yelled. A push on the plungers propelled thick ribbons of insecticide from the cans. Two jets of high velocity fluid sluiced into his mouth and eyes. He put an arm forward and dropped his head lower. Juliet adjusted her aim and tracked his mouth. Marietta's stream went straight into his eyes. Murphy ducked and weaved, yelling all the while.

Juliet swapped the spray can for the skillet and forced herself to take three calm steps forward. She drew back the heavy slab of cast iron and swung forward with all of her might. The flat of the pan struck him squarely in the forehead with a muted clunk that she felt all the way to her shoulders. Murphy dropped from the window and hit the ground with a thud.

Juliet pitched the skillet into a corner chair and tried to stop herself from shaking. She slowly became aware that the study was freezing cold. The air was putrid from the insecticide spray, a smell that engulfed her like a mixture of ether and hot asphalt from a new road.

Marietta moved to her side. "We need to go back into the living room and turn on the lights, Juliet. We close this room and wait for the police."

She shook her head. "He might get up again. We should stay here."

"*¿Para qué?* He won't get up, not for a long time."

35

The Plains had a late summer. The middle of May rolled around and Juliet could still see tulips and daffodils on the north side of the house. The weather seemed to confuse the migrating birds. They flew in all directions. Canada geese traveled from north to south, and then back again, loons scrambled overhead in worried circles, and large numbers of ducks flew past the house in fast formations, as if they'd just figured it out.

Juliet threw off her light jacket and let the morning sun soak through her thin, cotton T-shirt. She'd cut her hair, or rather Marietta had. Now she wore it in a short Latin or European style that had a cosmopolitan, upscale look. According to Nick, the new cut brought out her patrician lines, made her sexier in a whole different way. That was also news.

The day was warm and bright, and the soft breeze had a sultry effect on her bare arms and legs. She stood immobile, turned her face to the heat and light of the solar fire and let the tingle of the sun's rays wash over her, open her up like some erotic blossom. She gave herself a moment, let out a sigh, and picked up a twenty-pound bag of potting soil. The dirt from the bag was black and rich and she allowed the loamy contents to run through her gloved fingers as she dumped the payload into a brand new candy-red wheelbarrow. She tested the handles before carting the load along the hard dirt path to the garden in the side yard.

Today would be her final day at Lenny's house, and she wanted to get her hands dirty, mess around in the flower garden, and just enjoy herself outside. After all, it was their combined birthdays. Thankfully, the big meetings with lawyers and accountants were not scheduled until the following morning and afternoon. The weather was way too nice to stay cooped up inside on a day like today.

Juliet was pleased with her efforts around the place. In addition to caring for her brother during his convalescence, she'd brought order and cleanliness to the property just by virtue of living there. With Doris no longer present Lenny was more responsible and involved about what had become his house. There were other changes in her brother as well. He now wore braces on his teeth and he shaved every day. Some differences were subtler, but she could read them. He was not the same individual he had been before the incident in the well.

She dumped the wheelbarrow load, backed the wagon and parked it neatly upturned on its single front wheel. Doris had left unkempt rows of purple and white gladiolas, yellow marigolds, and pink and red snapdragons all scattered like roadside weeds. They were completely overrun by prairie grasses. Lenny had already departed in his new pickup truck for extra bags of mulch and topsoil. She had hoped to catch him early, maybe do a final brother-sister- breakfast-thing as a birthday present, but he was already on the road. He was actually setting an alarm clock these days.

The mirrored flash of a car windshield several miles away caught her eyes. Her focus tightened. Nick's car. She let out a sigh of contentment and anticipation. They could hardly stay away from each other, especially today, and her birthday was only one of the reasons. Tonight would be their first night alone together at Nick's place, or any place for that matter, and her insides went all fluttery in anticipation of the evening to come, the afternoon if they couldn't wait that long.

She shook the dirt from her gloves. So much had been going on since Murphy's recovery and his subsequent arrest that she and Nick had almost no time for each other. She had been busy caring for Lenny and living at the house, while both she and Nick were constantly being subjected to this or that legal deposition or summons, and all of this on top of Nick's occasional double duty covering for the missing deputy.

Her original criminal complaint was now in the hands of the State Attorney's Office, and fireworks of charges were going off left and right. She'd become something of a minor celebrity after two interviews on Channel 12, in spite of the fact that she refused to sink to the level of their prurient sexual interest regarding Clifford's abuse. She'd kept her comments above the belt and people seemed to respect that. In the process a strange thing happened: She came to realize that, except for Schwartzel—who was currently arraigned on federal charges—all of the principals involved were either dead or in jail. She was free to put everything behind her, to plunge forward into a new life, and she intended to do just that.

Marietta had become a close friend. Juliet had no reason to doubt Marietta's strict accounting of Clifford's hoard of cash and gold coins from the safe. But treasures of a different sort in his attic brought tears to her eyes. A steamer trunk held boxes of their baby clothes, silver rattles, and crib toys, all surely intended never again to see the light of day. The trunk had obviously been shipped to Clifford's new house and forgotten, forgotten in a way like the two lost orphans. Most heartbreaking of all were the books of photos, as precious as anything on earth to a mother and father. With both sadness and delight Juliet had exposed herself to small bits and pieces of the photo collection, a process so wrought with emotion that she was able to proceed only at a very slow pace. It was enough that the photo albums were in her possession, a tangible legacy of her family that she might pass down to her own children someday.

Nick's big Durango nosed into the front yard. He killed the ignition and seemed to study her for a moment. She returned his gaze with a steady, neutral expression, and then broke into a smile for this man she would marry. Together they represented the future. She could not live in the past any longer, and her parents would not have wanted her to.

Nick climbed out of the pickup and walked toward her wearing a faded blue T-shirt tucked into a pair of Levis. His jaw was covered with blond stubble from his overnight shift. He carried a bouquet of bright red roses at his side.

"Nick," she said with a tremor in her breath, "If you looked any more scrumptious I couldn't stand it." An ache of longing welled up as he stepped close to her.

"I thought about you all night," he said as he held out the flowers. "And God you're lovely. These are—"

"For me?" She laughed even as her respiration increased. She felt a rush of desire to touch him, run her hands under his shirt, fold herself into his bare chest and feel the sun hot on their naked skin. "Don't tell me. You picked them to go with the new wheelbarrow."

He grinned. "I had to break into three flower shops to match the color. Happy birthday."

"Nick." She allowed him to draw her closer still, enclose her in his arms. "But what about all the criminals you were supposed to be catching last night? Instead you were breaking into all these flower shops?" She moistened her lips, parted them slightly.

"I gave the criminals the night off. I told them it was your birthday. And I only smashed three florists' windows." He bent his head and kissed her straight nose and her closed eyes, and ran his lips lightly over her cheeks in a circular path to her mouth.

"Umm…Nick."

He hesitated just a moment, and then his lips were touching hers. She shivered, and as naturally as breathing opened her mouth to his and pulled him into her. She melded her body to his, ran a hand under his shirt, brushed his bare chest, and then to his belt. His hardness rose against her, a ridge of unabashed desire that matched her own sexual ache. She slid a hand over the rough denim of his jeans and cupped him. He parted his lips a millimeter and inhaled a quick beat of pleasure.

"I've wanted to do that for so long, Nick. Are we going to be able to wait until tonight?" She wore a microscopically short pair of cut-off bottoms, and the thin gauze of her panties underneath offered no impediment at all if he wanted to part the fabric and touch her. She imagined that and more and felt a flush in her cheeks and liquid smoothness lower down.

Marietta had likened the various complications and interruptions in the course of their romance to the Hoover Dam: A huge concrete barrier preventing the normal flow of a river. Well, that dam was about to break.

Nick glanced off her shoulder, then lowered his eyes and made a soft groan, "I think we have to wait. I saw Lenny pulling out from Plants 'n Plows as I passed. He can't be very far behind me."

Juliet threw her glimpse to the south. Her brother's vehicle was a hazy blue dot moving toward them. She inhaled deeply and released her breath in a long sigh against his chest. "Oh jeez, Nick. I don't think I can stand it."

"We have all night," he said. "And the next and the next…"

She gave him a slow kiss, a reluctant release as she reset herself, came down from the cloud of trembling intoxication. "And maybe every day after that?" she said.

He relinquished the bouquet of flowers. "And every day after that."

She drew in the sweet perfume of the roses and watched alongside Nick as her brother bounced his pickup along the furrows grooved into the final hundred yards to the house.

Juliet raised her head from Nick's chest and sipped chilled champagne as he tipped the goblet to her lips. "Careful, my darling," he said. Several drops escaped from the corner of her mouth and fizzed onto his bare skin. "Ah," he started. "A little cold."

"Umm…" she murmured as she licked the glistening pearls from his chest. She felt the slight touch of her silver pendant slipping between her breasts, a Greek letter *pi* on its chain of delicate, diaphanous silver. The necklace was the first gift of jewelry she had ever received from a man, and Nick had enclosed her birthday present in a small, silk sachet. *Pi* was their symbol now, from the crazy reference to her refrigerator magnet, to the classical mathematical formula, to the first letter of the word 'promise', and that was the meaning that had touched her. He'd said, 'This is my promise,' and that was all, but his four words carried their future together. She smiled inwardly. Would Nick ever tire of seeing her in just the necklace and nothing more? She didn't think so.

He leaned away from her, placed the glass on the bedside table, and came back.

"This is what I want," she said. "You." She ran her hands over his chest, put her nose against his skin and drew in the washed aroma of soap and the comingled scent of their perspiration. His smell was underneath it all, something that wasn't hers. It was heavier and carried the open-air flavor of the outside and maybe a sun-washed day on a beach. That's what she wanted, and she permitted herself to roam free around his bare frame.

She floated, allowed her thoughts and her languid, pleasured body to drift along as light as a vapor. Her mother again seemed to be near, a warm, ever-so-slight presence, and Juliet felt the family circle closing again, but this time with her own children, hers and Nick's. Did her mother smile just then? Maybe.

"Are you going to cook for me tonight?" she asked. "You promised."

"I would never break a promise, and we're going to need our energy."

She laughed a little as she walked her fingers lightly along Nick's ribs, a one-two-three tiptoe that ended with her palm flat on his muscled abdomen. She let her hand drift where it might, which was lower still. Juliet released a sigh. Here was a man who had mentioned marriage once already, casually, taking care not to spook her, as if it might.

After a long, dreamy period of silence she said, "So what did you decide about med school?"

"What?" He raised his head from the pillow.

"I know you want to finish, and I told you I'm going to get my credits in engineering and finish college. Maybe go to graduate school and teach." She pressed her lips into his chest. "We have the money. So much we could never spend it all, even if we wanted to."

"It's your money, my love. Not mine."

She could sense his smile, even though she knew he meant what he said. "What if I pay for everything?" she asked.

"I'm not sure how I'd feel about it."

"What if I made you earn it? Would you feel better about it then?"

"Depends on what I have to do."

She slid her hand between his legs and closed her fingers around him. "I see you're alive again, my Nicholas." She stroked his length up and down in a slow rhythm. "You have to make love to me again. Right now. And you need to get an A-Plus this time." Juliet pulled herself over his mid-section and allowed her legs to straddle him. She held herself just above his erection. The anticipation of his entry was intoxicating and sensuous, and to hold herself away from him even for a second was almost beyond her ability.

She placed her lips over his and touched his tongue, a flick of warmth, then more. A tremor rippled through her body.

He raised his head further, brushed his tongue over a nipple, and drew the sensitive puckering gently into his mouth.

"Mmm...God, Nick." The exquisite pleasure her body could deliver astonished her. Here she was at thirty years old, and only now learning about herself.

He murmured with slight puzzlement, "What did I get last time?"

"You mean, your score?"

He nodded.

"I gave you an A-Minus," she whispered, moving ever so slightly over him, holding back the moment.

She could feel the rumble of amusement in his chest. He said, "You're a tough grader. Can't you grade on the curve?"

She kissed him hard. "Only on yours, my love." She lowered herself onto him with a sigh and a moan that she barely recognized as coming from her lips. They began the passage once more, slower this time, with leisure movements that halted at intervals in a rapture of drawn-out pleasure. She became weightless in a world of exquisite sensation, eyes closed, her nerve endings split bare against his hardness.

At his final quickening she melted into him and locked herself to his rhythm. An instant later her world rose up and engulfed her in an airless pleasure so pure she could not breathe. And she could not stop. Tears came from nowhere. The moment was too sweet, the fire too hot. It might burn forever.

Sometime later she opened her eyes. Her legs and arms entangled him. The room had gone dark. At some point in the Dakota evening they'd missed dinner and now she was ravenous. "Nicholas?" She blinked an eyelash against his cheek.

He came awake and yawned. "Uhmm?"

"I'm hungry, my love," she said. "I'm *really* hungry."

ABOUT THE AUTHOR

William C. Walker started his writing career as a columnist for a regional newspaper. During a thirty-five year span as a military pilot and airline captain for Delta Air Lines he began writing short stories and novels. He is the author of five novels and has received numerous awards throughout the publishing industry. He lives on Florida's Treasure Coast with his wife and a fluff dog that likes him.